CLIO
IN THE
CROSSFIRE

PEGGY GARDNER

Clio in the Crossfire

Paperback: 978-1-64184-109-2

Ebook: 978-1-64184-110-8

Dedication

For my children, Morgan and Wade, and my sister, Patsy, who, in Auden's words, "can still persuade us to rejoice."

If ye break faith with us who die
We shall not sleep, though poppies grow
In Flanders fields.

—John McCrae

CHAPTER 1

June 8, 1942

If my Great-Aunt Norma Clower could have replaced Admiral Nimitz at the Battle of Midway, her voice alone would have sunk more than five enemy ships. "Clio, get yourself downstairs this instant. I will not have you lollygagging all summer long. Your music education begins in fifteen minutes. Downstairs now!"

Burrowing under the covers for a nice, little lie-in would be out of the question now that school was out for the summer and Aunt Norma had decided to take my education in hand. In Wolfe Flats, Oklahoma, a no man's land, where piano lessons and china painting are considered civilizing influences, I didn't stand a chance against enemy forces.

Almost three months earlier, my mother, Delia, had uprooted me from that great, civilized city of New York—when she wrapped a war correspondent band around her khaki sleeve—and shuttled me off to live with my two great-aunts, Norma and Harriet. Before I was dumped on their doorstep, I'd never seen these relatives.

This doorstep graced an elegant Queen Anne house that looked too fancy for this backwater town. The Muller's big white Victorian mansion stood next to it, adorned with more turrets than a medieval castle. Those houses were like a pair of prize-winning thoroughbred horses hitched to a dray, suffering the indignities of residing on a street called Choctaw, with modest bungalows a block away for their neighbors.

My mother had spent her childhood in this gigantic house with these hidebound aunts and never told me that she could watch the world through great humped windows, in a house with six bedrooms and a separate library, with floor-to-ceiling bookcases.

At the age of eighteen, without so much as a fare-thee-well-forever to her Aunt Norma and Aunt Harriet, my mother shot off for New York, finished a degree in journalism, married and divorced my father, and erased all traces of him by officially changing my last name—Licthmann—to Clower, her maiden name.

With World War II raging all about the edges of our country—Japanese patrolling the Pacific, Germans and Italians across the Atlantic invading their neighbors, and Russia dithering over its non-aggression pact with Hitler—Mother took matters into her own determined hands.

I can still see her small-boned frame moving effortlessly through the crowded aisle of the train that took us from New York City to Wolfe Flats. The perky beret smashed her auburn curls into submission, as one yellow-gloved hand jabbed in the direction of the only available space—somewhere over her head. Oddly, Mother's stiff, raised arm reminded me of the Statue of Liberty, her yellow glove beckoning me, like a floodlight in Lady Liberty's torch.

As I had shoved through the crowded train of soldiers, I couldn't get the Statue of Liberty image out of my mind. Unlike millions of immigrants buoyed by their first view of freedom in a new world, I was heading toward the worst kind of confinement: a tiny Oklahoma town with two gorgon aunts as my jailers.

Like one of those mythological storks that dump babies on the door stoops of unsuspecting parents, Mother left me on my aunts' front porch without so much as a "Howdy, here's my darling daughter Clio come to stay a spell."

My sudden appearance almost sent my dotty Aunt Harriet into a fugue state; she mistook me for my mother, as an eleven-year-old, until Aunt Norma straightened her out with the painful truth that I was to be occupying one of those extra bedrooms.

Aunt Norma had immediately set her sister straight, as she eyed my cardboard suitcase and sized me up as a Yankee and a carpetbagger. "A telegram let me know there was a possibility that Delia might be bringing Clio to visit. I didn't want to get your hopes up, Harriet, for good reason. Delia just headed down the street in Booger Allen's cab, without a word to us."

On her way back to the train depot that day, Mother had a few words with Lucinda, her aunts' long-time cook and housekeeper. Lucinda was part Comanche and might have been part Clower, but no one ever said. My middle name is Lucinda, because Mother said that Lucinda was the only person in her life that she could fully trust.

Trust was a word that left my dictionary when Mother headed down Choctaw Street in that cab to catch a train and hitch a way to Europe, leaving me so alone that I felt I could claim the word "solitary" as my very own.

Settling into a foreign country like Oklahoma would have tested the great Sherlock Holmes's aptitude and invention. But, when I discovered that three young women had gone missing during the past two decades, one as recently as the previous August, I immediately engaged my considerable intellect to find a serial killer.

Being a devoted student of the old master of sleuthing, I began to look for what Sherlock called the "veiled and deceptive nature" of things.

While Mother was tucked safely into a bomb shelter somewhere in the British Isles, I had made it my business to know what other people don't know. Sherlock said that. I have made it my mantra. My prime interest is detection; my hobby is map-making. The spatial distribution of every street and alley in Wolfe Flats is well known to me. Along with sleuthing and cartography, my vocation is solving problems, preferably those involving crime.

That's how I managed to nail Lester Lewin, nick-named Whitey, because his albino-phobic mother covered his face with talcum to protect him from the sun.

Her son wasn't an albino; his grandmother was; his mother feared UV rays were out to get Whitey.

People in Wolfe Flats seem to delight in latching onto infirmities and labeling children for life. Case in point: Shivers Johnson, Booger Allen, and my good friend, Manboy Muller, wear their nicknames without complaint. But, when young Whitey was tossed down a well by his great-grandfather for peeing in public, his psyche didn't recover—unless a weak bladder is an indication of future psychopathic behavior

If I were at the public library in New York City, I could research that question. The Wolfe Flats Library doesn't have a single issue of the *American Journal of Psychiatry*, so my research methods require what some might consider snooping.

Unfortunately, my sleuthing led me down a country road and smack dab into Whitey's ether gag. Lucky to escape alive, I've now added wariness to my bag of tricks.

Wolfe Flats may be backwards in many respects, but it offers considerable material for problem solving. Even a Methodist do-gooder like Whitey, beloved by the church ladies, couldn't hide from my considerable detection skills.

This talent brought me within a whisper of a watery death—and the gratitude of this entire community. I need to qualify "entire." I managed to get the worthless Sheriff McIver fired for brutalizing me in my hospital bed. And, Whitey's mother, Hedy Lewin, will never welcome me into Lewin's Department Store or talk Aunt Norma into buying for me those big cotton bloomers with rotten elastic waistbands. That's the upside of my sleuthing.

The downside of that night when Whitey nabbed me still visits me with nightmares. After he dumped me down the same well where his great-grandfather tossed him as a child, Whitey left me to float around with the body parts of those three missing women. Then, my friends, Jeremiah Whittaker and Manboy Muller, rescued me—not without collateral damage to my body.

For the past few weeks of what should have been a carefree summer, I've taken a brief respite from solving homicides—just to calm the anxieties of my great aunts and Lucinda.

In spite of a broken ankle and a bullet hole in my arm, I managed to recover for the celebration of my twelfth birthday last month, with so many well-wishers that my absent mother would have been amazed.

My journalist friend, Sally Tolliver, wrote a smacking good story for the Ft. Worth and Oklahoma City newspapers, but Aunt Norma put a damper on my inflated ego when she snapped at me: "Making headlines is vulgar, Clio. The Clowers prefer to keep a low profile."

My self-esteem might naturally get in the way of the Clower "low profile," but I have given considerable thought to Sherlock's belief that there is "nothing like first-hand evidence." After my near scrape with death, I will be a bit more careful in the future about actually tracking a killer to his lair. Getting first-hand evidence can be risky.

This morning, as I tried to ignore the trumpeting reminder from Aunt Norma about my music education, I thought about first-hand evidence, as I lazily stretched my skinny body in a four-poster bed that would have supported the bulk of Henry the Eighth.

Just last night, I had accidently stumbled on first-hand evidence in this very house. I wasn't quite sure about the exact nature of that evidence, but something in that old buckram journal in her bedside table had brought Aunt Norma to tears. Only toe-wedging with a medieval torture device that slowly prized off a victim's toenails could possibly bring my Aunt Norma to tears.

CHAPTER 2

"Clio, you have fifteen minutes to get downstairs, eat breakfast, and go to your music lesson!" Aunt Norma's voice rang out with the authority of a fleet admiral launching ships into battle. I could hear the banging of pots down in the kitchen; Lucinda waged her wars with the sounds of an opposing army whenever Aunt Norma nettled her.

I had allowed five minutes for breakfast and five minutes for a three-block walk. That left five remaining minutes to solve my music lesson predicament. Sherlock believed that learning useless things reduces a person's ability to remember useful things. His violin was his hobby, just as making maps is mine. I needed to help Aunt Norma refocus on what I considered useful.

Fishing under my bedcovers for yesterday's clothes, I found my yellow and brown plaid skirt—a fashion statement that would have sent Coco Chanel screaming from her atelier—and a white blouse with last night's potatoes glued to the buttonholes. Without unbuttoning the blouse, I yanked it over my head and thrust my legs through a rotten, elasticized skirt band that couldn't possibly outlast the war.

My cinnamon plaits hung limply, in need of a good wash, so I dunked my comb into the soapy sink and slicked down my part. If Aunt Norma would buy me Vitalis, as I asked, I could do the sixty-second workout for sleek hair, without tedious shampooing.

Loitering upstairs as long as I dared, I slid down the banister to save fourteen seconds, hoping to refocus Aunt Norma. Last night at dinner, I hadn't managed to shake her belief in me as a budding virtuoso.

In some ways, Aunt Norma is more devious than a methodical criminal. The minute Robert E. Lee Elementary let us out for the freedom of summer, Aunt Norma went on the culture warpath. She is determined to pop open every file cabinet in my brain and stuff the cavities with what she calls "refinements." At the moment, she is fixated on piano lessons, although I have not the slightest interest in pounding the ivories.

"Felicity Langston will have you playing Bach inventions before summer is over," Aunt Norma had beamed across the dinner table last night, as I lifted my wounded arm and groaned in protest.

"That's just a flesh wound, Clio. It didn't keep you from exposing your bloomers while you were doing cartwheels on the front lawn this afternoon, instead of weeding Harriet's zinnias. Imagine what a passerby would think of such an exhibition by a Clower!"

As I had reached across the dinner table for another spoonful of mashed potatoes, I tried not to visualize the undergarments of Aunt Norma and Aunt Harriet if they dared to do cartwheels: those peach-colored girdles, with garters dangling like desiccated claws; the flesh-colored stockings that pool around their ankles by the end of the day; and, the great, poufy bras that they hide inside of pillow slips on the clothesline.

Just as I was strangling back a giggle, while making a show of easing my wounded arm up on the table, Aunt Norma stopped it short. "You can get that sly smile off your face right now, Clio. Your biceps brachii injury has nothing to do with the motor skills needed for an elementary piano lesson. Felicity will be expecting you at nine o'clock in the morning."

With a set chin that resembled one of those busts of Napoleon as he outflanked the Austrian army, Aunt Norma continued: "Your summer will be regimented, Clio. You cannot run around Wolfe Flats like a hoyden, just looking for trouble. You might never have been found in that old well," she looked accusingly across the table at me.

"I blame myself for not providing proper guidance. You will not be left to your own devices, making those so-called maps of Wolfe Flats, riding your bicycle onto private property, and poking your nose into what shouldn't concern you. Now, that, my dear, is the truth of the matter."

Modesty has never been my strong suit. As I noisily scraped the bottom of the bowl of potatoes, I flashed a determined glare at Aunt Norma. My favorite detective,

Sherlock, says: "Eliminate all the factors, and the one which remains must be the truth."

Only a month ago, the process of elimination had led me to question suspicious people and explore secret places to find out why three young women had mysteriously disappeared.

If I hadn't engaged my Sherlockian brain, no one in Wolfe Flats would have ever known about bodies in a well. The next victim in Whitey's sights was yours truly. If you don't do considerable prying, you can miss what might be looking right at you.

I shoved a platter of gelatinous meatloaf toward Aunt Norma and stared her down. It is simply the "veiled and deceptive nature" of certain things to stay hidden, especially in old houses filled with old people trying to conceal what might be of interest to a detective.

At what appeared to be a perfectly normal meatloaf dinner downstairs, secrets were hiding themselves upstairs in closed drawers in my aunts' house. Hush-hush things from the past tucked themselves into the minds and hearts of Aunt Harriet, Aunt Norma, and even Lucinda, who claimed she despised secrecy. All three of them had managed to conceal the reason that Mother took off like a scalded cat from Wolfe Flats.

Mounding my mashed potatoes into a small tower, I flattened the top, like the Devil's Kitchen structure at Lake Murray—the place where Manboy found my bleeding mother.

"Do not play with your food, Clio," Aunt Norma chided me.

If my architecture skills didn't throw her off track, my saccharine smile might, as I tried to time travel back to that night when my mother had been attacked and beaten within an inch of her life at a Methodist Church wiener roast.

After Manboy took Mother to the hospital in Ardmore, Aunt Norma and Aunt Harriet had convinced the doctor to keep his mouth shut about her bodily injuries. So no one investigated the criminal act against her.

Furious with her aunts' hypocrisy, my mother didn't return to Wolfe Flats until she had an opportunity to start a new career as a war correspondent.

With just a tad of modesty, I can say that within a week I had started my new career by solving Wolfe Flats' crime of the century—three missing girls, lost for a decade and a half, with not a clue as to where they'd gone.

They'd gone into a well behind Whitey Lewin's famous frontier home, built by his great-grandfather, the old rapscallion who lowered Whitey into the same well to cure him of a leaky bladder.

If he hadn't kicked the bucket three years ago, Dr. Freud might speculate on why Whitey became fixated on popping bodies of young women into that well. You can be certain that the locals in Wolfe Flats would never consent to one of their own being psychoanalyzed to assure that their ids, egos, and superegos were in sync.

"Do you know that the moon is in opposition to Jupiter tonight, Clio? It's a waxing crescent —a meaningful moon, because it is partly hidden," Aunt Harriet's voice, from the far end of the dinner table, came out of left field, as I was forking furrows into my potatoes.

Planetary alignment carries more weight in Wolfe Flats than Dr. Freud's theories. I could speculate for hours about how the deviant criminal mind becomes so quirky, but psychology isn't my strong suit. However, I can search for clues until the cows come home. (That's a little phrase I picked up in Wolfe Flats.) Speaking the local lingo helps a New Yorker like me to blend in with the natives, so that my eavesdropping is not obvious.

Aunt Harriet's observations often startle me, as though she's able to see inside my head. Aunt Harriet probably knows that I have a magnetic attraction to anything that seems to be hidden, purposefully concealed. For instance, consider that suspicious top drawer of the bedside table in Aunt Norma's room, where she keeps an odd, water-stained journal. I long to flip that thing open, to find out why Aunt Norma keeps it so close to her dreaming head. I saw it for the first time yesterday morning, when she sent me upstairs to get her white gloves for church.

Last night, after dinner, I sat in the backyard swing with Aunt Harriet to watch the cresent moon, hoping a "meaningful moon" would loosen her tongue. It didn't. But when I tiptoed downstairs last night to raid Lucinda's cookie jar, I passed by Aunt Norma's bedroom. Through a slightly ajar door, I could see her sitting on the side of the bed, her mouth slack with pain, her eyes flushed with tears. She was turning the pages of that old journal, as though each page held bad news but she couldn't stop turning the pages.

What were the secrets that Aunt Norma was keeping to herself? What so distressed her on the pages of that water-stained book?

Her composure would return. I was sure of that. Tomorrow morning, she'd be as bossy as ever, forcing piano lessons on me. But I would remain disturbed. I had seen another side of Aunt Norma. The strangeness of that *other* weeping woman inside of my no-nonsense aunt unnerved me. I'd do us both a favor to get to the bottom of what upset her. If it meant prying into her bedside drawer, then so be it.

Those old circus tricks of lying on a bed of nails can't compare to a bed of peanut butter cookie crumbs. I flopped around in my four-poster half the night, thinking about secrets in this old house. My dreams were cluttered with hidden crimes and Aunt Norma's tears.

CHAPTER 3

My slide down the bannister had irritated Aunt Norma but not moved her from the beaten path. Unlike my proclivity for solving crime, playing a musical instrument is not a gift of mine. Yet, Aunt Norma had plotted a dreadful morning for me with a piano teacher named Felicity Langston. Once downstairs, I drifted like a shadow through the kitchen door so that I could grab one of Lucinda's sausages wrapped in a buckwheat pancake and be on my way before Aunt Norma nabbed me.

Aunt Harriet beat her to the punch. "Clio, I wonder why Winky is delivering ice this early in the morning." Blissfully unaware that she had sidetracked my escape so that I could unmask further criminal acts, Aunt Harriet pulled aside the kitchen curtain and looked down the street at the iceman's wagon.

"Felicity Langston has been a friend to your Aunt Norma and me since we were children. She and I played duets at the soirées our mother hosted every Wednesday. That was before the Great War, when small social gatherings were the heart and soul of Wolfe Flats. Winky's truck is belching out dreadful puffs of black smoke."

As though nothing had intervened between Aunt Harriet's odd comment about the "soul of Wolfe Flats" and Winky's smoking truck, Aunt Norma stepped through the kitchen door and took up the thread of Aunt Harriet's dialogue with an edgy tone to her voice. "We made a considerable effort to renew that tradition of musical evenings when Delia was a teenager. I remember that evening when we invited several friends to hear Delia perform a Schubert duet with Felicity, but . . ."

"Delia started walking her left hand up and down that keyboard as though she were in a honky-tonk. I think they call that kind of playing boogie-woogie now. It didn't have a name back then. Felicity didn't seem the least bit shocked." Aunt Harriet glanced apologetically across the room at Aunt Norma. "Delia wasn't overly fond of Schubert. Sister and I never held another musical soirée."

"Praise the Lord," I muttered over a hastily downed sausage-in-a-blanket, settling into a chair closest to the back door. I needed to strategize a way to avoid piano lessons with a woman named Felicity who was sure to be joyless. That's the way names worked in Wolfe Flats; they either publically nailed a person's deformities, like Shivers or Winky, or were the polar opposite of their dispositions. Someone named Felicity was sure to be a grouch.

Tucking my bare feet under my chair, I reached for the syrup pitcher and upended it on my buckwheat pancake to get Aunt Norma's attention. The regular sale of sugar ended on April 27th—and War Ration Book

Number One, the "Sugar Book," was distributed the first week of May.

Even with an allowance of half a pound per person per week, Aunt Norma feared that no ships from Hawaii would bring sugar when they were needed to transport soldiers and weapons. "Without sugar, making our summer jams and jellies will be a thing of the past. War means no more jam," she had warned Lucinda.

Although more than a month had passed since Aunt Norma's ominous "no jam" edict, Lucinda—as was her habit—picked up the thread of that previous conversation out of the blue and said: "Japs is responsible for no jam on the table. They cut off all them supply ships when they chased General MacArthur out of the Philippines and left Amaday's daughter Opal behind to nurse soldiers. I suspect Opal is fearin' fer her very life while the general is safe with the kangaroos. I'll sacrifice our last two jars of sand plum jam. Hep ease Amaday's mind."

Clutching the last open jar of sand plum jam in one hand, I dared not question why sacrificing our small store of my favorite jam could in any way help Amaday Terrill's daughter escape the Japanese.

With an enthusiastic nod toward Lucinda, Aunt Norma appeared to be in perfect agreement with her plan to spirit away our only remaining jam to relieve a neighbor's grief. I drooped my mouth into what I thought was a classic despondent expression and shoved the jam jar in Aunt Norma's direction, so that she could share the last smidgen of tart sweetness.

After Aunt Norma's threat to fill my summer with cultural activities, I had spent a sleepless night testing the best arguments for my freedom to explore Wolfe Flats in order to find the 6.4 percent of citizens guilty of homicide out of a population of 1,837. Back in early April—as soon as Mother told me I was being banished to her hometown in Oklahoma—I had gone to the New York Public Library to get crime statistics.

Surely, denizens of Wolfe Flats were no more law-abiding than the rest of the nation. If I eliminated the children, there remained a tidy number of suspects primed for murder.

The threat of criminals on the loose in Wolfe Flats wouldn't sway Aunt Norma. Principles of logic would be the only way to make her backtrack on her plans for my musical education, so I could have the entire summer to suss out murderers.

Reaching across the table for a second buckwheat pancake before I hustled out the back door, I set forth my argument: "I really don't have any aptitude for musical instruments. My skill set is in cartography. I'm thinking of asking Manboy to tutor me in German. If we are invaded by the Third Reich, I'll need to know the language to be an effective spy." I flashed Aunt Norma an innocent smile, confident that she would be impressed with my thirst for learning a second language.

"It's not likely that the Office of Strategic Services will be recruiting children as spies." Aunt Norma clamped down like a dog with a bone on my Mati Hari fantasy as a seductive spy who could outwit the firing squad.

Knowing that I had to capitulate a tad if I wanted to move Aunt Norma off dead center, I said brightly: "Thanks to my old friend Mr. Abrams, I have a fondness for geometry—Euclid, you know, if I'm forced to study the classics," I added, thinking that might throw Aunt Norma off the scent, as I propped my bare feet up on the stretcher board that braced the table's legs.

"Members of this family do not go barefooted in public like peasants. You don't have to wear shoes inside the house or yard. Otherwise, I do not want to see you without them. Get shod, Clio."

As I limped back down the stairs in my vise-like Mary Janes, Aunt Norma added insult to injury. "I will be forced to lock you into your bedroom with bread and water if you don't get yourself down the street to Felicity's house this instant," Aunt Norma said, frowning at the empty syrup pitcher. "You can call her Miss Langston; that's proper since she is your elder by a number of years."

"If you really want to be proper, you shouldn't," Lucinda contradicted Aunt Norma. "During the war, that other war, she married one of them Jocund boys from the West End three days before he shipped out. He didn't make it home, so Felicity took back the name her daddy give her. More uppity. Langston. That certainly ain't a West End name. Not the one that give her daddy heartburn."

Like one of those googly-eyed dolls, I could feel my own eyes beginning to roll. Lucinda could wind out the social fabric of Wolfe County faster than Mrs. Lewin could unfold a bolt of gingham for the poorer customers of Lewin's Department Store.

At that moment, I felt just a frisson of regret for Hedy Lewin, whose only son was roasted in a burning pickup shortly after he put a bullet through my arm. I take full responsibility for Whitey's demise—with just a modicum of pride for my sleuthing. Needless to say, Mrs. Lewin continues to shun me in public to demonstrate her grudge.

"I'm sure that Clio can ferret out local gossip about Felicity's widowed state without our help, Lucinda. Go to your music lesson now, young lady."

Ferret my foot. Aunt Norma purposefully compared me to a weasel just to get my dander up. So, I lollygagged along the sidewalk toward Felicity Langston-Jocund's house just to spite my aunt, dragging a stick along a row of picket fences to annoy any late-sleeping neighbors.

Maybe I hadn't asserted myself strongly enough. Too much fawning, too much toadying to an adult, even if she is a great-aunt, can drive a person haywire, set her moral compass spinning like a top so that nothing seems normal.

CHAPTER 4

"Hey! Wait up, Clio!" Two blocks behind me, I could see my friend Jeremiah Whittaker popping wheelies as he sped up the street. Spinning sideways and bouncing up the curb next to me, Jeremiah blocked the sidewalk.

"I haven't seen you since school's been out. I'm helping at the blacksmith shop in the mornings after I get chores done. Mr. Nebojsa pays me, so Pa says it's OK to help when I earn money." Jeremiah's chest might have puffed out just a tad.

"Marek helps me with math when we take a soda pop break. Actually, he's helping me understand physics. We're having a whale of an interesting time. Marek says the field of physics is the future for boys good in math like me."

That thatch of chestnut hair glistening in the morning sun and those wide-open eyes of my best friend Jeremiah couldn't counteract the force field of electricity buzzing around me: his charge was a red positive and mine was a blue negative.

"A future for boys skilled in math? What about girls?" I could feel testiness erupting like hives after I'd eaten walnuts.

"You, too. Clio. Marek says you're the best girl at math he's ever taught." *There was that qualifier again. Taking the edge off but not quite removing the stigma of gender. I shouldn't be surprised. Wolfe Flats segregated its schools, neighborhoods, churches, and drinking fountains by skin color. You couldn't expect them to put boys and girls on a level playing field. They had even managed to segregate the future of physics. That took some doing.*

"Why don't you come to the blacksmith shop with me. Say hello to Marek and his dad? They said they haven't seen you for a coon's age."

I know for a fact that neither Marek nor Mr. Nebojsa said that.

As Czech refugees, "Coon's age" wasn't in their lexicon. Mr. Nebojsa's son Marek speaks excellent English. He substituted for Mrs. Wallace when Jeremiah gave her a bouquet wrapped with poison ivy—after she made him swallow a wad of tobacco in front of our class. Jeremiah said he'd swallow an entire pack of Red Man to keep Marek as our teacher.

No such luck. Mrs. Wallace had returned to the classroom with chalky calamine coating her nose and cheeks, and we were back to doing stupid story problems in math. The last woman killed by Whitey Lewin was Mrs. Wallace's niece. Frankly, I don't think she gave her missing niece a second thought, until I found her bones in that well. Then, Mrs. Wallace trotted out her slinky black dress.

The school board wouldn't hire a teacher full-time with "foreign credentials," even a war hero like Marek. After a German Messerschmitt had branded Marek with a red-puckered scar that ran the length of the right side of his face and had given him a permanent limp, he and his father left England for Oklahoma and opened a blacksmith shop in Wolfe Flats.

"Why Wolfe Flats?" I had asked Mr. Neboja, after he and Marek became two of my good friends.

"It's about as far from the Germans and Japanese as we could go," Mr. Neboja had shouted over the roar of the piston bellows he was using to fire up the forge. Then he had flashed a grimy smile. "We were flung out of heaven like Hephaestus, the blacksmith of the gods. Wolfe Flats was as good as any place to land."

Later, Marek told me that his father just liked teasing me. Mr. Neboja's cousin lived in Ardmore, twenty-five miles up the road, and had heard that the only blacksmith in Wolfe Flats had to retire with serious eye problems. "Papa and I both needed work. The war needs metal workers, but Papa likes working independently. So, we chose a rural community that needed a blacksmith. A safe, bucolic place."

I had to go look up the word "bucolic," although I nodded and plastered on my intelligent face for Marek. Fields of Indian daises and wild milkweed make a stunning carpet of the most glorious oranges and yellows on the prairie. But Wolfe Flats is anything but bucolic, as Mr. Neboja and Marek can attest. They had both been involved in my rescue and helped cause Whitey's fiery crash.

"Are you woolgathering, Clio?"

"Am I what?"

"Daydreaming. Spaced out. Vacating the old noodle." Jeremiah giggled. "I just asked if you'd like to come out to the farm tomorrow. Pa said it's OK if your aunts agree. Think they will? Pa says we can pick you up when he brings the eggs and milk into town tomorrow. Pa got a letter from Mom yesterday, and he's in a good mood." Jeremiah's freckled face flushed with pleasure.

Just like my mother, Jeremiah's mother had dashed off to the war. *Unlike* my mother, who was interviewing soldiers in foxholes and writing about the misbehavior of Nazis, Jeremiah's mother, a botanist with expertise in fungi, was somewhere in the South Pacific checking out foot rot. Sensitive to Jeremiah's feelings about our mothers' very different careers, I smiled back at him.

"I'd love to see your farm tomorrow. I can talk Aunt Norma into it, since I'm doing exactly what she wants me to do today." I squinted up at the sun that was hiding behind darkening clouds. "I'd better get going. Felicity Langston is giving me a piano lesson this morning."

Just as I turned to sprint on down the street, I could hear a snort of laughter. "You taking piano lessons from Felicity Langston? That woman is over-the-top strange."

Did that snide remark bother me? *Not at all.* When I first met Jeremiah less than three months ago on my first day of school, he spent every recess scraping the mortar between bricks on the side of the building so that the entire wall would collapse in a strong windstorm. On my first day at school, Jeremiah swallowed a wad of tobacco in front of a classroom of awe-struck kids, without flinching.

Later, I joined Jeremiah every day at recess, scraping mortar as though the furies were after me. Strange is not an unusual word to describe people in Wolfe Flats. Shaking my head to clear away some odd notions that bombarded me, I picked up the pace down the remaining block toward the house of Mrs. Felicity Langston Jocund. I stopped dead in my tracks and stared at what waited on her porch.

The tightly clustered red curls atop a rather woebegone face were the exact color of the crimson wool on the Raggedy Ann doll our New York neighbor, Mrs. Abrams, made me as a going-away present when Mother hauled me down to New York City's Grand Central Station and away from civilization as I knew it.

The odd, limp doll with garish wool curls and shoe-button eyes reminded me of myself that morning we boarded the train for Wolfe Flats. I had been trying to hide a shameful expression—scorn that Mrs. Abrams would give an eleven-year-old a baby toy and anger that Mother was taking me away from everything I loved.

As I crept up the sidewalk toward a modest Victorian house painted three shades of olive green, the Raggedy Ann standing on the front porch thrust out her hand with an audible sigh. "I was so fearful that you wouldn't come, Clio. Your mother often played hooky from her lessons. Even when she made it on time, she'd rather talk than practice. She called it 'interviewing,' preparing for her journalistic career."

Swinging the porch screen door wide, Felicity bent over with a great, sweeping bow to direct me past potted eruptions of Boston ferns: "Enter the inner sanctum, Clio."

The roots of her red curls were as white as Aunt Harriet's. The skin on her thin neck reminded me of the curdled film on Lucinda's clabber. Behind those shoe-button eyes brewed mischief of some sort.

"I made hot chocolate for us and cake with butter cream frosting. We can visit before we start your lesson. I want to know all about Delia, about her war effort. Your aunts are so close-mouthed about family. They always have been, even as girls. Sit down, Clio, and help yourself to treats." She pointed toward a Victorian loveseat flanked by two red-velvet, spoon-backed chairs, much too posh for me.

The bronze bust of a surly man glowered at me from a pedestal near one of the red chairs. "He looks like . . ."

"Beethoven. A man of genius. Papa bought that for me when I was only ten years old as a reminder that I needed to practice under a watchful eye."

I had just started to say that he looks like a man with severe gastric problems, but was, happily, saved from my observation by the dotty expression on Felicity's face as she stroked an excess of beetling brow on the statue's head.

I edged next to the high armrest on the peach satin loveseat to get a closer look-see at the adjacent low table. The silver coffeepot with steam rising from its spout wasn't nearly as enticing as a huge, iced cake, banked by two stacks of glistening fudge squares.

Like a bee off to the hive, I buzzed over toward entrapment, turning my back to a gleaming black Steinway that took up half the room. Before I grabbed a month's ration of sugar, I remembered my manners, trying to sort out what Lucinda had told me about Miss Langston's widowed state. "Do I call you Miss Langston? Or Mrs. Jocund?

"Neither. Call me Felicity. Not Felicity Jocund. When I first went out with Luther, your Aunt Norma told me that I'd be a tautology if I ever married him."

Knowingly, I nodded my head. I'd need to look up "tautology" in the dictionary to see what Aunt Norma had against her friend marrying a man called Luther Jocund. I reached for a second slice of cake to fortify myself in case tautology meant something really bad.

"My honeymoon lasted only three days. My husband, Luther, left with the other two Musketeers to train at Camp Lewis near Tacoma, Washington," Felicity reported with a deadpan expression. "Norma and I learned that our Musketeers would leave for France sometime in mid-July of 1918."

If a ragdoll could blush, she did. "We tried to hide our heartaches behind flippancy. We made stupid jokes about the characters in Dumas's novel."

Felicity stared into space for a moment, and then snapped her head back toward me. "Norma said she'd never forgive herself for that silly quote. I don't think she ever has. Our last words to the dead haunt us forever."

Felicity pursed her mouth as though no silly quote would ever come out of it.

"Have some more cake, Clio. I don't know what got into me. Here I am telling you sad stories that happened a quarter of a century ago, and you must be worried sick about your mother, wondering where Delia might be in a war that's happening right now. Let's forget war. Let's sit on the piano bench." Felicity hopped up and said: "Bring your cake. I'll show you some easy scales."

I watched Felicity moving across the room, just like a rag doll, arms akimbo and knees gyrating in diverse directions. I held my breath in amazement as she made it to the piano. The moment she sat down, her body collected itself, like fall leaves raked into a perfect mound. An invisible wire traced down her stiffening spine and brought her arms into perfect alignment. Her fingers chased an eerie melody up and down the keyboard. "I don't know which scales you prefer, Clio, but I find an A Major scale most comforting."

Sugar overload must have hit me as the time-for-truth-telling popped open the left hemisphere of my brain. "Truthfully, Felicity, I like to listen to music. I like to dance to music. I even like a couple of those Methodist hymns. But, I'd rather be drawn and quartered than spend time practicing the piano. Especially that classical stuff."

"Exactly your mother's opinion." Her eyes hazed over, as though monkey business fulminated behind them, not daring to surface.

Felicity patted the tufted piano bench. "Sit by me, Clio. That *was* your mother's opinion until she realized that Beethoven's 32nd Sonata has the same heavy syncopation of that eight to the bar she was hearing in those juke joints down by the river."

She paused to release a half-hearted sigh. "It was a bit tacky of your mother to turn our Schubert duet into her version of boogie-woogie. Norma said she spoiled the soirée. That night marked the end of Delia's music lessons."

With a flourish, Felicity chased an oddly comforting scheme of notes up the keyboard. "That's the A Major scale. But we'll start with C here in the middle of 88 keys. Place your thumb here, Clio. Just let it rest and move your other fingers gently against the keys. Your fingers are long. I think you'll be a natural."

I listened. I thumped. I liked the touching the ivories. They were real. As I was walking my right hand up the keyboard, I had an uneasy feeling that I was fondling the tusks of dead elephants. So, I moved my fingers up to the black keys for comfort. After about fifteen minutes of scales, my eyes began to cross, so I stretched my toes down toward the brass pedals, forcing the entire keyboard to shift at my will.

"I think that's enough for today, Clio. I'm sending this little book on scales home with you. Half an hour a day on your Aunt Harriet's piano should be more than enough to satisfy your Aunt Norma that your intentions are good. You won't turn into Horowitz with that schedule," Felicity added, with the flash of a wink.

Reaching for my hand, she said: "Let's sit on the front porch swing for a spell, before it gets too hot. Something is brewing with that purple cloud mass to the north. Rain would be nice."

CHAPTER 5

N ow that I had softened up my new music teacher with fifteen minutes of pounding the keys, and we had retreated to the front porch swing, I put on my wistful expression. It was time to pry into that little slip Felicity had made when she said: "Our Musketeers," with a reference to some quote of Aunt Norma's that she had regretted.

"Would you tell me about your Musketeers? Who were they? Why did you call them that? What happened to them?"

"They were classmates of mine and Norma's in high school: Lawrence Bresant, Luther Jocund, and Lester Smith. We might have called them the three "L's," but back then Dumas's *Three Musketeers* was on our required reading list; those boys seemed like the characters in the novel," she giggled softly.

"Lawrence, always called Larry, was, of course, Athos, the aristocratic nobleman, who had been married to the wicked Lady de Winter. Norma claimed that she could imagine herself as the seductive Milady de Winter with a *fleur de lis* branded on her shoulder, marking her as a felon, an expert with poisons."

Noting my raised eyebrows as I tried to imagine Aunt Norma having any life outside the Methodist Church and her zillions of committees, Felicity tentatively touched my wounded arm. "We were just silly girls, Clio, making up lives that seemed more glamorous that we could imagine. But your Aunt Norma was fearless as a girl. She rode her horse at breakneck speed and jumped any fence in sight."

Trying to imagine Aunt Norma hoisting her arthritic knees up to straddle a horse taxed my imaginary powers. I wanted to hear more about Aunt Norma, but Felicity was back in the swing of her story, as she urged the porch swing to move at a fast clip.

"My Luther was Aramis, brought up in a monastery, wanting to be a priest, not a swordsman. That left Lester Smith to be Porthos, the Musketeer who loved fancy clothes and good food. Come to think of it, he still does. He wears that ridiculous trilby hat and a cravat instead of a tie to church."

"He didn't . . . I thought they all . . ." I stuttered, trying to sort out how a soldier could rise from a grave in France to wander around Wolfe Flats wearing a trilby.

"You thought Porthos died in the War? The one in Dumas's novel married a rich woman and lived off her wealth. Lester Smith, our Porthos, wasn't so lucky. He came back from the battlefield to take over his father's feed and seed store, but not before he had said the wrong thing to Norma."

"What? What wrong thing?"

"I don't know. Norma wouldn't say. After he came back from the war, Lester got off the train and went to her house. He hasn't been invited back. I'm getting ahead of myself, Clio." Felicity shook her head in frustration. "I was almost back there in that time when we were so young, with no idea of what was coming in the war that was supposed to end all wars."

I took over the rocking of the swing, digging my heels into the front porch boards to ease the pain of tight, patent leather shoes grinding my toes into a bloody pulp. Felicity took up her story again.

"As I told you, the three boys, Norma, and I were classmates. Harriet was three grades behind us. The Bresants and Clowers had been friends for generations—lived in the Territory long before statehood. The Bresants owned the bank. The Clowers owned half the town. Larry and Norma were just a given back then. You didn't see one without the other. Larry was her beau." She paused and stared into a space that was not of this time and place.

My Aunt Norma had a boyfriend? I tried to control my rolling eyes so I could keep Felicity on this interesting track. "So, what happened to Aunt Norma and this Larry person?"

"College happened first. Then the war. Larry had no interest in being a banker like his father. He liked languages, perhaps because his grandfather was French. He went to Oklahoma University that summer, right after he graduated, to get a head start with a tutor in Latin before the fall semester started."

"And Aunt Norma?" I knew that she tried to get my mother to go to the university in Norman instead of New York to keep her close to Wolfe Flats. Mother didn't talk much about life with her aunts, but she did talk about getting away from them, very far away. They had done something to make her really mad, but she wouldn't tell me what it was. I got an earful about it from the serial killer just before he tossed me in the well.

After my mother was attacked, her aunts—fearful of public exposure—refused to file a police report. If they had, Whitey Lewin might have been caught and jailed before he murdered three young women.

The steady rocking of the swing caused my mind to drift—something that rarely happens to me—as I remembered Mother putting up a weekly typewritten quote on the door of our Frigidaire. "This one is the most important one, Clio. Alexander Hamilton: 'The first duty of society is justice.'"

Mother had frowned as she used our last roll of cellophane tape to place the quote squarely in front of me. "We have a duty to justice, Clio. That's something about which your aunts and I could never agree."

At the time, Mother's comment about my aunts had sailed right past me, but the frown between her eyes lasted until one of her headaches came on, as they often did when she talked about those Oklahoma aunts of hers.

To lighten things up, I remember finding a quote by Oscar Wilde and pasting it over the Hamilton quote. Oscar's "Be yourself; everyone else is already taken" had sent us into spasms of giggles for a week, until it fell off and that prissy Hamilton quote underneath brought on another headache.

"Norma's father was determined to put some miles between Larry and his daughter, so he sent Norma off to college in Denton, Texas." Felicity's soft voice broke my reverie. For a moment, I flashed to the miles between Mother and me—about 4,300 as the crow flies. She was probably questioning Scots about kilts being banned from the battlefield, not thinking at all about me. I shifted my attention back to Felicity.

"Girls, like your Aunt Norma and I, were expected to get more than a high school education before we considered marriage. My father disliked Luther and hustled me off to the teachers' college in Denton with Norma. Norma and I were both exiled, so to speak. Neither of us had any interest in becoming teachers. But, North Texas State Normal College had a good music program and was implementing baccalaureate degrees. Your Aunt Norma was an enthusiastic reader. She still is."

I restrained a heavy intake of breath and steadied the front porch swing. People in Wolfe Flats had such a penchant for digression that it took all of my willpower to keep a conversation from wandering into the middle of nowhere. "The Musketeers, Felicity. What happened to them?"

Felicity's head wobbled a bit, as though the threads holding it in place were wearing thin. "Oh, the boys. Luther and Lester enrolled at Oklahoma University for the fall semester. They would naturally follow Larry. No one thought too much about the war then. It was being fought far away, across the Atlantic. President Wilson wanted peace. Then he didn't."

She paused, twisting her head, as a brisk breeze moved those tight little red curls like lollipops, rooted to her scalp by white paper stems.

"Luther's parents were farmers in the West End. Well-off farmers. No kin to those no-account Reeves out there." She paused, as though I might need time to sort out the social classes of Wolfe County. I nodded affably, as though I knew those "no-account Reeves" couldn't possibly be kin to Luther.

"Luther's folks wanted him to go to the university to 'better himself.' That's what they told me. Imagine that. Who could have been better than Luther?" She waved distractedly at the iceman, who had just stopped his pickup at the house across the street and was balancing a giant block of ice on a leather pad across his back.

"You'd think Mrs. Davis would invest in a refrigerator after all this time. But, no. She still has an icebox. Smelly old thing. Like blinky milk."

"You were telling me about the Musketeers. Aunt Norma's beau. Your husband, Luther." *This woman really needed to focus.*

"Well, when Luther started his junior year at Wolfe Flats High, his folks sent him into town on his mare that could sugar foot like no horse I've ever seen. That's a kind of trot that makes a ride a comfort. Back then, the black-smith offered students who lived out of town the use of a corral for their horses for next to nothing. Luther had been going to a small school out by Rubottom. His folks wanted a better school for him."

And I wanted to know why Aunt Norma sat in her bedroom crying over an old buckram-bound journal.

"So the three Musketeers went to college in Norman?" I asked brightly, although I didn't give a fig about their education.

"Yes, after they became best friends in high school. Luther used to stay over at Larry's house, if the weather was bad. He was in our drama club and played right guard on the basketball team. So, he spent more and more time at Larry's house his senior year. And more and more time with me," she added, with a sly grin.

"So, they all went away to college together, and then what?" I wasn't my mother's daughter for nothing. I had the "who" down pat. It was hard to nail down the "what" with a Raggedy Ann who seemed to have cotton wool between her ears.

"Then, the war happened. The Great War. Camp Lewis sent out the clarion call, and our boys couldn't ignore the sound of a trumpet. So they left that summer in 1918. Larry came back to see Norma, and Luther came to see me. He was honest to a fault. Except."

Felicity's dark eyes flushed with tears as the word "except" hung in the air, solemn as the knell of a far-off church bell. "He neglected to tell me before we eloped that we'd have only three days of married life. He said that he felt obliged to serve. He couldn't have known what it was like over there. Those naïve boys thought they were going to ship out, defeat the Austro-Hungarian Empire within weeks, and head back home—not slog through muddy trenches to their deaths."

As her head drifted sideways, I reached for Felicity's hand and squeezed it. She squeezed back.

"You have worries enough with your mother overseas, Clio. She didn't have to make that choice, but, knowing Delia, that's exactly what she would do. Not my Luther. Those war posters of Uncle Sam in a white stovepipe hat, pointing a finger and saying 'Enlist' wouldn't have persuaded him."

Felicity sniffed and wiped her eyes with the same kind of dimity handkerchief that Aunt Harriet carries, useless for nose blowing. "Luther showed me a poster that had convinced him to go. It depicted a soldier standing on the island of England, reaching across the Atlantic to a young man and saying: 'Come, lad. Slip across and help.'"

Felicity shoved against the floor with her feet and sent the swing into great swoops that caused the eye screws to scream against the beaded board porch ceiling. "Luther loved Wolfe County. He had no desire to go abroad on a troop ship. He got seasick in a rowboat on Red River. Luther could have better served the war effort by working on his father's farm. He was a farm boy at heart. Not a traveler."

Felicity spoke with nostalgic fondness when she talked about a boy named Luther, as though he had taken a wrong turn and wandered out of the county by mistake. She was a rag doll again, collapsing into the porch swing.

"You mentioned a third Musketeer, Felicity. Lester Smith. The feed and seed man's son. What happened to him?"

The look Felicity gave me was troubled, but she soldiered on, whacking the floor with the soles of her feet as the swing charged back and forth, and I began to feel as queasy as Luther in a rowboat.

"Lester came home. He told me where he thought Luther might have been buried, in a grave with many others. He'd just been to see Norma. I don't know what he told her. He gave her some kind of journal that Larry kept."

"Like a diary?"

"I don't know. Lester said he picked it up and hid it in his knapsack when they took Larry away."

"What do you mean? Who took him away? I thought he died."

Felicity planted her feet, bringing the porch swing to a screeching halt. "He did. We're just not sure how. Something to do with a German, just a boy, he found in Belleau Wood in France. All I know is that Norma hasn't spoken to Lester in twenty-four years, not since that day he gave her Larry's book."

She eyed me with a sheepish expression. "You are most certainly Delia's daughter. You have her ability to draw out information, Clio. I haven't talked about the war in years. It was a terrible time. Now, we're doing the same war over again. I shouldn't say anything else. I don't think Norma would want me to say as much as I have."

Felicity couldn't stop now. Not with something fishy happening to Aunt Norma's beau on a battlefield in France.

Felicity Langston, aka Mrs. Luther Jocund, collected her arms and legs, and rose as though a puppet master might be pulling her heavenward. She stared down at me. "I'll tell you one other thing, because I find it puzzling and troublesome. Norma only talked to me once about her reaction when Larry told her he had enlisted and would soon be leaving for France."

Holding the swing chain to steady her legs, Felicity bent over and whispered as though no one else should hear her. "Norma told me that a quote from *The Three Musketeers* popped into her head and settled in her mouth like ashes, and she said it to Larry: 'You are very amiable, no doubt, but would be charming if you would only depart.'"

As the screen door closed behind Felicity, I sat on the porch swing without so much as a wiggle, wishing this conversation could have continued. Maybe my investigation into the three Musketeers had made Felicity too sad to talk to me.

Usually, making an effort to be sociable in Wolfe Flats can be tedious work for someone like me who thrives on purposeful dialogue. But not here. Not with this woman with eyes that catalogued more pages of secrets than they might ever reveal.

"Clio, I wrapped the last of the fudge for you to take home." Felicity pushed the screen door open and handed me three squares, wrapped in wax paper. "Next week? Same time? I'll expect progress on those scales."

She touched my cheek hesitantly, as though I might rebuff her touch. "We had a good visit this morning. You are so like your mother. Delia and I were good friends, just as you and I will be."

CHAPTER 6

As I trotted towards home on Choctaw Street, my Mary Janes were murdering my feet. When my everyday Buster Brown shoes crushed my toes past recognition, I had pushed them to the back of my wardrobe and brought out my Sunday best shoes.

Now, a growth spurt in my phalanges and metatarsals was crippling the best sleuth in Wolfe Flats. Without ration coupons for new shoes, I would soon join the ranks of those Chinese women with bound feet, who lost any desire to walk. All this rationing, this demand for coupons to buy shoes, must be a Nazi plot. A cheery thought popped up. I could ask Manboy Muller, our neighbor, who had helped Jeremiah rescue me from the bottomless well.

A lawyer by trade, who was fluent in German, Manboy had been recruited to interview incoming German prisoners of war over at Camp Houze. Camp Houze was a POW camp just across the Red River that separated Oklahoma from Texas. Manboy could sneak in a few questions about this rationing business for me. In the war footage I saw at our local theater, those Nazi Storm troopers wore handsome knee boots. You didn't see any of them limping around in too-tight shoes.

I circled around the house to the back door and shuffled off my shoes on the stoop. Gingerly pulling open the back screen door, I listened for the usual morning sounds: Aunt Harriet on the piano; Lucinda banging pots and pans; and, Aunt Norma on the phone, reading the riot act to unruly committee members.

For once, the house was strangely silent, infused with an odor like singed hair. Aunt Harriet's old-fashioned curling tongs lay ajar on the kitchen cabinet. She had been torturing her locks again.

"If you want curly hair, Harriet, go down to the beauty shop for one of those Victory perms. You are getting third-degree burns on your scalp with that iron. It's downright dangerous," Aunt Norma had cautioned her sister.

For once, I was on Aunt Norma's side. Fried hair was not attractive. I picked up the curling iron by one thin tong and shoved it under the counter, far behind Lucinda's galvanized zinc canning pot.

Another big pot simmered on the back burner. A note with Aunt Norma's careful cursive script held center stage on the counter: *"We've gone to see a farmer in the West End about produce and dairy deliveries to the house. Lucinda left chicken soup on the stove for your lunch. I expect you to start on the summer reading list I gave you. We should be back by two o'clock."*

Oh yes. Aunt Norma's reading program. After her initial tizzy over something she caught me reading last week, she came up with two pages of what she called "the Classics."

"We don't want your mind stagnating during the summer, Clio. Your Aunt Harriet and I will take turns discussing these books with you. I've put a little star by the ones that I think are most important, but you can decide. We won't require written book reports," she had added with one of those saccharine smiles to let me know that she and I weren't on the same page.

We weren't even close to the same book. The first book on the list with a little star was John Wesley's *A Collection of Different Forms of Prayer for Every Day in the Week.* I usually spent six days of the week figuring out how to avoid the Methodist Church on Sunday.

I had already read all of Jane Austen on the list. I might try Harriet Beecher Stowe's *Uncle Tom's Cabin* again. Mother and I read it out loud and giggled in all the wrong places, as Eliza leapt across ice floes to save her child from being sold down the river. Those heavenly visions that came to the slaves just in the nick of time seemed a bit overdone for people who had spent their lives in a hellish place. However, what got me into this pickle with Aunt Norma made *Uncle Tom's Cabin* look like great literature.

When I was casually flipping through the magazine rack at Selvidge Drug Store, I felt compelled to buy a fat, pulp magazine called *Ranchland Romances* for fifteen cents. On the cover, a bosomy blonde straddled a bale of hay. She exhibited no obvious discomfort as stalks of straw skewered her bare legs. Frankly, my main interest was to find out why this young woman was wearing cowboy boots and a skimpy bathing suit inside a barn.

The first story was downright silly, with cattle thieves rustling around the clock and the rancher's daughter dithering over the villain, rather than the handsome hired help. I wouldn't have read another stupid page, but Aunt Norma snatched it away and held it aloft by two fingers, as though I had brought *Yersinia pestis bacterium,* the plague, to our house.

"Trash!" Aunt Norma's "shush" at the end of that word rattled the rafters more than the thump of the magazine landing dead center in the waste paper can.

The next morning, a tidy list of books, ranging from Austen to Wesley, was propped by my bowl of oatmeal. So far, I had taken all of the books on the list from Aunt Norma's considerable library and stacked them by my bed to demonstrate just a tad of compliance on my part. The books made a nice bedside stand for my evening cocoa.

Glancing up at the Ingraham Regulator oak case kitchen clock with smudged Roman numerals, I noted that it was only 10:30 in the morning. The piano lesson had not been a waste of time. I usually considered any effort to be social with the natives as a tedious undertaking. But not with Felicity, not sitting on the porch swing with a woman who had eyes the color of buckeyes that hid much more than they revealed.

Felicity had given me names, dates, places, and a considerable puzzle to solve about the death of Aunt Norma's beau, Lawrence. I just needed to double check Felicity's statements with a reliable source—Sally Tolliver, *Wolfe Flats Messenger* reporter extraordinaire.

Sally, my mother's childhood friend, might know what really happened to the Musketeers who didn't return to Wolfe Flats. Sally and I had developed a close relationship after I gave her a feature story about the hours I spent in Whitey Lewin's well, continuing to plot his destruction, while wondering if I would survive.

Actually, I had to give some credit to Jeremiah and Manboy for their daring rescue of me from a well full of body parts of murdered girls. Manboy's expert driving saved us, but not before I took a bullet in the arm.

Giving Sally the scoop, with all the embellishments that only a budding reporter could provide, had endeared me to her forever. Now, it was payback time. Time to hustle down to Sally's office at the newspaper, cover my tracks from Aunt Norma, and make it back home by two o'clock so Aunt Norma could find me in bondage to Harriet Beecher Stowe.

Looking down at the dirty socks on my feet, I knew that I had to make a major adjustment to my Mary Janes if I were to follow Aunt Norma's edict about wearing shoes in public places.

Taking Lady Macbeth's words "Screw your courage to the sticking-place" to heart, I spooned soup juice into a bowl, dumped it down the drain, and left a dirty bowl beside the sink as evidence that I had eaten lunch as directed. Then, I unwrapped Felicity's three fudge squares and chomped away. Heading out the back door, I snatched up my Mary Janes and talked to those shoes, apologetically, about the joy of transformation.

CHAPTER 7

The two-story garage behind my aunts' house held a wondrous supply of rusted tools, menacing clippers, hoes, and one thirty-inch rip saw. An old post vice, that hadn't been used for a century, was clamped to a worktable covered with sawdust. Easing one shoe, toe-up, between the four-inch jaws of the vice, I sawed carefully through patent leather that had seen better days, and peeled a slab down to the sole. The next one was easier.

The well-worn strap held my foot in place; the ends of my toes made comforting contact with the pavement, as I headed downtown toward the newspaper office. Sycamore trees, with meaty, green leaves the size of a coolie's hat, flapped in the mid-morning breeze, as purple clouds provided a fierce backdrop to towering grain elevators north of town.

Walking down the streets of Wolfe Flats, I felt a sudden surge of affection for this flat landscape. No skyscrapers interrupted the horizons—the sweep of wheat fields surged on and on beyond the city limits.

Inside the town of Wolfe Flats, spaces closed themselves into postage-stamped lawns, cordoned off by rows of zinnias, marigolds, and limp dahlias, too modest to lift their heads. The odor of cut grass perfumed the day. In the distance, to the south, a whisper of hilly land sloped into shades of green.

In my real home of New York City, tall buildings formed giant canyons where you could lose yourself if you weren't watching the street signs. Buildings there were so tall and expensive that they held offices, not households of people. No tire swings dangled from shade trees on those streets.

In Wolfe Flats, a few big houses congregated at the end of one block; then, houses tapered off into modest bungalows. Some had little blue stars—or the occasional, dreaded gold one—on felt banners in the windows for sons in the war or sons who would never return from the war. These stars marked a visible absence. Not the dark hole my mother had left when she rushed off to write about the war.

I tried to curl my toes upward as I walked, imagining that I was a court jester with long, pointy-toed shoes, not shod in these butchered Mary Janes, with wads of wet socks where sleek patent leather once protected my toes.

Just as I neared the end of the residential block, a blast of wind whipped the diseased elms along Choctaw Street, as though trying to perk up their maimed branches. An old woman ripping billowing sheets from a clothesline planted her heels into the ground, skidding forward like a jumper, wrestling with his parachute.

I paused, ready to help the woman, just as an image flashed into my head of Mother, as a paratrooper, leaping out of a British Whitley bomber. The woman snapped the sheet into flat, neat folds, shook her head at me, and pointed to the threatening sky. So, I hustled on down the street, hoping Mother knew how to scrunch up a parachute quickly, so the enemy couldn't spot it.

Just before taking a right-hand turn toward the *Wolfe Flats Messenger* building, I made a detour to check out the World War I Memorial, a brass plate with a roster of names, plastered low on the wall of the County Courthouse.

I traced my fingers along the words: "In grateful memory of the men who gave their lives for freedom and honor in the Great War." Just below, five names marched across in three straight lines. No Lawrence Bresant. Aunt Norma's beau was missing. But beside a Harris and Henry, the name of Luther Jocund blazed, as though a rag doll with the fingers of a pianist polished it daily.

Feeling sadder than I wanted to about something that had happened before I was even a molecule in the universe, I walked up half a dozen steps to peer through the plate glass window of the newspaper office. There was Sally, at her desk, banging away on her old Royal.

She'd be happy to see me, the person who nailed Whitey Lewin as the serial killer, brought about his fiery death, and helped rid the town of a worthless sheriff. Not many girls could survive near-death, as I did, surrounded by floating tibias of murdered women, and perk up to give a top-notch interview.

"Clio, get in here this instant! Can't you see that sky? It could be full of funnels!" Sally flung open the door, looped me tightly against her, and glanced into those dark clouds behind me with a fearful face.

"Come on down to the press room; it's no storm shelter, but it is halfway into the ground, safer than standing by these windows."

Clattering beside me down a short flight of stairs, in sensible, black suede, lace-up shoes with high heels, Sally stopped and stared at my feet. "Butchering your shoes out of boredom, Clio? It's summer. Tell your aunts to get you some decent sandals."

"I outgrew both pairs of my shoes. Aunt Norma says I can't go barefoot in public. Mother didn't leave me a ration book for shoes," I added missishly.

"Your Aunt Norma can get you shoes without coupons. Lewin's Department Store just got in a nice selection of summer sandals." Sally halted, took a breather, and offered a retraction. "Considering your recent run-in with the Lewins, I think you'd better shop in Ardmore. If your aunts won't take you, I will."

In front of us, the two Linotype machines sat like hulking word monsters, hibernating, until the operators awakened them. I knew exactly how that 90-character keyboard worked as the operator entered the text; then the machine took over, humming, grinding. The presses in the back of the basement were quiet this morning. I loved to see pages whipping out like a flashcard shuffle. All those words. Magical.

Most of all, I longed to see my name in 72-point type, the biggest that the *Messenger* could make. Sally told me they were saving that sized headline for the end of the war—or when the Nazis invaded, whichever came first.

Sally pointed to the linotype operator's stool, knowing how I loved to be so near a machine that could spew out enough words to fill an entire newspaper. "Now, what brings you out on a stormy day like today, Clio?"

"An A major scale," I responded testily. "Music lessons from Felicity Langston. Aunt Norma is forcing me to learn."

A happy thought hit me. "Felicity makes good fudge and told me things, very interesting things, that I thought you might verify."

"Things? Like what?" That same crinkly, curious expression I had often seen on Mother's face lifted the corners of Sally's eyes.

I needed to get answers, not give them. "I think we were talking about books, about Jane Austen. Jane says there are secrets in all families." I smiled with what I hoped was a coy expression.

"Yeah, and Ben Franklin says 'Three may keep a secret if two of them are dead.'" Sally matched my coy expression with a coy expression. "My brain jingles with quotes. I'm like a bird that picks up bits of things and tucks them away. I manage to slip them into an article now and then. Exactly what secrets are troubling you, Clio?"

I might as well let her have it. Reporters have a way of prying things out of the unwary. "Lawrence Bresant's name is not on the War Memorial. It's missing."

"Not missing. It was purposefully left off. That's something no one ever talks about around here. With old families like the Bresants, staying on the QT rules." She paused and gave me a quizzical look. "He and your Aunt Norma were close friends. What exactly did Felicity tell you?"

"Just about the classmates that she and Aunt Norma called the Musketeers, who went off to war and were killed in Belleau Wood in France. Not much really." *Like a savvy interrogator, I was keeping my cards close to my chest. Mother says to let the person being interviewed fill in all the blanks.*

"World War I was a quarter of a century ago, Clio. Delia and I were just children. However, I've done a bit of research about how that war affected Wolfe County." Sally launched those overstuffed archives in her brain at me full force: "Of those 1,811 Americans killed at Belleau Wood, five were from Wolfe County; twenty-five percent of the men between the ages of eighteen and thirty were serving in the military; between the mustard gas and the mud . . ."

My eyes were glazing over, so rudeness intervened: "I can read about that in a history book, Sally. I want to know some particulars about Aunt Norma's beau, Larry Bresant. How was he killed? Why isn't his name on the county memorial? Felicity told me that one of the Musketeers came to see Aunt Norma after the war, to give her something that belonged to Larry, and she hasn't spoken to that man since then, even though he lives right here in Wolfe Flats."

"Yours are the same questions that Delia asked when she was about your age. She'd heard rumors about the Bresant boy and her aunt. His folks moved away from Wolfe Flats after the war, so Delia couldn't question them. Believe me, with her nose for news, she would have." Sally shook her head slowly, as though trying to dislodge the notion of "nose for news" from the idea of nosiness.

"I can't quite visualize him as a Musketeer, but I know the man and a little bit about the situation. Lester Smith is a World War I vet who goes to the Methodist Church. Norma has been snubbing him for over two decades. That's my church, too. Anger between members of the congregation bothers me. It's not Christian."

I wasn't Christian either, although I was considering baptism in the Methodist Church so that I could have a sip out of those tiny glasses of communion wine that went around the first Sunday of every month. Aunt Harriet told me that the drink was "magic" and would keep me from "the dark place."

Terrified by those gap-jawed monsters in Hieronymus Bosch's painting of Christ entering Hell in the Metropolitan Museum, I was willing to try anything as simple as grape juice and crumbles of soda crackers to ward off monsters in the afterlife.

Sally stretched back against the wall and heaved a painful sigh, as though I might be giving the torture rack one twist too many. "I've been told that Lester Smith had a crush on your Aunt Norma in high school, but she and Larry had been a couple since the beginning of time. Personally, I think Norma's angry because Lester came back from the war instead of Larry. Why don't you ask your Aunt Harriet?"

I fixed a gimlet eye on Sally. Aunt Harriet often let tidbits of information slip, but never about her sister. Thoughts might pop in and out of her head willy-nilly, but never about family. Those memories were locked away in cupboards under that frothy white hair.

"Bad idea, Clio. Best not to trouble your Aunt Harriet about things that happened so long ago." She stopped and gave me a quizzical look.

"Don't you ever stop?"

"Stop what?"

"What you are doing now. Interrrogating."

I reflected a minute before answering. "Nope. I'm basically a curious person. When people try to hide things from me, I become more inquisitive."

"Did you ever consider that some people keep secrets for a good reason?"

"Sure. Like Whitey. He got a *secret* thrill out of keeping secrets about girls in a well."

Sally flushed bright as a beet. "Oh well. I might as well tell you what I know, Clio. Whatever happened to Lawrence and a young German in Belleau Wood probably had nothing to do with Lester Smith. He simply brought Norma the bad news. As a reporter, I can identify with someone hating the bearer." She peered past me out a grubby window at ground level. "I don't like the look of that greenish sky. The wind was blowing hard; now, it's too quiet."

CHAPTER 8

The shuffle of footsteps sounded just above us, and the hint of a shadow I had been watching by the doorway arch shifted. Turning toward me, looking a bit embarrassed, Sally blurted out: "Your Aunt Norma is a very private person, Clio. When she headed up the fundraising committee for the new wing on the church, she wouldn't allow her name to appear in the paper. She was not happy with me for writing that feature story about you. Your Aunt Norma has a way of gouging out a groove in a person without ever raising her voice."

"Cain't nobody say that about you, Sally." The shadow moved into the room, blinking at us through squinty, lashless eyes. He was a short, muscular man with cracked black wingtip shoes and suspicious yellowish spots on his tweed wool pants. The skin on his face and arms resembled a newly dipped and scraped pig, taut with recent pain.

Watching us too intently, he moved across the room, dragging one stiff leg, as though it were an uncooperative crutch. Leaning against the corner of the Linotype machine, he lit a cigarette and cupped his hands furtively around it.

"Jake, you know you can't smoke in here! Harold will skin you alive if you damage his Linotype. I'm not covering for you this time. You messed up the auxiliary rail last time you fooled around with that machine. We *occasionally* need words in italics." Sally stepped over and smacked his hand off the machine. "You need to get those rolls moved out of storage by tomorrow. The ad pages are set. Go! Get it done!"

We watched in silence as he continued puffing away and limping up the stairs. "Sorry about that, Clio. I should control my temper with Jake, but he pushes the envelope constantly. It was rude of me not to introduce you, but Jake brings out the worst in me."

She plopped down in a chair. "I've never heard anyone call him by his real name. He goes by Jakeleg. His last name is Simmons. He sneaks around, eavesdrops, and never gets things done. You have to feel sorry for him. When he was just a kid, a team of mules bolted, with him holding the reins, while his father was unloading fence posts. Flipped the wagon and butchered his leg. They say his father was angrier about the crippled mules than his son. Called him Jakeleg after that."

I let out a snort of displeasure. These Wolfe Flats nicknames had a downright wicked edge. Shivers, Manboy, Winky, Booger, and now Jakeleg.

Sally flashed an embarrassed grin. "I think his Christian name is Robert, but everyone calls him Jake. He's a drop-the-reins kind of fellow."

Sally's smile didn't quite reach her eyes as she searched my frowning face. "I suppose it is crass, but people around here have a habit of putting a life-long name to physical conditions. I guess they find it comforting, in a way, to face disabilities head-on by naming them."

I didn't want to criticize Sally. Or anyone, for that matter. I wanted people in Wolfe Flats to feel comfortable around me, to accept me as one of the community. That's the only way I could get them to confide in me. Whenever I tried to get information, I often felt an invisible barrier rising. In Southern Oklahoma, a Yankee is still a Yankee, even with family roots here that reach down to the earth's molten core.

I still had questions, because, in truth, Felicity had said very little about Aunt Norma's almost-fiancé. I didn't dare ask Aunt Harriet or Lucinda. "Nosy Parkers don't need to know," Lucinda had cut me off at the pass when I asked about why both my aunts were spinsters. That reluctance to share, to talk about my own relatives was a kind of meanness in itself. It forced me to investigate, to find out important things on my own.

Sparks glittered like flint against stone in Sally's gray eyes, as she gripped my hand and whispered: "I don't know why people have to be so mean. We should help each other. Truth to tell, Clio, your Aunt Norma's friend Larry was helping a wounded German escape and got shot."

"What do I have to do to get some help around here?" As though one of those claps of thunder had burst into the newspaper office, a booming voice shouted down the stairs: "Why is no one working in this place of business?"

"Good grief. Speak of the devil. That's Lester Smith. I need to go upstairs to see what he wants. You'd better stay here, Clio. That's a tornado sky if ever I saw one. Back in a jiffy."

Sally dashed up the stairs. My brutalized Mary Janes made odd, slapping noises two steps behind her. On the other side of the counter that was meant to keep the riff-raff out of the newsroom stood an ancient man, pounding on the countertop. He yanked off his hat, exposing messy tufts of white hair that longed to be hidden under his trilby.

I was staring at the third Musketeer, Lester Smith, the man who might have answers about Aunt Norma's beau, Lawrence Bresant, one of the two Musketeers who didn't return from France.

"It's about time you showed up, Miss Tolliver. Had to catch you before the paper goes to press. I have an excellent idea. I might have dreamed it. I want to change my advertisement this week."

"The ad pages are already typeset with your usual promotion, Mr. Smith. You'll have to wait until next week if you want to change it," Sally's smile did not quite expose her teeth.

"Smith's Feed and Seed has been a customer of this newspaper for longer than I've been on this planet." He fingered a small paisley scarf, tucked around the neck of a shirt that had seen better days. "I think you can make an adjustment for one of your best customers. Just hear me out."

I wanted to hear him out. This was a former friend of Aunt Norma's that she had snubbed for a quarter of a century. With little rivulets of red veins chasing across his cheeks, he appeared to be just this side of apoplexy.

"You know how the Brits are making their people plant Victory Gardens in their backyards for the war effort? Well. I came up with a great idea and a catchy phrase to go with it. Victory Chickens." His smile was so wide that his dentures shifted and clicked with a resounding pop.

"I've got lots of chicken wire, nesting boxes, and incubators that my father kept in storage. I don't exactly know why, since we all thought the Great War would be the last one," he mused. "I expect everyone in Wolfe Flats will want a coop of Victory Chickens."

"Isn't Victory Chicken a contradiction in terms?" I asked, trying to be helpful.

He glowered down at me. "It's part of the war effort, little lady. Nothing contradictory about raising chickens and feeding your family eggs out of your own chicken coop." He stared down at my odd shoes. "Are you from around here?"

"This is Clio Clower, Mr. Smith. She's Delia's daughter, living with her aunts while Delia is overseas. Covering the war," she added smugly.

Realizing that this was a perfect moment for an exit, I nodded at a frowning Mr. Smith, did not offer my hand, raised my eyebrows at Sally and dashed for the door with a mumbled: "Got to get home. Before the storm. See you later."

Within two minutes, I had whipped back around the corner, heading for the courthouse. I wanted to jot down the names on that memorial. Maybe some of the relatives of those dead soldiers still lived around here and would be up for an interview.

As a few drops of rain splashed the sidewalk in front of me, I froze in my tracks. A humongous spider, big as a dinner plate, stretched across the pavement, oblivious to the rain. Most girls would be terrified of something that big and hairy. Not me. I was simply taken aback by seeing this creature outside the glass aquarium where Billy Foster kept it, in the apartment next to ours in New York.

Great, dark cumulonimbus clouds to the north were taking on that anvil-like shape that meant they were up to no good. I knelt down closer to the tarantula. Out of 900 species, it was questionable that I could identify this one. Billy Foster's spider was a male. He had explained to me in great detail how two of those six-sided appendages connected to the thorax—near the mouth—were really little "pee-pees."

Billy used that term. Not me. Mother told me to call things what they were. Billy said that male tarantulas deposit a special sauce in their web, dip those appendages into it, then they stick them in the female's belly to grow baby tarantulas. Billy was hoping they could get a girl tarantula, but his mother refused to have anything reproducing in their house after his father ran off with their pregnant housekeeper.

I thought about scooping up this tarantula and taking him back to the house with me, but Aunt Norma has a particular dislike of living under the same roof with "creatures that belong outside." That included cats, dogs, birds, and, I assume, spiders.

Tempted by the stock-still spider, I considered giving it a brief touch to encourage it to move out of the storm. Tarantulas can bite, but usually don't. If they do, they cause only a small sting.

Just as I extended my hand toward that faintly trembling torso of the tarantula, my arm was snatched up and yanked hard. "Into that little cave under the courthouse stairs! Now! It's here!"

Before I could gather my thoughts to make a smart-ass remark about "it" having no referent—a pet peeve of Mother's—I found myself squatting next to Lester Smith in a damp, dark place under the courthouse stairs, watching the world come to an end.

CHAPTER 9

G reat cylinders of oil drum trash cans spun end over end down the street, while leafy branches of trees swept up wads of trash that sailed into a purplish sky. Mr. Smith pulled me down, wrapped both arms around me, and wedged his feet against the concrete stair ramp. He shouted over the sudden roar: "It's right overhead. Hang on to me. The suction might be fierce."

The odor of camphor can be fierce. Witch hazel smells like raw beef going bad. In this cramped, moldy space beneath the courthouse stairs, I was doomed to be asphyxiated by Lester Smith's favorite aftershave, or die in a twister.

The great stillness that fell about us might have sucked all the oxygen out of the world; or, I had simply stopped breathing. I struggled to stand up. Claustrophobic after all those hours spent down Whitey Lewin's well, I was determined to sprint for home before the storm kicked up again.

"We must be in the eye of the tornado. It hasn't touched down, or we'd see uprooted trees and roofs flying by. Stay right here. A funnel can suck us into the next county." With arms surprisingly muscular for such an old man, Mr. Smith pulled me back down and pointed to an odd, metal sphere rolling down the street. "That's the top off the clock tower of the fire station. That's on Seminole near the end of Main. The tornado must have dropped lower there. We need to wait it out, little missy."

Great sheets of dull, gray rain fell steadily, but only small branches and paper trash whipped about in the dwindling wind. It might be safe to leave this shelter, but such an auspicious moment rarely presents itself to a sleuth. *Time to hit the nail on the head.* "I think you know my Aunt Norma, Mr. Smith. Norma Clower."

If I had smacked him with a hot iron, Mr. Smith couldn't have moved faster, as he jerked back from me. "What the . . . who . . .?"

"I'm Clio Clower, Norma Clower's great-niece. I met you when you were in the newspaper office, talking to Sally Tolliver about your victory chickens. That is an ingenious idea. I think the people in Wolfe Flats will *flock* to Smith's Feed and Seed when they see your new ad." *I simply couldn't help a little wordplay to lighten things up.*

In the darkness of our little storm cave under the courthouse steps, I could see a parade of emotions traveling across Mr. Smith's face: surprise, irritation, vexation, and, finally, curiosity. This was the time to set the hook.

"I'm very interested in World War I history, Mr. Smith. Sally told me that you were a highly decorated veteran of that war." *I was lying like a cheap rug.* Anything to get this man to open up after I had linked myself to Aunt Norma.

"You're Delia's girl, the one who collared Whitey Lewin. I thought I was saving a helpless girl from the tornado," he snorted with a grinding noise that appeared to be laughter trapped somewhere between the hard palate and the trachea. "You probably don't know, but Delia interviewed me about the war for the school paper when she was in high school." He rubbed a patch of silvery whiskers on his chin. "That was a long time ago. So was the war. One of your relatives can't seem to forget that."

Beyond the purple and yellowish mishmash of clouds above, I could see a faint ray of sun. *Time to get to the heart of my interview while I had an old soldier in my sights.*

"I'm interested in Belleau Wood and the boys from Wolfe County who fought there and didn't come back, particularly Luther Jocund and Lawrence Bresant. Felicity Langston Jocund, Luther's widow, is my piano teacher," I added, hoping to make a connection that didn't involve my kinship to Aunt Norma.

"It's a strange thing to be sitting in the middle of a twister with a girl who looks like Delia Clower, talking about a war that is too painful to remember. It hurts my head. What did you say your name was?" He frowned, heaved himself to his feet, and bent over to keep from bumping his head on the low-hanging structure.

"My name is Clio, Mr. Smith. Sally introduced us at the newspaper office. I don't mean to give you a headache, but when I ask questions about that war, I just get half-answers. Not real ones. Felicity told me some things.

Sally told me something else. I don't dare ask Aunt Norma. I want information from someone who was actually in the battle at Belleau Wood."

Like a blast from a foghorn sending a warning signal, that strange, muffled snort of a laugh practically deafened me. Then a solid, ham-like hand settled firmly on the top of my head. "The rain has stopped. I think we can sit on the courthouse bench over there while we talk."

As we walked over to one of the benches that lined the sidewalk by the courthouse, Lester Smith paused and fiddled with his neck scarf—his "cravat," as Felicity called it, tying and retying it, shoving it into the neck of his shirt, then pulling it out again.

An uneasy feeling crept into my noggin, one of those intuition things that Aunt Harriet natters on about. Something was bothering Lester Smith. He was stalling for time, as he prettified his cravat—and preparing to hide something from me. I didn't know what, but the clairvoyance, the second sight that Aunt Harriet claimed, wafted around me like a whiff of doubt. At that moment, I realized that my aunt and I were cut from the same genetic cloth.

Levering myself down on the soaked boards of the bench, I put on my best hanging-onto-every-word expression, and said: "You were going to tell me about Lawrence Bresant, Mr. Smith. And Luther Jocund." I added Felicity's late husband just to head him off at the pass before he balked at my directness.

"It's easier for me to remember the war chronologically. The specifics get muddled sometimes. The Brits were underfoot; then the Marines showed up. Nobody where they said they would be. Not my fault. I was good with my Trench Transmitter, little lady." Mr. Smith flashed a sly smile at me before spurting out more directions than Aunt Norma on one of her bossier days.

"There was nothing easy about managing that 30-watt transmitter. It had a single valve for the transmitter and receiver circuit. Had to keep her dry, with mud up to my knees and nothing but staples holding that waterproof flap. I was a natural though. As a young man, my father operated a telegraph before my mother inherited the feed store. He taught me Morse when I was just a kid." Mr. Smith's face flushed with pride.

"Most operators had to train for three or four months to get up to twenty-five words a minute. I could outpace them all and assemble and dismantle in record time. With my special training, I never imagined Larry and Luther and I would end up in that miserable bog together." His face flushed with irritation.

"The front lines got all the credit, but I had to carry the box and my mat, set up my aerial, and stay close to the boys to send and receive. Communication is what wins war. Don't let anybody ever tell you any different, missy. Now, let me explain exactly how to assemble a Marconi 1½ K. W. in the field."

"Fascinating, Mr. Smith." I remembered my mother's favorite punch line when the technology of something overpowered the sense of it. "Girls like me just don't have the kind of head you do for mechanical things," I simpered. "I'm really more interested in the battle at Belleau

Wood. What happened to your high school friends there."
I could remove, adjust, and oil my bike chain faster than any
boy in Wolfe Flats, but I played the helpless girl card.

"Started with those war posters," Mr. Smith said huff-ily. "They can incite young men to do their duty when it isn't even their war. It is now that those Japs bombed Pearl Harbor. If I was a young man today, I'd . . ."

"Be right in the thick of it," I interrupted quickly, with a sympathetic pat. I needed to get Mr. Smith back on track. He'd just skipped over two and a half decades to the present war. I wanted him to focus on the First World War. "Think back to those trenches in Belleau Wood. Tell me what it was like. Make me see it through your eyes." There. That was another of Mother's interviewing tricks, that old "through your eyes" gambit.

So, for the next ten minutes Lester Smith talked and I listened. He told me how a "patch of forest" like Bel-leau Wood was full of pitfalls and ambushes. Through his watery, red-rimmed eyes, I could almost see the mud-covered men hunkering down in their trenches, then moving ahead into low-lying patches of mustard gas that they couldn't see or smell before it claimed their eyes, their skin, their lungs.

"The orders came to move forward. We knew the gas was out there, but orders were orders. I hung back, trying to get a different order. Have you ever seen a butterfly come out of its chrysalis, its safe shell? Butterflies were all I could think of as I watched our men crawling out of the trenches into enemy spotlights."

He shuffled his feet and looked off toward the roof-less fire station. "Some people think that radio operators stayed behind the lines and were safer. Not true. Some of us saw too much. I saw what I think must have been Luther. A flying pig hit, then someone was screaming. It wasn't Luther's voice. I was able to tell Felicity that Luther didn't feel a thing. I didn't give her details. I couldn't burden her then. They don't matter now."

At that moment, the vertebrae in Mr. Smith's spine belonged to a hundred-year-old man with a century of wars weighing it down and down. I did what Aunt Harriet always did for me when I drooped. I reached over and rubbed the muscles between his shoulder blades, searching for knots, or "trigger points," as Aunt Harriet called them.

Slowly, very slowly, Lester Smith leaned forward and stretched. "Don't know that my back has felt that good in forever and a day. Sitting hunched over in that cubbyhole under the courthouse stairs, waiting for that tornado just about did me in. You have a magic touch, Clio."

He eased himself to his feet and hesitated, as though trying to find better words. "I know you want to know about Larry. You mentioned his name twice—just a bit too casually. That means you *purposefully* want answers. You're kin to Norma Clower. There's nothing casual about that lady."

Mr. Smith turned his head away so that I had to strain to hear his next words: "Larry's mother and father cried so hard, while I tried to say what I couldn't say. The words felt like stones in my mouth. They said that their lost boy

Lawrence would never. Just that word 'never,' hanging in the room like a hangman's noose." Mr. Smith fiddled with his cravat, as though the fabric resisted his fingers. "Larry always got what he wanted, for sure. Had the best of everything. Money. Looks. Brains. Not that day."

Mr. Smith clasped my hand and pulled me to my feet. "Your Aunt Norma was the worst."

I dropped his hand and stepped back. Harsh words about Aunt Norma could come out of my mouth, not someone else's, especially someone she shunned for some mysterious reason.

"That's not what I mean, Clio. I mean that telling her was the worst, the worst thing I've ever had to do. In the middle of that horrible, bloody wood, something happened that wasn't supposed to happen. Because of that boy. That German boy. When that happened, something else happened. Larry . . . he . . . made . . . a . . . a . . . a . . ."

Like one of those caged hamsters that can't seem to get off the wheel, Mr. Smith was trying to find a word, a word that doesn't want to be said, a word that can't be translated, because it lies in a dark place where light doesn't dare shine.

So I said the word: "Sacrifice." I set free the possibility of his unsaid word, so that somehow Aunt Norma's friend Larry could be safe from whatever kept his name off the memorial plaque to war heroes.

Lester Smith heaved a sigh that moved the weight of the world just a fraction off his shoulders. "Perhaps. That's a good word. Sacrifice for a German with a mangled foot. The enemy. Doesn't bear remembering. I need to go check on my store. You've talked me out, Clio." Lester Smith lifted his right hand up to touch the brim of his trilby hat in a half-hearted salute and headed down Main Street at a fast clip.

CHAPTER 10

Heading home, I splashed through pools of water down Choctaw Street sidewalks that buckled as though pools of lava simmered below; in the distance, I could see Manboy scooping up armloads of branches in his front yard. With my socks lapping over the toes of my butchered shoes like sacks of wet sand, I hopped toward a flat piece of sidewalk concrete, slipped, and sprawled headlong into the Muller's driveway.

"Are you OK, Clio? Your knee is bleeding. What in the world do you have on your feet?" The sympathetic face bending over me might have come right off one of those German propaganda posters—blue eyes, bright blond hair, squared-off chin, and perfectly aligned white teeth. The rest of Manboy's body would have qualified him as an undesirable to be "purified" off the planet with gas by the Nazis.

Scooping me up with his two foreshortened arms that were strong as a forklift, Manboy set me gently on my feet; we eyed each other on the same level. "I didn't tell your Aunt Norma that you weren't in her storm cellar.

I had no idea where you'd gone. She called me a little while ago from the store out at Rubottom."

"I thought she and Aunt Harriet and Lucinda were going to see a farmer about getting home deliveries of food. Her note said they'd be back by two o'clock. That's why I was hurrying to beat them home when I tripped on that stupid sidewalk. Sidewalks in this town are a disgrace. New York city has the best . . ."

"The Rubottom store is twenty miles from here, with the only phone in that part of the county," Manboy interrupted just as I was winding up to catalogue the merits of my city versus this hick town.

"Your aunts and Lucinda are frazzled. They were trapped in Oscar McNair's cellar for over two hours. They'll be here soon. Your Aunt Norma sounded frustrated because you didn't answer the phone."

"Well, I was somewhere else. The tornado threat happened when . . ."

"You have just a few minutes to get your story down pat, Clio. Your mother could rarely out-maneuver Norma when it came to explaining why she wasn't where she should have been. Now, let me see that knee."

Manboy led me limping over to his porch steps, squatted down, and examined my knee. "Skinned a bit. Wait here." When he pushed his screen door back open, he had two Nehi strawberry sodas in one hand and a brown bottle of something lethal in the other.

"Leg up. This won't sting. It's just hydrogen peroxide. Your Aunt Norma would douse your knee with alcohol.

That would get your attention. You want to tell me where you've been before your aunts and Lucinda get here?"

I watched peculiar little bubbles of pinkish blood bubbling on my knee as I gulped down slugs of strawberry pop. Two shades of pink. One painless, and the other absolutely heartening to someone who hadn't had anything but fudge and cake since breakfast. I smiled genially over at Manboy, considering how much of my day I wanted to share with him.

Spilling secrets is what people in Wolfe Flats do best. When I tell Manboy something, he, occasionally, tells his mother, a very nice lady that I call Aunt Claire. She tells her best friend, my Aunt Harriet. Then, confessing under duress, Aunt Harriet dumps everything on Aunt Norma. The only person in this town who could absolutely keep mum was the town's serial killer.

I managed to suss out Whitey without so much as a hint or clue from anyone in this little one-horse town. I guess that's the cosmopolitan side of me, a big-city outsider who can get answers without asking too many questions.

"There's a question I want to ask you, Clio." Startled that Manboy seemed to know what I was thinking, I jerked backwards and snorted, as fizzy strawberry soda went up my nose.

"Sorry, there weren't any cold ones in the fridge. We need to talk before your aunts and Lucinda get here. They'll want an explanation about why you weren't home where you were supposed to be." He gave me one of his eagle-eyed lawyerly looks.

Moving to the side of the porch steps that were not soaked with strawberry pop, he continued: "I'll stay out of that discussion, Clio. Just keep the whoppers to a minimum if you want to be believed. There's something else bothering me. It happened this morning when I was over at the POW camp at Camp Houze."

"Did a POW escape?" I asked, blithely, hoping to throw Manboy off the scent of where I had been while a tornado was spinning over Wolfe Flats.

"No. Don't be flippant. This is serious." Manboy twisted his hands. "I want to ask you about something that might be upsetting to your Aunt Norma."

The loud, scraping sound of a Pierce Arrow front bumper peeling off a yard of concrete curb should have been upsetting to Aunt Norma, but she wheeled into the driveway, swung open her door, set both sensibly-shod feet on the ground, and strode purposefully across the Muller's yard toward me.

"Your Aunt Harriet and Lucinda were so worried about you that I just ran the only stop sign in Wolfe Flats." She pointed a spindly finger at my lukewarm Nehi soda. "I see that you've imposed on Manford and are busy stripping the enamel from your teeth. Let me see that knee." She grabbed my mutilated shoe, lifted my leg, and peered over the top of her glasses at my oozing knee.

"Superficial," she snorted. "Lucky you're not a Jehovah Witness in need of a blood transfusion. I feel a migraine coming on. I'm going to lie down and hope that the stress of worrying about you doesn't make it worse. Your Aunt Harriet will see to you, Clio."

Without another word, Aunt Norma stalked across the yard, stepped dead center into a soggy flowerbed, and left muddy prints across the front porch.

"What was all that about, Lucinda?" Manboy stared at Aunt Norma's retreating back.

"We been locked into a dirt cellar for nigh on to two hours with them Jehovah Witnesses. Oscar McNeil and his missus—the farmer we went out to the West End to see about gettin' regular deliveries of meat and eggs and summer vegetables."

Lucinda shook her head in disbelief. "Them folks didn't keep enough coal oil in the cellar to light the lantern for more than a few minutes. Pitch black and no way to get the door to raise up. Miz McNeil went on and on, praying to the Archangel Michael to save us. Folks that don't pray to Jesus ain't likely to be saved from a tornado. Don't know that we want their produce."

"Yes, we do, Lucinda. It wasn't that bad. The top of the silo blew down on the cellar door and trapped us inside. A neighbor came by to check on the McNeils and heard us shouting. He had to hitch up a team of mules to pull that big pile of metal off the cellar door. It took awhile. Mrs. McNeil is expecting her first child and was unduly excited. We were never in danger," Aunt Harriet's thin voice chimed out reassuringly.

"Yer Aunt Norma got plumb distracted, because you didn't answer the telephone when we phoned from Rubottom, Clio. When she worries, her tone gets a bit sharp. Worryin' brings on them headaches." Lucinda inspected my knee, while Aunt Harriet stepped away from the porch, flexing her fingers along the top of her stiff, brown envelope handbag, as though she might be warming up for an attack on a C Major scale.

"Could I have a word with you, Manford?" Aunt Harriet moved over by her zinnia bed, inspecting the footprints that Aunt Norma had left.

I watched her reach into her bag and fish out a clutch of bills, whispering all the while, just out of earshot. Manboy took the money and grinned over at me. He and Aunt Harriet looked like co-conspirators, not guilty, just very pleased with themselves.

Aunt Harriet beckoned to Lucinda. "Let's go fix Norma a nice tisane with rose hips. We need to head off her migraine before it gets any worse. Manford and Clio are going to run up to Ardmore for a couple of things." She grabbed Lucinda's arm and said something out of my hearing; then, they disappeared around the corner of the house, giggling like wayward children.

"Ardmore?" I asked. Twenty-five miles north, Ardmore was a metropolis compared to Wolfe Flats, according to my aunts. Lucinda said it has a real department store with an elevator that boasts brass grill accordion doors. Lucinda said: "You never seen the like. An operator wears a little monkey hat and white gloves to work the lever and calls out: 'Floor one and floor two.'"

Well. I certainly had seen the like in New York City at Sak's Fifth Avenue, but I didn't want to mention it to a travel-deprived person like Lucinda. She'd never been out of Oklahoma, except across the river to Gainesville, Texas.

Every Memorial Day, half the people in Wolfe Flats cross the Red River to stick little Confederate flags on graves in Fairview Cemetery, while someone plunks out "Eating Goober Peas," as the sound track, while they dig into a shared potluck feast.

Manboy drove my aunts, Lucinda, his mother, and me over for the flag ceremony this year. I felt it was my civic duty to give everyone in the car a little history lesson about how some citizens in Gainesville had hung 41 suspected Union sympathizers during the Civil War.

You could have cut the silence in the car with a knife, until Manboy cleared the air with his lawyer panache. "The legal proceedings were certainly questionable, Clio, but it's not what people want to remember as they are bumping elbows to get to Lucinda's chocolate cake."

So, I ended my little tutorial in the car. When we arrived at the cemetery, I studied the words on headstones while the locals planted miniature Bonnie Blue and Confederate flags on top of dead rebels. As I circled to the far side of the graves, my interest in the propped up stones above the dearly departed put me in a primary position to be first in line at the graveyard buffet.

From the back of a long, winding line with my aunts, Lucinda, and his mother, Manboy had raised one hand in a half-salute, as though he could see into the cubbyhole in my mind where no Bonnie Blue flag would ever wave. Being first in the food line trumps misguided patriotism any day.

CHAPTER 11

Now, as I pushed myself up from the porch steps with a wounded knee and mangled shoes, Manboy sauntered down the sidewalk, dangling his keys. "Hop into the car, Clio. We're heading north."

Wiping the toes of my muddy socks along the running board of his car, I hesitated. The spotless interior was off-putting. After massacring my Mary Janes with Aunt Norma's saw, I had managed to scoop up enough mud through the open toes to dam up Red River.

"Don't worry about your shoes, Clio. Nadine will sort that out."

"Who's Nadine?"

"Nadine Jennings. She works in Daube's Department Store. Nadine is the best person there. Knows where to find everything—usually before you ask her. She'll locate what you need before I'm done with the Geneva Convention work."

"Work?" My voice sounded a bit quivery, as I envisioned being dumped on someone named Nadine while Manboy went off to some convention.

"My office is just down the street from Daube's. I need to review the Geneva Convention guidelines about working conditions for POWs. The Major General plans to use the prisoners in Camp Houze to dig Lake Texoma, but the working hours and living conditions have to meet international guidelines."

"Oh," I sighed. *Manboy wasn't deserting m*e. "That convention. The official papers that say you can't torture or mistreat prisoners. Mother told me Germany supposedly follows the rules but Japan doesn't. She heard rumors about mistreatment of prisoners but said they don't like to put stuff like that in the papers. Upsets the relatives."

With his eyes fixed ahead, down a road that went straight as a string, alongside cow pastures and nothing else of interest, Manboy seemed quieter than usual. Maybe the idea of going shoe shopping with an adolescent girl wasn't his idea of a jolly afternoon. I could liven it up.

"You said you wanted to talk to me about something that happened at the POW camp this morning. Did you uncover a nest of Nazi spies? You told me that most of the POWs are conscripted Germans who didn't want to go to war. Jeremiah says there are more Nazis in Camp Houze than you can shake a stick at."

"Jeremiah's father spots Messerschmitts overhead every time he goes to milk his cows," Manboy retorted snidely. "Most of the POWs at Camp Houze didn't go to war because they had a choice. They're not political. Just ordinary men caught up in a terrible war. Their stories are painful to hear. No different than our own soldiers."

"George Whittaker thinks you're on a government watch list because you speak German, but Jeremiah says his father is wrong. He said the Office of Strategic Services hired you to nose out SS officers from the regular German soldiers. Jeremiah is one hundred percent sure that you are an excellent interrogator," I smiled encouragingly over at Manboy, because he appeared a bit miffed.

"Name, rank, and serial number, Clio. The POWs tell me more, but they don't have to. That's their choice. Both Jeremiah and his father are wrong. I'm there to help civilian contractors determine the best prisoners for work to dig Lake Texoma. The prisoners will be paid eighty cents a day and have decent housing and food."

"That sounds like boring work. I thought you'd be into espionage. Something interesting." I heaved a sigh, as I stared at fields of knee-high wheat, rippling in the spring wind. "I guess what you wanted to talk to me about isn't all that interesting."

"It is, and disturbing. But we're here. It'll have to wait." Manboy turned the car expertly off Highway 77 and down a street lined with diagonally parked cars. "That's Daube's." He pointed toward a two-story building with big glassed-in display windows.

"It isn't Sak's Fifth Avenue,"

"No. I suppose it isn't, but it's better than the devil you know."

"What are you talking about, Manboy?" I turned a surly face to him.

"Just reminding you that shopping in Daube's will be a treat after Lewin's. I shouldn't be reminding you of Whitey. Sorry, Clio. I just remembered that old idiom 'better the devil you know than the devil you don't know.' Tactless of me."

I narrowed my eyes at Manboy, my brain churning out idioms faster than Lucinda could crank her Daisy churn. "No point in beating around the bush, Manboy. I can add insult to injury faster than you can. Actions always speak louder than words."

The snort of laughter from Manboy broke the tension as he whipped the car between a rusty pickup and sparkling clean DeSoto sedan. "Let's go shopping."

As I pushed against a swinging glass door, I froze in front of the counter facing me. The woman behind it bore an uncanny resemblance to Mrs. Wallace, my sixth-grade teacher, who was the aunt of one of those murdered girls. Same form-fitting, dark dress. Same sliced-down-the-center hair, with neat little poufy mounds on each side of the head above the ears. The mouth was different. A kind mouth.

She wasn't Mrs. Wallace, but she resembled her—and that Duchess of Windsor woman who lured England's playboy king off his throne. The Duchess's angular face had a hard-edged look about it, as though it had started to be pretty but veered off track. I call it a missed-the-mark face; I'm always trying to figure out what would make that kind of face beautiful.

Then I knew. It was a smile that lit up the room, as Manboy said, "Nadine." She rounded the end of the counter and thrust her hand out to Manboy. "Mr. Muller. I haven't seen you for ages. I was going to run down to your office and let you know that the tailor will be finished with your suit by the end of the week."

She held her palms up in a helpless gesture. "Our tailor had a problem finding that shade of gray wool you wanted. Quality wool is scarce with the war. Almost all the good wool is going for uniforms. He finally found a tailor in Oklahoma City who had a nice bolt of lightweight wool."

Standing by Manboy, watching little rivulets of water oozing out of the toes of my wet socks onto the highly polished wood floors, I saw Nadine looking, not at me, but at my feet. The faintest frown was beginning to lock itself between her eyes.

She recovered and said brightly: "Who is the young lady with you?"

"Clio Clower," *I muttered frostily. I could say my own name. Usually introductions take place before a treatise on the scarcity of wool.*

"Clio is the great-niece of the Clower sisters in Wolfe Flats. She's living with them while her mother is in England."

Manboy nudged me forward, so I offered a limp hand. She could either shake it or kiss it if the spirit moved her. I wasn't exactly feeling like royalty in this sleek place, with racks of interesting clothes lining the walls. My plaid skirt from Lewin's department store was just the other side of hideous. My blouse had last night's mashed potato stains on it. My shoes would make a third-world peasant weep.

The arms that circled me were, surprisingly, loving. "I know about you, Clio. Your aunts have been shopping here for years. Your mother was one of my favorite customers." Nadine tilted my face toward her. "You are Delia in the flesh. You have Delia's nose—just a tilt at the end. Celestial is what we call it."

Linking her arm through mine, she said, "I read that story about you in the *Daily Oklahoman*. You must have been terrified. You are a real heroine."

"A heroine badly in need of shoes, Nadine. Sandals and church shoes, her Aunt Harriet told me. Can I leave her in your hands? I have a bit of work to do in the office. I'll collect her in an hour." Just as Manboy pushed out the swinging door, he added: "Oh, yes. She needs a bathing suit. Clio doesn't know how to swim, and I promised to teach her."

A frisson of irritation swept over me. Manboy could have talked all day without letting it slip that I couldn't swim. Everyone in Oklahoma knows how to swim by the time they are out of diapers. That's what Lucinda told me. "It's a survival skill. I can't imagine Delia not tendin' to that part of your learnin'."

I could. Swimming pools were available in New York City, but I couldn't go alone. Mother said she'd try to find a pool close to our apartment, but she never did. Then, there was the polio scare one summer, with all kinds of rumors about viruses growing in heated pools. I understood. A crippling virus was a good excuse. Time was the

real issue. My mother was trying to support us in a pro-
fession where men were hired full-time and women sold
news stories by the line—or worked on the advertising
side, a job she despised.

CHAPTER 12

As Nadine steered me past tables with sensible, squared-off oxfords clumping their way into my worse nightmare, I began to get a sinking feeling that this shopping trip would be worse than the one I took with Aunt Norma to Lewin's Department Store in Wolfe Flats. Aunt Norma pounced on ugly plaid skirts, prim buttoned-up blouses, and cotton underwear that scratched worse than a monk's hair shirt.

Like someone with a shoe fetish, I snatched a red high heel off a display table; I could actually hear myself purring as I stroked the sleek, rounded toe. How could the skin of a dead cow transform itself into something so lovely?

"You can wear shoes like that in a few years, Clio. Those are exactly what your mother would have chosen. I don't think they are quite what your aunts had in mind, do you?"

Glumly, I put them back. In those shoes, I could have danced up Choctaw Street, just like Rita Hayworth. What my aunts had in mind were the shoes that the Wicked Witch of the West wore in the *Wizard of Oz*. Sensible.

Black. Laced to my knees. I'd rather be squashed like that witch than wear the kind of shoes my aunts wore.

The Land of Oz popped up before me, as a giant red goose filled the frame. The good witch Glenda was speaking: "These, I think, would be good dress shoes for you. We just got in a new Red Goose shipment."

Without a word, I snatched the shoes from Nadine's hand, and clutched them to my chest. Even if they didn't fit, I'd pretend they did. I'd amputate my toes to wear these shoes. They were smooth, soft, black leather with a t-strap and clever little cutouts across the toes. The heels were slightly raised, not quite Cuban, but almost.

"Red Goose shoes are built for action—and your feet can breathe with the nice cutouts. The insole gives you support and freedom." I smiled genially at Nadine, as she gave me cue after cue to convince my aunts that these were sensible shoes.

Leading me over to a line of chairs against a far wall, Nadine moved a fitting stool in front of me. I shuffled out of my raggedy-assed shoes and peeled off muddy socks. She anchored my bare foot onto a cold, metal plate.

"Size six and a half or seven. I'll bring several different sizes from the back room. And get you some socks." She eyed my Mary Janes, picked them up by the straps, and tossed them, along with my holey socks, into a nearby trash bin.

Returning from the storeroom with a stack of boxes and a cluster of socks, Nadine whipped thin socks on my feet before sliding them into heaven. "Girls wear these thin, white cotton socks with dress shoes. Not those heavy socks you had. I brought a six-pack so you'll have plenty of extra."

She pressed down on the toes. "About a thumb's width of space. Now, walk around on the carpeted area, Clio. We've ordered one of those x-ray machines for shoe fitting. I don't know when it will be here. You can actually see your bones inside the shoe. It's a wonderful invention."

I knew all about it. They had those machines in shoe stores in New York City. I longed to see my metatarsals and phalanges under the skin of my feet. Mother wouldn't hear of it. "Dr. Muller says that exposure to radiation makes flies sterile," she told a shoe salesman. "Don't get that device near my daughter." So we left a harried salesman behind and me wondering what fly fertility had to do with the bones in my feet.

At this moment, the bones in my feet were shouting Hallelujah! When Nadine came out of the storeroom with a pair of sandals, so far removed from what the Brown twins wore the last day of school, I almost wept. Constructed of two-toned fawn and beige leather, the sandals sported a wide band with a gold buckle over the toes and a substantial ankle strap to hold them in place.

They were hand-tooled with what appeared to be Gnostic symbols on the toe band. "I don't know if your aunts will approve, but these are very nice imported sandals. They've been in the back for a while. We don't get imports with the war. We only have the one pair, but these are in your size. They might have been a salesman's sample."

Nadine smiled, as she snapped the buckle snugly across my toes. "I can give you a good price on them. The quality is superb. Remember to show your aunts how supple the leather is and how well the arch support fits your foot."

Just the idea of walking around Wolfe Flats wearing Gnostic symbols gave me such a sense of pleasure that I clutched Nadine's hand, as though she had become my new best friend. I hoped the library had something resembling a reference book on ancient signs and symbols. Seeing me strolling along with mysterious signs on my shoes should put those Brown twins in their place.

"I've bagged your dress shoes and the socks. You should just wear the sandals. That way, your aunts can't return them," Nadine grinned at me. "We'll take the elevator to the upper floor."

With Uncle Remus. I gasped as we stepped through ornate doors. The elevator operator's face was the color of polished ebony; like patches of little white clouds, his grizzled hair pooched out from the side and back of a silly round hat.

"Meet my friend, Mr. Baudeen Harris, Clio." Nadine patted the elevator operator's arm. "Mr. Harris worked for my parents for years and told me the most marvelous stories."

"Yes 'um. I did that all right." Mr. Harris smiled at me, so I stuck my hand into his white-gloved hand and smiled back.

It was the oddest thing. Just yesterday morning, I had found *Nights with Uncle Remus* in my aunts' library and propped it up by my oatmeal bowl when Aunt Harriet noticed it. "That's a first edition, Clio. It has lovely gilt lettering. Treat it carefully." She shoved it back from a puddle of milk and added: "Joel Chandler Harris wrote the most charming folk tales. You'll love them."

I knew how to take care of books. I don't crack their spines or get grease stains on their buckram bindings. Librarians at the New York City Library would have skinned me alive for being careless with their books. I didn't need a lecture from Aunt Harriet about book care. I might have been a bit snarky with my response.

"Mother says Uncle Remus stories aren't politically correct."

"Oh. And why's that? These are just little animal stories," Aunt Harriet said.

"Out of the mouth of a former slave. That's what Mother said," I popped a spoon of oatmeal in my mouth to keep from saying anything else. Aunt Harriet tended to side with me against Aunt Norma. No point in needling an ally.

The elevator ride in Daube's was short. Nadine propped her back against the door, as though to delay us. "Mr. Harris grew up in Wolfe County. He probably knows your aunts. The Clower sisters, did you know them, Baudeen?"

Mr. Harris shoved a big, round, brass lever into the locked position and spoke to me. "I grew up out in the country at Jimtown. As the crow flies, that's not far from Wolfe Flats. I knew *of* your aunts. Nice ladies from all I ever heard, Miss Clio."

"Just Clio, Mr. Harris," I said, trying not to cross my eyes as I thought about the deferential respect in the word "miss." *This is the Twentieth Century.* I tried to be conversational. "I've never been to Jimtown, but I know where it is. I've been mapping Wolfe County, mostly Wolfe Flats. If you blink, you could miss Jimtown."

Mr. Harris didn't blink, so I struggled to say something nice. "Cartography is my hobby. That's map-making. It's a very old craft."

"Yes, miss. It is. My son sent me a framed print copy of Mercator Gerhard's map of the world. The original map dates from the 1500s. It makes me want to travel. See sights I've never seen."

When a dinging sound went off in the elevator, Mr. Harris grabbed the brass wheel. "I have a customer downstairs. I'll let you ladies off now."

There was something very special about that moment in the elevator. I learned not to underestimate a person, just because he wore a silly hat and cranked an elevator. This man could remember the name of one of the greatest mapmakers ever—Mercator Gerhard. I also noticed how gently Nadine brushed the gloved hand of Mr. Harris when we stepped out of the elevator. It was the kind of understated caress that we give someone without anyone else knowing how much we care.

"Swimsuits are straight ahead, past table linens, over by the dressing room. A woman here in Ardmore makes the knitted ones. They might be a bit revealing, but they dry quickly." I passed by a half-mannequin with something lumpy and peculiar stretched on it. It looked like gray mold was taking over an unwilling human form.

"What about this? It's perky." Nadine held up a navy blue slithery swimsuit that could be described as flimsy. I couldn't see anything perky about it.

"These just came in last week. They are rayon jersey with a knit cotton lining so they stretch a bit." She fingered a strip of ruffled white. This little skirt goes all around the bottom. It's supposed to be slimming.

That's not your problem, but I think it makes a slender girl look more substantial."

Substantial. That's exactly how I wanted to look when Manboy tossed me into Lake Murray to drown. A substantial object would be easier to spot in the depths of a murky lake than a flimsy one. That white ruffle would be a perfect SOS alert. In front of a full-length mirror, I held it up in front of me, wrapping my plaid skirt tightly so I could see what my shape might be if I had any shape.

"You'll look smart in that, Clio." The reflection of Manboy in the wavering glass of the mirror startled me. He resembled a sturdy tree trunk with a nice head on it. I looked like skinny branch of a tree with something navy and white caught on its limb.

"One of those rubber caps, too, Nadine. Clio's mother wore those to keep her hair dry. Sometimes the Lake has algae close to the shore where we'll start her lessons. Clio's a fast learner. Before you know it, she'll be swimming out to the float. They've just replaced the diving board on the end of it. Delia was a good diver."

Manboy was getting ahead of himself. I wasn't my mother. I hadn't had a swimming lesson in my life. And, I had great fear of going into deep water feet-first. The very idea of plunging into a lake headfirst brought on heart palpitations of the first order.

Chapter 13

With a box of new shoes, socks, a bathing suit, a rubber swim cap in my arms, and the most fashionable sandals I'd ever seen on my feet, I was practically euphoric as Manboy pulled his car onto Highway 77 heading south.

"It's like this, Clio. When the POW told me about Larry Bresant, I almost fell off my chair."

Whipping around to face him, I almost slid off the front seat of his car. Usually stories don't start in the middle. "You mean Aunt Norma's Larry?"

"Yes. Lawrence Bresant, who didn't come back from the Great War. The man your aunt never, ever talks about, but never forgets." Manboy slammed on his brakes to avoid a tractor that pulled off a side road in front of us. Then he slowed down and took the story back to where it started.

"I was interviewing a POW named Lorenz Weber for the Texoma Lake project. If I share something about who I am, what I'm there to do, how the project will be run, it seems to help the men be more forthcoming. We don't want any prisoners who are intent on escaping at the work site."

Now, I was getting too much background information. I wanted to know how a POW knew about Aunt Norma's beau—immediately, so I could find out why Larry's name wasn't on the county War Memorial and why nobody would give me a straight answer about a local soldier who didn't return from the Great War.

"When I told him that I lived in Wolfe Flats, this young man became excited and began questioning me. He asked if I knew Lawrence Bresant's family. Then, he said: 'Is his beautiful friend, Norma, alive?' I'll tell you Clio, I felt as though I'd just walked into a different universe. Here's a German POW talking about my next-door neighbor as though he'd stepped back into time. It spooked me."

"Well you're spooking me! How did this guy even know Aunt Norma's name?"

Manboy glanced in the mirror at the road behind him, signaled, and pulled off onto a side road. "I need to concentrate on what I'm telling you, Clio. Frankly, I don't know if I should be. You weren't even a gleam in anyone's eye when it happened. I feel as though I'm invading your aunt's privacy by saying anything."

It was time to set him straight. "I know some things about Larry Bresant and Aunt Norma that you probably don't know. She hurt his feelings when she saw him off to France with a stupid quote from *The Three Musketeers.*"

"We're not discussing a Dumas novel here, Clio. I'm trying to sort out why Lorenz Weber wanted to tell me something that happened to his father a quarter of a century ago. Me? A stranger?"

"He's locked up. Who else could he tell?" Having answered that question, I went on to the next answer. "I've been talking to Felicity Langston about Larry and Luther and Lester—the three 'L's,' aka, the three Musketeers. That probably doesn't ring any bells for you," I added smugly.

"You asked me what I was doing while that tornado was whipping overhead this morning? I was investigating Wolfe Flats's Musketeers. Felicity Langston talked to me about her husband, Aunt Norma's beau, and Lester Smith." I paused and took a deep breath.

"After I picked Felicity's brain, I went to the newspaper office to question Sally Tolliver and just happened to run into the third Musketeer, Lester Smith, who told me even more." I paused a moment. I wasn't sure that Lester had told me much more than what a great radioman he was and that Larry had been "taken," after helping a wounded German at the Battle of Belleau Wood.

"I should have known you wouldn't let sleeping dogs lie, Clio. You have a categorical spirit."

"What do you mean by that?" I asked, huffily.

"Nothing negative. You like to break things down into components, look at those from every aspect. That kind of analysis can seem invasive to a person like your Aunt Norma, who values her privacy. I don't think she'd want you snooping around her past. She has never discussed what happened to Larry with my mother—and they are good friends. That fact alone tells me that your Aunt Norma doesn't want to discuss Larry with anyone."

"She grieves. Aunt Norma cries at night in her room. I saw her through the crack in the door reading an old journal. I think it might be Larry's. If you can't get the right answers, it makes you sad forever. Aunt Norma doesn't deserve to be sad for so long. I can help her." The end of my little speech sounded plaintive, as though I doubted that I could help her at all.

"I had no idea that something so far in the past continues to trouble her, Clio. Norma appears self-sufficient. She's one of those people who never asks for assistance, never needs help, because they are in absolute control. Maybe she just hides her sadness better than others do."

"Doesn't mean she isn't sad. She is. I think that sadness makes her mean sometimes, even when she doesn't intend to be," I tried to cover for Aunt Norma's habitual, in-your-face rudeness.

"Delia often told me that Norma would fit comfortably in the tribunal of the Spanish Inquisition. But, that was the opinion of a hardheaded, independent teenager, who battled her aunt every inch of the way. Raising Delia was a struggle for both of your aunts and Lucinda, no matter what your mother says. I lived through it. Oil and water never mix."

I didn't want to hear about my mother's trials and tribulations with her aunts. Surely, I had enough problems of my own with them, trying to keep a low profile in a house with people who were constantly on alert for human flaws.

To get Manboy back on point, I put on my inquisitor face: "So, what did this Lorenz person tell you? Specifically about meeting Larry Bresant in the war?"

"He's too young to have known Larry. It was his father who had an interaction with Larry in Belleau Wood."

"And so?"

"So . . ." Manboy let the conjunction drift out and away as he appeared to be ordering his thoughts. "Lorenz told me that Larry found his father bleeding from a partially blown-off foot. He said his father was a fifteen-year-old from one of the *Jugenwher* camps."

"Jugenwhat?" *I wish Manboy could control his German vocabulary. What did a camp have to do with anything?*

"During World War I, Germans didn't go into the military until they were twenty years old. But, they had *Jugenwher* camps, youth camps where boys were trained to use rifles and machine guns. Lorenz said his father was tall for his age and managed to talk his way into a Landsturm. That was a term used for groups of semi-skilled soldiers."

With a small sigh of frustration, Manboy continued: "According to his son, Dieter Weber ended up in the wrong place at the wrong time. The Landsturm were supposed to bring in supplies and help the regular troops move forward through all that mud in Belleau Wood. An artillery shell exploded next to Dieter and blew off part of his foot." Manboy glanced down at my sandals and seemed relieved that all ten of my toes were in place.

"Can you imagine the terror of a fifteen-year-old boy caught up in the middle of that messy, bloody war?"

Well. Yes I could. Mother had taken me to war mov-ies since I gave up my pacifier. Dieter Weber sounded like a first-class idiot. He could have avoided enlisting until he was seventeen—even then, he wouldn't be sent into the field until he was twenty. What sane person would go into the middle of a battlefield to bring in supplies?

"Lorenz told me that his father couldn't remember being hit, but when he woke up and tried to stand, a piece of his foot wasn't there. That's when Larry came upon him. Lorenz said his father told him that he was crying out for help and trying to run, but he just struggled in the mud. Lorenz used the word *aufwühlen* and moved his feet back and forth, as though they were churning mud when he told me about his father."

"But what happened then?" Frustrated by Manboy's use of a German word to describe churning feet, I wanted to move the story along, not have a vocabulary lesson.

"It gets a bit confused, Clio. You have to remember that Lorenz is telling a story that his father told him. His father, Dieter, was young, seriously wounded, and in a lot of pain. What he told his son would have been convo-luted, at best."

"I can unravel. Tell me," I demanded.

"Lorenz said his father told him that an American soldier came out of the shadows like a *barmherziger Samariter*, a good Samaritan. The American carried Dieter over behind a big tree. With all the firepower blasting, I doubt that many trees were standing in Belleau Wood by that time," Manboy paused and stared through the open window at a field of ripening wheat. "After the war, the French made that area a permanent memorial to American soldiers. They probably replanted trees," he added.

Frustrated with this digression into a horticulture lecture, I thumped Manboy's arm harder than I meant to do. He didn't flinch.

"This is where the confusion comes. Lorenz said that the American Samaritan stayed behind the tree with his father for most of the night. He took off Dieter's boot, lifted his leg to slow down the bleeding, bound it with his own undershirt, and talked to him in French. Dieter thought that Larry was French, until he started telling him about his home in Oklahoma."

"Why French?"

"Larry was fluent. His grandfather was French. Larry grew up speaking French. He had been studying languages when he was at OU, before he left for the war, but his German probably wasn't very good. According to Lorenz, his father spoke French. The Germans might have been planning to use Dieter in some other capacity. He wasn't where he was supposed to be—behind the action with the rest of the Landsturm. Only experienced German troops were used on the front lines in Belleau Wood. Many of those troops had fought in Russia until the Brest-Litovsk Treaty."

Talk about getting twisted up in your underwear. Manboy might spout the entire history of the Crimean War before he got to the point of what happened to Lawrence Bresant. I sighed, audibly.

"I know, Clio. Who, what, where, when, why and how. You are Delia's daughter. No confusion about that. You want everything packed into the first paragraph. Lorenz told me that his father's Samaritan wouldn't leave a boy to suffer alone; he stayed there with Dieter, talking to him, comforting him, telling him about his own life in Wolfe Flats."

CHAPTER 14

Manboy rolled down his window and took in a deep breath, as though he needed to restore the vigor sapped by his story. "Wheat in Wolfe County has such a nice, earthy scent, just before it is harvested." I didn't move a muscle—even to breathe. I know all about diversions in this part of Oklahoma; they serve to distract or redirect or create a smokescreen. Lawyers like Manboy cut their teeth on digressions. I could wait him out.

"Lorenz said that Larry told his father about a little church outside a nearby village where the wounded were being taken. He said he would try to carry Dieter toward the village road and flag down an ambulance. They had to wait, because there was continual fire of shrapnel and high-explosive shells in the area."

Manboy sighed, took his foot off the brake, shoved the gear into neutral, and gunned the engine. "I doubt that Larry told Dieter that the makeshift hospital was only for Americans, French, and Brits. Ambulances wouldn't be picking up wounded Germans."

"Medics take care of anyone wounded. They couldn't refuse. It's a Hippocratic Oath thing," I said with the assurance that wounded enemy would be treated as kindly as our own. *Didn't our POWs get good food and beds? And couldn't they make eighty cents a day working on the Lake Texoma project, if they didn't try to escape?*

"From everything I've read about Belleau Wood, it was a nightmarish battle, Clio. Not that all battles aren't gruesome, but the Germans were using mustard gas. Under those conditions, I don't think a wounded German would be triaged like an Allied soldier."

"Then why would Larry try to get that boy to a hospital?"

"I don't know that Larry believed he could. Maybe, he was just comforting a wounded boy, trying to give him hope, getting his mind off his terrible pain. That's probably why Larry told Dieter about Wolfe Flats, about his life there, about his girlfriend, Norma. Anyhow, that's just my guess."

Manboy whipped the steering wheel sideways. "There's no way we'll ever know what Larry was thinking or intended to do. We know what Dieter thought about Larry. He named his only son after him—Lorenz. German for Lawrence." Manboy eased the gear into first, glanced to the left, and pulled back out on the highway.

"Don't leave me hanging in mid-air!" I screeched. What happened to Larry?"

"That's the part that troubles me the most about Lorenz's story. He said another American, a radio operator who knew Larry, came up with two other soldiers.

The soldiers wanted to finish off Dieter with a clean shot. End his suffering so to speak. Lorenz said his father could hear them arguing, but he didn't understand English. He did understand the pointed guns. Lorenz said Larry stood between his father and the soldiers and yelled at them."

Zing went that synapse in my brain. That "categorical spirit" that Manboy accused me of having was sorting and arranging at a fast clip. "Lester Smith was a radio man in Belleau Wood! He was with Larry's unit. He told me this morning when we were hiding from the tornado. He said something about Larry's sacrifice." I stopped and let out a huge intake of breath.

I retracted my words. "He didn't say that. Lester was fumbling for words. He seemed really upset to be talking with me this morning about that battle. I'm the one who used the word 'sacrifice.' Lester looked like a sad, worried, old man. I thought he needed a good word to use. So what happened next?"

"If you can believe what his father told Lorenz, those soldiers dragged Larry away, yelling and protesting. Lorenz said his father was picked up the next morning by German soldiers when they left their Southern defensive line."

"So that's all? We don't know what happened after that?" I threw up my hands in disgust. Stories without a complete ending frustrate me.

"We know that there was a rumor in Larry's unit that he had aided the enemy. That's what Lester Smith told Larry's parents. Lester didn't say that he was there when it happened. He claimed to be back in the trenches when Larry was brought back from the front lines. All I know is that Lester told Larry's parents that he was never sure what had happened." Manboy had a disbelieving look about his mouth.

"This is second-hand information, Clio. My father was a friend of Mr. Bresant's. He helped find a buyer for the bank when the Bresants left Wolfe Flats after their son's death. It was a very bad time for them."

Time to get Manboy back to the main sticking point. "And Aunt Norma? What did Lester tell her?"

"That is the only thing Norma did tell my mother. She said that Lester Smith brought Larry's journal home from the war. He told Norma that he grabbed the journal and hid it in his pack before some other soldiers took Larry away. Lester told Norma that he saw Larry leave willingly with two soldiers from their unit late in the afternoon. He never saw him again. He said there was talk that Larry had aided the enemy."

"Helping a boy with a shot-off foot is aiding the enemy?" I protested.

"The Espionage Act of 1917 lists treasonable acts and speech, but the intent wasn't to address soldiers in battle—President Wilson wanted to put a lid on protests against America's entry into the war. Field conditions were terrible in Belleau Wood. Who knows what rules, if any, were followed," Manboy added.

That kind of answer with a question that wasn't a question always gets my back up. "Parents have the right to know. People back home have a right to know. Aunt

Norma had a right to know." My voice tapered off into a mouse-like squeak.

Manboy sighed and said, "My father told me that Mr. and Mrs. Bresant got an official Army form saying that their son died in Belleau Wood. The typed letters SP CMO followed that statement."

"SP CMO means what?"

"Special Court Martial—but that's from Canada's Army Act. Basically, our military operated off the 69 Articles of War, established by the Second Continental Congress in 1775. World War I was supposed to be the Great War to end all wars. Congress wasn't interested in the legalities of a court martial for its own soldiers. Now that we're in another war, considerable discussion is taking place in legal circles about the need for a uniform code of military justice."

If I were commanding a firing squad at this very minute, I'd be aiming for that self-satisfied lawyer sitting beside me, who was fulminating like a legal beagle at the top of his form. *Control, Clio. Control.*

"Sorry, Clio. The history of law is a passion of mine. Because military justice is not part of the federal judicial system, it has been sadly neglected. You want to hear about Lawrence Bresant. I'm trying to remember what my father told me—I simply haven't thought about that sad time for years."

"Doesn't mean that Aunt Norma doesn't," I squeaked out through gritted teeth—muffling the words that I really wanted to scream.

"You are right, of course. The problem is that any military file that might exist on Lawrence would be closed. The Bresants were told that no more information was authorized. Only the soldiers who were involved would remember any details. They might not have survived the war. Sorry, Clio. I was young when my father told me about the Bresants. They sold the bank and left town. Then the gossip ended. Looks like the case is closed."

"But Lester Smith was there! Lorenz's father saw him."

"That was a long time ago. Lorenz said that his father described one of the American soldiers as a 'radio man.' That could have been anyone. Lester told the Bresants and your Aunt Norma that he was behind the troops with radio equipment when Larry's unit left for the front lines. He hasn't changed his story in twenty-five years."

As he drove, Manboy tapped the steering wheel in an annoying way. "Whether it's true or not, Lester probably believes he said the right thing at the time. He wouldn't have wanted to cause any more grief for Larry's parents— or for Norma. After all, Larry was his friend," Manboy added. *Without much conviction, I thought.*

Time to stick my oar into these muddy waters. "Did you know that Lester Smith had a crush on Aunt Norma? Felicity told me that he did."

"So did every teenage boy in Wolfe Flats, according to Mother," Manboy said, dismissively. "Your aunt was the town beauty. But she and Larry were a couple. No one thought otherwise. In retrospect, they were like star-crossed lovers. The town's Romeo and Juliet."

"Romeo is pushing up daisies somewhere in a remote French forest, and Juliet sits in her bedroom crying at night. That's not Shakespeare's ending," I said, testily.

Manboy spun the car off Highway 77 to cut a nice slice out of the loop into Wolfe Flats. "No, it's not. But your aunt's life has been a good, productive one. She does a lot of community and church work. Always has. She never complains. She raised Delia, and now she's trying to do her best with you, Clio. I think that we should just keep quiet about Lorenz and Dieter. Don't you?"

Never let it be said that I would close the door on an interesting case without getting all the answers I could. So, I answered Manboy with a faint "Hum . . um . . .um" like a strangling, operatic soprano, who might never hit that high note again.

I decided to hit a low note. "Do you know anything about the science of physiognomy, Manboy?"

"Do you mean that pseudo-science that pretends it can judge a person's character by facial characteristics?" Manboy scoffed.

"That very science," I said defensively. "I found a book called *Practical Character Reader* in the New York City Library that gave me a leg up on sorting out good from bad people based on their eyes, noses, chins, and mouths. I never saw more suspicious eyes than Whitey Lewin had."

"I won't dispute you on that statement, Clio. But physiognomy is pure hokum."

"It isn't. It may not be *pure* science but it isn't *pure hokum*." After hearing about a WWI radio operator who was where he said he wasn't, I examined Lester Smith's face in my head and let go: "Lester Smith has what is defined as a 'deceitful mouth.' That means his upper lip is tucked in below his lower lip. And his chin sticks out too far. That's considered a deceitful chin."

"Or, it's the result of ill-fitting dentures. Really, Clio. Can a girl as smart as you believe anything so stupid as physiognomy?"

That put a sock in my mouth. I didn't even mention Lester's deceitful, droopy nose. Lester Smith was now on my radar screen. From the set of Manboy's chin (not deceitful in the least), I figured that I'd keep my opinions to myself for the time being. That's Lucinda's favorite phrase. It means now. Or temporarily.

Dinner that evening, served on the winged griffon mahogany table at 170 Choctaw Street was pleasant, as dinners at that address sometimes are. Aunt Norma wobbled down the stairs with a damp cloth pressed to her head, declaring that no migraine would upset the order of regular meals.

Lucinda served up collard greens with ham hocks— the greens were over-cooked into a soupy mess, flavored with lots of pig fat. Just the way I can tolerate green things on my plate. Lucinda passed around a platter of sensible, well-trimmed pork chops, with gravy made from the "leavins.'"

When chefs scrape the bottom of the pan for gravy or sauce, Mother says they "deglaze" the pan. When I told that to Lucinda, she said: "Leavins' is somethin' left behind that tastes really good. Deglaze is an empty, silly word." *You don't argue with an expert maker of gravy.*

I didn't even have to argue with Aunt Norma. When I stuck out my foot for a new shoe examination, Aunt Harriet giggled and declared: "They look like winged sandals, with all those little squiggles like feathers on the sides. Shoes that Hermes, the messenger of the gods, might wear."

Not feathers, I wanted to tell Aunt Harriet. Gnostic, secret symbols that I will eventually translate.

Aunt Norma peeled a sandal off my foot: "The leather is very good, with a nice, sturdy insole. Not like those flat, cheap things I saw in Hedy's window."

The church shoes and swimsuit got the same once over. "The heels are a bit extreme for a young girl, but Nadine knows the current fashion. I certainly don't," Aunt Norma added, pressing her fingers between her eyes, as though she might squeeze the life out of a migraine.

"That bathing suit won't cover anyone with glory, but as long as you aren't going out in public in it—just to Lake Murray for swim lessons, I guess it will have to do."

Aunt Norma had just given my new swimsuit the only blessing she knew how to give—a reluctant one, when Aunt Harriet stuck in her oar.

"But, Sister, we talked about Clio joining the MYF. They take the young people to the Lake for wiener roasts and swimming. She'll have to wear it in public. Remember, we both talked about Clio needing more friends.

MYF is a good option. The Brown girls from her class belong."

MYF. Methodist Youth Fellowship. I'd rather join the POWs at Camp Houze than spend a minute with the Brown twins. Time for a diversion.

I sliced an offending piece of fat from my pork chop, pushed it to the side of my plate, and said, cheerfully, to no one in particular: "I met a very interesting man in Daube's today. Mr. Baudeen Harris. No kin to Joel Chandler Harris, but Baudeen Harris looks exactly like Uncle Remus—and he tells stories."

After half an hour of discussing the merits of *Aesop's Fables* versus the "folk tales" of Uncle Remus, Aunt Harriet exhausted the topic, and I traipsed upstairs to bed, determined to take another look at an Oklahoma map with Jimtown on it so that I could find where Baudeen Harris had lived. I'd add the location to my map—put it "straight as the crow flies" from Wolfe Flats, just as Mr. Harris had described it.

CHAPTER 15

The iron knocker on the front door could wake the dead. Or maybe it was Lucinda's hesitant welcome that alarmed me. "How you, Jeremiah? Didn't expect to see you here." Then some garbled words and a shout up the stairs. "Clio, get down here! Jeremiah says you suppose' to go to his farm today."

Scrabbling for the birthday playsuit that Lucinda had made me out of an old linen tablecloth and my beautiful, new sandals, I smashed my hair into order and dashed down the upstairs hallway. How could I have forgotten?

Yesterday morning, Jeremiah had asked me to spend the day at his farm. He said his pa would come with him to pick me up if my aunts agreed. I had forgotten to ask them.

Hopping down the hall with one sandal off and one on, I made it to the top rail of the landing. "I'm coming. Just a minute."

From the open door, I could see George Whittaker in his pickup with the motor running. His posture was not that of a man who tolerated waiting.

"I forgot to ask Aunt Norma, Lucinda. All that shopping in Ardmore went to my head. I lost track." *It wasn't the shopping. It was what that POW had told Manboy about his father, Dieter Weber, and Lawrence Bresant in Belleau Wood.*

Last night, Aunt Norma had been so low-key about my new shoes and swimsuit that I couldn't get my mind back to everyday wheedling; my wheels must have slipped a cog. When Jeremiah had invited me, I knew that considerable wheedling must take place before Aunt Norma would let me leave with George Whittaker. She holds a considerable grudge about his friendship with my mother when she was in high school.

"Yer aunts went to church early this mornin' to help with the rummage sale. They said you was to go around noon. To learn about community service."

Jeremiah shuffled back a step and said, "Well. Maybe we . . ." I could see a flush of disappointment turning his russet freckles a nice, bright hue. *Time for me to put Lucinda in the catbird's seat.*

"I wouldn't want to bother my aunts when they're helping with the sale, Lucinda. That's a big money raiser for the church. You told me that Mother put you in charge of me, along with my aunts, when she stopped by your house the day she left me. She visited with *you*—not the aunts. You should decide more things."

If the chest of a plump woman can poof out any further, Lucinda's did. "You hit the nail on the head. Delia did say she depended on me. It's a courtesy to ax yer aunts first, but beins' they ain't here, I should decide."

She swung around and grabbed Jeremiah by the arm. "Clio can go on one condition. You see that she's back here afore dinner. And, don't let her get near that mean dairy bull. I heard tales about it. No floggin' roosters either. Wait here. I just frosted a chocolate cake. You youngins can take it with you."

A mile-high chocolate cake with frosting dripping on the front of Jeremiah's shirt instantly put his father in a better mood. When he turned his smile on me, I could see exactly how Jeremiah would look in twenty years. I knew that my mother could not have been immune to the charm George was turning on me as I slid into the front seat between him and Jeremiah.

"Well, Clio. We're pleased that you can visit the farm today. A big-city girl like you might find it interesting." He glanced at my feet. "Nice shoes. You might want to wear some of Jeremiah's boots that he's outgrown. Yesterday's rain mucked up things. Jeremiah thought you'd like to see the new dairy calves—and check out the steers we just bought. They're fattening on wheat pasture."

"I guess the steers need to put on weight before they can produce much milk," I said, conversationally. I had the sense that Jeremiah's father was trying to be civil but would rather be somewhere else.

The snort of laughter that erupted in the front seat of the pickup from both of the Whittakers almost spun the vehicle into a ditch. Jeremiah couldn't stop giggling, but his father recovered enough to offer an explanation for my stupidity and a subtle criticism of my mother. "You're a city girl, Clio, but I'm surprised that Delia didn't tell you about country life. She spent a lot of time on the Clower Ranch."

"The Clower Ranch?"

"Your aunts lease their family ranch. I don't think they ever go out there. The folks that lease it used to keep Delia's horse. The place is not far from Jimtown. Good wheat land with big pecan trees along the bottoms. Fellow named Blake leases it. You should check it out. When his lease is up, I might be interested. Tell your aunts."

The dazzling smile he flashed might convince someone else to plead his cause, but not me. This was the man who had smacked Jeremiah across the face; this was the man who hid letters from Jeremiah's mother so that her son thought she had run off without any concern for him. This was the man whose bad temper probably drove Jeremiah's mother to join the war effort, not because she had a thing about studying fungi in tropical lands.

Jeremiah's last letter came from the South Pacific. His mother wrote reams of information about how certain kinds of fungi deteriorate clothing and equipment. Much of her letter was inked out. I don't know why anything related to mold and mushrooms would interest the enemy, but the censor's office apparently did. Jeremiah wouldn't have known that she was in the Pacific, but she gave him a clue by naming tropical plants that only grow there.

Mother's last letter was two short paragraphs, saying that she missed me, was grateful to the aunts and Lucinda, and that I should try to get my hands on a copy of the *New York Times* in case they published her feature stories about life behind the front lines.

Ink marks crossed out half of the paragraphs, but Mother managed to stick in one clue about her location that the censor missed. She wrote: "Shy bairns get nowt." That's an idiom from the northeast part of England. Mother put it on our apartment refrigerator with her other quotes as a joke. It was definitely a clue. No question about me speaking up for myself.

So, as we neared the Whittaker house, I spoke up again and, this time, I really meant what I said: "That is an absolutely charming farmhouse, Mr. Whittaker. I love that long, wraparound porch, with those Queen Anne posts and railings." The only reason I knew that they were Queen Anne was that Aunt Harriet had taken me on an "architectural appreciation" walking tour of Wolfe Flats.

After listening to Aunt Harriet blather on about Arts and Crafts bungalows, catalog homes, gables, and shingles for an hour, as we tromped up and down Wolfe Flats streets, I stopped the conversation with my dotty aunt. "None of these houses has more than two stories and an attic. The Empire State Building has 102 stories. They had 3,400 people working on it, many more than the entire population of Wolfe Flats." That bit of information put a sock in Aunt Harriet's mouth.

From the expressions of pride on both Jeremiah's and his father's faces when I complimented their house, I decided to leave the Empire State Building in New York City and concentrate on praising their house.

"Some of the farm houses I've seen don't have any shelter around them, just bare ground. Yours is landscaped beautifully," I beamed over at Mr. Whittaker, knowing full well that his botanist wife Sonya had done all the landscaping. Jeremiah had told me. I was hoping George Whittaker might let something slip about why his wife flew the coop without a word.

"My wife is responsible for the landscaping. I can't take credit for any of that," he flicked his hand, dismissively. "Landscaping is a luxury most farmers can't afford. If it doesn't produce a crop or a calf, we don't keep it around."

That statement was so in-the-face utilitarian that I knew better than to comment. As I slid out of the pickup on Jeremiah's side, an Irish setter squeezed past Jeremiah to sniff at my sandals.

"That's Caedmon, Mom's dog. I take care of him. He's a great hunting dog. Like Dad says, he has to earn his way."

Caedmon circled the pickup, lifted his leg, and pissed on the back tire on Mr. Whittaker's side. I didn't so much as lift an eyebrow, but I thought that Caedmon was giving me a dog's opinion of the master of this house.

"What about we cut into that cake of Lucinda's?" Mr. Whittaker thumped Jeremiah between the shoulders. A bit too forcefully, I noticed and nodded agreeably. I had dashed out of the house this morning without Lucinda noticing that I hadn't eaten breakfast.

"I'll let Jeremiah be your tour guide, Clio. The rain has washed a gully along the fence on the north forty. I'll be working with the front loader out there all morning, Jeremiah. It's a two-man job, but we want to show Clio a good time. I'll manage alone."

I watched Mr. Whittaker lift Lucinda's cake from Jeremiah's calloused hands and stalk toward the back door. That man could lay guilt on a saint. I could cheer up a saint. "Your mother's landscaping is stunning, Jeremiah. It's considerably different from what she did in the Muller's backyard. She made such a beautiful retreat for Manboy's mother."

"Yeah. It was no retreat around here when she was working on the Muller's yard, I can tell you. Pa let Mom do that job for the Mullers, because they paid her—he doesn't have much use for Manboy. Goes back to when they were younger, I guess. Don't know what caused the rift," Jeremiah mused. "Manboy's always been nice to me. Mom became good friends with both the Mullers. Spent too much time there, Pa said. He raised a ruckus about it."

I was still hung up on that phrase, "Pa *let* Mom." Sometimes I didn't miss having a father around at all. No one but my mother decided what she would do. I stood a bit straighter as Jeremiah and I walked up the front steps, feeling stoked that I'd inherited Mother's backbone.

In the living room, bright chintzes on the sofa and chairs, soft, thin curtains over the windows, and muted tones of an old Oriental rug transported me to what might have passed for a country home in England. There was no sign of the heavy Eastlake and spindly Victorian furniture that my aunts and Claire Muller seemed to favor.

Holding my arms wide, I admired every stick of furniture in the room. I might have been overdoing it a bit—furniture was something to plop down on, not wax on and on about—but Jeremiah was pacing the room, house-proud, straightening picture frames and rearranging cushions. "I keep it real clean, Clio. Just like Mom did. Pa tends to be careless with his muddy boots now that she's away. He comes in tired at the end of the day."

And still pissed off at your mother, I thought. "Well, it's a beautiful house, Jeremiah. Mother and I lived in a crummy apartment in New York. You wouldn't believe the mold problem around the bathtub. We drew straws to see who had to clean it."

I tried to smile at the memory. Then, I remembered how often Mother cheated when we drew straws. "Long one wins! No, short one! Long one won last week." Mother's idea of cleaning was to remove pictures from the wall so she could put up more maps of the European and Pacific war zones.

CHAPTER 16

One-third of the chocolate cake was gone by the time Jeremiah and I got to the kitchen; Mr. Whittaker had gone to the north forty—whatever that meant. Jeremiah poured two glasses of milk for us; I cut a tiny slice of cake and a three-inch slice for Jeremiah, to make him more receptive to a few questions.

"So. That giggling fit when I commented on your cows in the wheat pasture relates to what?"

"Basic anatomy, Clio. They aren't cows. They're steers, and you said 'steers' when you made the comment about milking them."

"So, they're boy cows. Everybody knows you can't milk bulls."

"That's true. And, no they're not. Steers are castrated. That means their balls ..."

"I know what it means. If they could sing, they'd be mooing like a castrato."

Jeremiah sniggered. "I wish Pa were in here. He gets a kick out of your sense of humor, Clio. Did you hear him laughing in the pickup? I haven't heard him laugh like that in ages."

Reaching across the table for another slice of cake, Jeremiah kept talking with his mouth full: "We raise steers for beef. When they've put on enough pounds, they'll go to the slaughterhouse."

I pushed my leftover cake toward Jeremiah. Images of great haunches of bloody meat on hooks popped into the picturesque frame of adolescent bovines peacefully chomping their way to certain death in green pastures. I might never be hungry again.

As though he were reading my mind, Jeremiah said: "This is a working farm, Clio. Most of our stock aren't pets. We don't give names to the animals that are heading to a butcher. Mother always had a problem with that part of farming. She only named animals that we keep, such as the milk cows and our horses."

"Horses?" That got my attention, especially after what Mr. Whittaker said about my mother keeping her horse at the Clower Ranch, a place my aunts rarely mentioned.

"Yeah. We're going to ride back to Wolfe Flats this afternoon. You sit here for a minute while I go upstairs to see if I can find a pair of boots so you don't ruin your new sandals."

Jeremiah knelt by my foot and stretched his thumb and little finger alongside the sole. "Big feet for a girl. Mom's feet are small. I think you can wear the boots I had in the fifth grade."

Gratified that Jeremiah didn't hang around to register my shock, I began cataloging the reasons why I would never get on a horse. With Mother's encouragement, I'd touched the muzzle of one that pulled carriages around

Central Park. It snorted something so slimy on me that I could literally see *E. coli* multiplying on my hands.

"It's just oats, Clio," Mother had made light of my immediate health risk. "Horses are wonderful. We'll rent some and ride in Central Park one of these days."

We never did. Mother was good at coming up with things we should do. I might have had a bit of practice, gotten my sea legs, so to speak, before being told that my transportation home would be a huge, snorting beast. I'd call Lucinda before that trip could take place. She'd save me.

A rough, mannish pair of lace-up boots plopped down by my feet. Jeremiah held up thick socks. "We're going to check out the dairy calves, Clio. Pa and I did the milking early; the bucket-fed calves are in the corral. We have twin baby calves on the bottle out in the barn. Their mother died having them. Pa thought you'd get a kick out of feeding them. They're bull calves. We usually castrate them within a day or two, but these had a hard birth, so we'll wait until they're stronger."

Still talking as he scrubbed our cake plates and stuck them in a rack to dry, Jeremiah pointed to the boots. "Better get those on. Those prissy sandals won't last a minute in the muck."

As I clomped past an unsightly heap of manure-coated hay at the side of an enormous barn, I gave Jeremiah a quick thumbs down and pointed toward the boots. Expecting his puzzled look, I enlightened him: "Roman gladiators got a thumbs down when they performed well—thumbs up meant they were toast. Reversed in translation, I suppose." I tend to rattle on when I'm out of my element.

With double doors on both ends of the barn flung wide to the streaming sunlight, this huge structure appeared forbidding. Nooks and crannies everywhere sheltered unfriendly creatures, perhaps spiders and vermin so deadly that they were yet to be classified. To combat my general uneasiness, I moved over to a row of empty stalls and let my hand dangle casually over the top board.

A fat, sandpapery slab encircled two of my fingers and began sucking, as I screeched like a banshee.

"For crying out loud, Clio. Pa probably heard you clear up in the north forty. It's just a baby." He handed me a big bottle of milk with a weird rubber spout. "Cattle have powerful tongues—they don't have any top teeth in front of their mouths. They just rip up big hunks of grass with their tongues. They aren't carnivores," he added, giggling unnecessarily.

"I know that. They are ruminants with four stomachs. I was just startled when that one latched onto me." I tried to glare down at the offending calf, but the little fawn-colored creature was looking at me with big, innocent eyes. I unlatched the gate with a bit of bravado, just to show Jeremiah. Wham! Two calves hit me, their sharp hooves battering my boots as I held the bottle aloft.

In desperation, I lowered the bottle to the greediest mouth I've ever encountered; the other mouth butted the guzzler, the bottle, and me. Simultaneously, if that is possible.

"If you feed them outside of the stall, you might survive, Clio. These little orphans think you're their mother," Jeremiah laughed.

Thrusting the bottle at Jeremiah, who had begun feeding the other calf through the slats, I eased out of the stall, checked the playsuit for calf slobbers, and gave Jeremiah the most cutting remark I could think of: "I don't think we should be talking about mothers or orphans, considering our own situations."

With that, I turned on the heels of Jeremiah's boots, intending to stride purposefully out of the barn, but tripped over a bale of hay and sprawled chin-up against an adjacent pen. Red-rimmed eyes glared down at me past a wet, black nose with an enormous ring through it. Mountainous dark shoulders rammed against the flimsy board stall.

The snorts that came out of that beast would have shamed a freight train on its huffing best day. The arms that lifted me up and backwards would have my eternal gratitude. "What in the world is that kind of cow?"

"That bull is a descendant of Majesty, a very famous Jersey from the Channel Islands—that's where the Jerseys came from. Mother named him Prince Albert, for Queen Victoria's husband—not tobacco. That is the kind I was chewing the first day you came to class."

As he leaned nonchalantly against the corral, Jeremiah ignored a beast with shoulders as wide as a freight train bracing itself for an onslaught that would surely take out those rickety boards and mangle my good friend.

"Get away! Get away! He's going to strike!" I tried to muffle a near-scream, as I tugged on Jeremiah's arm.

"He would if he were a rattler. By the way, we need to look out for them today, Clio. Snakes are coming out of hibernation. Pa saw a two-footer yesterday. Bulls gore. They don't strike." The grin on Jeremiah's face irritated me past any hope of civility.

I brushed off the straw clinging to my playsuit, stalked out of the barn, and ran smack dab into something with feathers that jabbed me in the leg; then, it held its wings down and did an odd little dance around me while I screamed in pain and fear.

Within a flash, Jeremiah snatched up the rooster and hurled it into the sky. It landed with a thump, righted itself, fluffed out its feathers, and strolled away, still looking like the cock of the walk—or barnyard, as the case may be.

"Sorry, Clio. That one did strike. Actually, he flogged you. Pa and I wear long pants, so Foghorn can't get us with his spurs. Your bare legs were a temptation. We'd put him in a pot, but Mother likes his crowing, says it reminds her of a far-off foghorn."

Kneeling down, Jeremiah lifted my leg and touched a small puncture wound. "He got you, Clio. That's for sure. It's just barely bleeding. Sometimes, a rooster's spurs gouge really hard. Good that you're OK."

Well. I wasn't. Every creature I'd encountered this morning had an overdose of testosterone: baby bull calves that tried to butt me into a pulp; a monster Jersey bull that ached to gore me through a rickety corral; and, now, a flogging rooster that had actually stabbed me.

This farm was a medieval torture chamber. "I know exactly how it feels to be on the Catherine Wheel," I muttered.

"The Catherine what?" Jeremiah questioned.

"The Catherine Wheel was a medieval torturing device, named for Saint Catherine. They strapped a victim onto the wheel and slowly rotated it while a man with a hammer smashed bones. Then, while the victim was still alive, they left what remained for the birds to peck."

"Honestly, Clio. For a girl who outwitted a serial killer and survived being thrown down a well with his other victims, I'd think a little rooster's gaffs wouldn't phase you at all," Jeremiah said.

A bit testily, I thought. Time to keep my opinions close to the chest and give the farm a chance to be the idyllic country retreat that Jeremiah needed to pretend it was.

"So, show me something that doesn't butt, gore, or flog."

Jeremiah opened the door of a chicken coop and pointed inside. Dozens of tiny yellow chickens drank purplish water from an upside-down fruit jar on a circular trough, while others scratched and pecked pale dirt.

"Chicken mash. We buy it from Lester Smith's Feed and Seed. These chickens just hatched yesterday. I was hoping they'd hatch before you got here." He scooped up a fluffy mite and put it in my open hands.

Its tiny feet peppered my palms in the most restorative pattern I could imagine. This was idyllic. No other word for it. When Jeremiah mentioned Lester Smith, I thought about his idea for victory chickens, a coop in every backyard in Wolfe Flats. Then I remembered those hesitant half-truths he had told me about Aunt Norma's beau.

"I met Lester Smith yesterday. We hid under the courthouse steps while the tornado twisted overhead. He told me about the war." I revealed just a vague bit of information about my meeting with Mr. Smith. So far, I hadn't told Jeremiah anything about my Aunt Norma's beau, one of the two Musketeers who didn't come home, and the only one not listed on the WWI memorial on the outer wall of the courthouse.

"Why in the world would Mr. Smith be talking to you about the war?" Jeremiah asked as he latched the chicken coop behind us. "He's ancient. Probably older than your aunts."

"He was in the Battle of Belleau Wood in the Great War, along with a few other men from Wolfe Flats. If you knew your history, you'd know that Belleau Wood was an important battle in World War I. The Marines saved the day. Now, that place in France is a memorial to American soldiers."

"You got all that under the courthouse steps?"

I could tell when Jeremiah was peeved. He read all the war histories he could get his hands on. His brother, Luke, was in the Navy, somewhere in the South Pacific. He'd never let on, but Jeremiah was a bit envious that my mother was at risk in Europe interviewing soldiers, while his mother was studying mold somewhere safe in the tropics.

Circling back into the barn, Jeremiah grabbed wire cutters and cut through a bale of greenish straw. "I'll show you the horses. They'll come when I throw alfalfa over the fence."

Alfalfa was a word I knew. Mother loved the Our Gang movies, so we hadn't missed a single one in the series. The child star who played Alfalfa sported two black wings of hair, clipped above his ears and parted neatly down the center—as though a blackbird had landed on his head and been whacked in half.

I didn't know that the character Alfalfa was named for a bale of hay.

That made sense, considering that his best friend was called Spanky, another curious name. Mother laughed at everything in those movies—bullies picking on Spanky, fake love notes, and frogs being stuffed into a dancer's tights.

Growing up in Wolfe Flats in Mother's generation must bolster a sense of humor. Just look at how George Whittaker split his sides laughing at me this morning, because I didn't know that steers weren't cows. Considering the lack of entertainment in these parts, I'll admit that there's not much to laugh about in Wolfe County.

CHAPTER 17

I moved unreasonably close to Jeremiah as four horses thundered across the pasture; they were clearly intent on flattening us before we could scoot under the fence. Like small miracles, flimsy piles of alfalfa hay stopped them short. Jeremiah walked around those huge huffing beasts with no more concern than if they were fuzzy chickens.

"Pa's horse is this buckskin. He's called Buck, not a very inventive name. Buck's as good a cutting horse as you will ever see. Pa competed when he was younger."

From a safe distance by the fence, I glanced at an ecru-colored horse with a dark stripe down his back. I wasn't about to ask what a "cutting horse" did. I had already shown my color as a greenhorn.

"This little chestnut mare is Mom's. Her name is Marguerite, for the Scarlet Pimpernel's wife. Mom and I love that book," Jeremiah paused and cocked his ear toward the horizon as though listening for his mother's confirmation. "The two geldings are mine and Luke's. My pinto is named Percy; he's the Pimpernel. Luke's horse is

Skipper. I wasn't sure why he named it that, but when he ran off to join the Navy, the name made sense."

Flinging his arm over the neck of Marguerite, he walked the horse toward me. I stood, rooted to the spot, with a nonchalant expression on my face, keeping my eye on an escape route. "Does she bite?" I asked, taking note of her great, square teeth chomping down green hay.

"Yeah. Grass and the other horses, if they bother her. She's female, snappish if she doesn't get her way." Grabbing her mane with one hand, Jeremiah effortlessly swung up to her broad back and smiled down at me. "This afternoon, you can ride her to Wolfe Flats. I'll take Skipper. He hasn't been ridden for awhile."

"I'm not accustomed to riding horses, Jeremiah. Subways, buses, and cars are the preferred modes of transportation for New Yorkers. I'm still a New Yorker at heart." I tried to let a dismissive tone override the considerable panic I was experiencing. Lucinda could pick me up in her old truck. She'd rather collect me in one piece than with multiple fractures.

"This old mare is so gentle that she could rock a baby to sleep. You don't have to be *accustomed* to ride Marguerite." Jeremiah slid off the back of the horse. "Pa told me to check out the steers to be sure none of them have grass staggers. Let's walk over to the steers, the milkers," Jeremiah giggled.

I wasn't about to be fooled twice. "There is no such thing as 'grass staggers,'" I said archly. "I may not be schooled in the rural lexicon of animal husbandry, but I can recognize a put-down."

"No. Really, Clio. New wheat can cause low levels of magnesium in cattle. They have to be checked for signs of it. We lost a couple of steers last year. Pa would be pissed off if I don't check them. There's a spring-fed pond just beyond that pasture with the steers that you'll want to see. I fixed up a great rope swing."

I'd show interest in anything to get Jeremiah off the subject of me riding a horse. That wasn't going to happen.

What happened next restored my belief that rural life can be pleasant and bucolic. We walked through a field of steers, so busily chomping on wheat that they didn't cast an eye in our direction—and not a single one staggered about or fell into a cow coma.

Following a pair of ruts through the pasture, we climbed a small hill and came upon a pastoral scene that stopped me short. Great swaths of wildflowers swooped ahead of us toward a small crystalline lake, dimpling in the morning breeze, with a magnificent, branching tree beside it. Nothing that I had seen in Wolfe Flats, or, for that matter, out the train window while traveling through the entire Midwest, could top this scene for beauty.

"Poppy Mallow," Jeremiah announced, pulling up a handful of white flowers tinged with pink. "Mom told me that wildflowers are temperamental. They grow when and where they want to. Sometimes they don't come back for years. Then, they do."

Jeremiah had the saddest expression on his face, as though he wasn't thinking of wildflowers at all.

He broke of a fernlike stem with compact heads of flowers. "This is Wooly Yarrow, *Achillea lanulosa.* I know the common names and the scientific ones. I cut my teeth, so to speak, on botanical names. Mom knows more about wildflowers than anyone on the planet."

He crumbled the stem in his hand and sniffed it. "Yarrow has lots of medicinal uses. It's an analgesic, an anesthetic, and an anti-inflammatory. The Indians and pioneers used it for lots of things."

We circled the pond and came up on the far side of the tree. "This tree is a bur oak, *Quercus macrocarpa*, the only one on our place. Pa says this one is well over a hundred feet high. Mom made lots of sketches of it. She loved this place."

Jeremiah unwound the end of a thick rope, tied far up in the tree, let it dangle free, then swung from branch to branch, using it to go higher and higher.

A grinning freckled face looked down at me. "Watch me launch off this branch, Clio. In summer, you can drop into the pond, but it's too cold now, so I'll just swing like Tarzan. Then you can do it."

Or not. The city fathers in New York do not take kindly to people climbing trees along the sidewalks. The city doesn't have very inviting trees, except for the tall, friendly American elms in Grand Central Park. With millions of visitors a year and police on patrol, I learned to be a quick and invisible climber. This tree, with its symmetrically tiered branches, seemed to be laying out a welcome mat just for me. Kicking off Jeremiah's boots so that I could get a good grip with my toes, I swung up to the first forked branch. Then, staying fairly close to the trunk, I went from limb to limb to limb without the aid of a rope.

The sensation was dizzying. Not nauseous dizziness, but the kind of gasping breathlessness, tinged with terror that makes an experience exhilarating. I could see the soles of Jeremiah's boots on the branch over my head. He might need to use the rope to climb, but I didn't. I was a born tree squirrel. Climbing always seemed second nature to me.

"You are some kind of monkey, Clio. I don't think I've ever seen a girl climb so fast. Come to think of it, I don't think I've seen anyone climb better." Jeremiah scooted along a fat branch and held out a helping hand.

I took his hand, just to be courteous, swung up and wrapped both legs around the branch on which he was sitting. The rope was knotted on a limb just over our heads.

"Later in the summer, we can swim in this pond. It's spring-fed from artesian wells way down deep in the earth. So it's always cold. By July, it'll warm up to be tolerable. Never as warm as Lake Murray. But cleaner water. From here, you can swing out and drop pretty near dead center of the pond." Jeremiah wiggled the rope. "This time of year, I just swing out and rappel down the side of the tree like a mountain climber."

"You go first," I grinned at Jeremiah with a confidence I wasn't feeling. I liked clutching branches with my hands and feet.

Just as Jeremiah swung out, popped back, jarred the tree with his big boots, and did it again, I heard the racket of a tractor grinding down that rutted path. Hanging about thirty feet above his father's head, Jeremiah looked a bit sheepish. "I was just showing Clio the pond, Pa. She can't swim."

Well. Did he have to spread that around?

"Manboy Muller will give me lessons. I have a new swimsuit," I added confidently, as though a fragment of rayon might keep me afloat.

Then, with more courage than I was feeling, I dropped down a branch, landing on both feet, and swung down a tier of branches faster than I climbed them. Within seconds, I was on the ground, while Jeremiah was still hanging off the end of his rope.

I thought that George Whittaker had only two expressions—grumpy and stoical—but he showed a third one. It was a cross between disbelief and envy.

"You made it down that tree in ten seconds flat, Clio. I'd say that's a record. Climb aboard. I thought you two might like a ride back to the house for lunch."

Standing on the back of a bumpy tractor with two big wheels threatening to grind me into oblivion if I fell in their path was not my idea of a good trip. I did like the way that Jeremiah gripped my arm. I wasn't too keen about leaning into his father's sweaty back.

Letting the tractor idle, while we hopped down, Jeremiah's father barked out orders: "Jeremiah, you can pan fry the hamburgers with onions." He handed me my boots. "It's a good idea to wear these around here, Clio. They might not be good for climbing, but I killed a copperhead in the front flowerbed this morning. Bare feet and snakes are not a good combo."

CHAPTER 18

L unch was a hamburger patty on a slice of home-made bread with a pickle and onion on the side. Iced tea with too much sugar made me gag, but I was hungry, so I made fast work of the hamburger. Dessert was home-canned peaches, floating in whipping cream.

"Mom did all the canning. We're rationing the jars until she gets back. Her peaches are a special treat for you, Clio. I hope she's back by late summer. That's when the peaches will be ripe."

I didn't want to throw a wet blanket on this nice lunch, but considering that Burma fell to the Japanese two days ago, and Mexico declared war on the Axis early today, we appear to be in this war for the long haul.

My mother wouldn't be getting on a troop ship home from Europe as long as an Allied soldier was left for her to interview. Jeremiah's mother might be getting tired of mold and foot rot, but I doubt if watching jars seal in boiling water while the heat is 115 degrees in the shade would lure her to Oklahoma in the summer.

I watched George Whittaker and his son chewing companionably.

Jeremiah would be an important reason for his mother to return. His good-looking father might be another reason, if he weren't so handy with his fists.

I cast my eyes down to my greasy plate, for fear that Shakespeare's "green-eyed monster of jealousy" might be flashing in my peepers like a go light. Even a testy father is better than no father at all. When Mother got rid of mine, she wiped the Licthman name off my map.

"The day is getting on. Why don't you show Clio your mother's sketchbooks? Sonya has a real talent for drawing, Clio," he added with just an echo of melancholy—or maybe regret—in his voice. Mr. Whittaker shoved his chair back from the table, walked toward the kitchen door, and barked out: "Kitchen duty, Jeremiah. You should give those twin calves another bottle of milk before they go in with the other calves tomorrow. No more pampering. I'll get the cows in while you're taking Clio home."

Jeremiah's father had an odd way of saying that my visit was coming to an end. I needed to get to a phone to call Lucinda so that she could rescue me before my equestrian skills were made public. A black wall phone hung beside the back kitchen door. As soon as Jeremiah disappeared up the stairs, I picked it up and told the operator, Rayleen, to connect me to my aunts' number: 405.

After half a dozen rings, Rayleen came back on the line and snapped at me: "No one is answering at your aunts' house. You need to hang up, Clio. The Whittakers are on a party line. Someone needs to use the phone." *As if I didn't. Alexander Graham Bell must be turning in his grave to know that ill-mannered operators had taken over his invention in this undeveloped part of the world.*

Jeremiah came into the room holding two portfolios. "Pa thought you'd like to see Mom's drawings. Who were you calling?"

"Just checking in with Lucinda. No one answered. My aunts keep me on a short leash." I threw in a zinger, so he wouldn't suspect I was trying to arrange sensible transportation home.

"With good reason. You almost rode the pale horse after tracking down Whitey Lewin." Jeremiah smiled at me. "Revelations 6:8. I can quote biblical passages, but only interesting ones. You know something, Clio? Helping Manboy pull you out of that old well, then being chased by Whitey in his pickup was the most exciting time I've ever had. I'll remember that all my life. Shots fired. A pickup exploded in flames. It was better than a movie."

Jeremiah could have talked all day long without bringing up the pale horse of death, considering what might be waiting for me atop a fat mare named Marguerite. Staring him down, I settled onto the stiffest chair in the room and tried to repress memories of my near-death night. I recalled an ether-soaked rag in my mouth, waking up halfway down a well, sprawled on top of my bicycle above a bottomless pit of water, and wondering when my bones would join those of the other girls in the well.

Except for the setbacks of a bullet through my arm and a broken ankle, I came out of the entire experience with a considerably inflated ego. By situating my wounded arm atop the sizeable cast on my foot, Sally Tolliver got a riveting news photo. Aunt Norma said I looked like an acrobat who fell off the beam. However, I was the town hero—for about a week. Wolfe Flats isn't a place that is overly mindful of gratitude.

"You're not nervous about riding a horse home are you, Clio? I'll get you back by three o'clock. I need to help Pa with the milking—keep him in good spirits. I can use a lead rope on Marguerite if you think she's going to bolt."

I didn't think any such thing. Or, if I did, I'd keep it to myself. I opened one of the sketchbooks of Jeremiah's mother and began praising her drawings to high heaven, just to stay on Jeremiah's good side. To put his mother in good company, I told him about the greatest museum in this country.

"Do you know that the Metropolitan Museum in New York City has over 17,000 drawings? Da Vinci, Raphael, lots of the Old Masters—and tons of newer artists. Our neighbors, the Abrams, took me to the museum almost every week. They said that when the Nazis invaded Poland in 1939, they snatched up art objects from public places and private citizens. They're a bunch of goose-stepping thieves."

Just at that moment, thinking about Mr. and Mrs. Abrams brought on a sad feeling. They'd be missing me something fierce. Mr. Abrams taught me more about math and geometry than our sixth-grade teacher, Mrs. Wallace, could imagine—with her silly word problems. I guess I hold a grudge against her for not missing her vanished niece. The fact that Mrs. Wallace let that murderer Whitey teach her how to drive her niece's car was salt in the wound.

"This one puzzles me." Jeremiah held up what appeared to be a segmented tree. "I keep looking at it over and over. This is that old oak we climbed, but Mom drew it with odd cubes and squares and circles so that it looks like a geometric maze with leaves—not the tree at all. It's like she was trying to get to the soul of the tree—not what it looks like but what it is."

"That drawing is very modern, Jeremiah. Like Klee and those artists at the Bauhaus. That was a famous German school of art before the Nazis decided what was good art and what wasn't. They had a big bonfire of what they called 'degenerate' art. Mr. Abrams almost hyperventilated when he talked about it."

I flipped through another sketchbook, hoping to find other examples of his mother's modern art. Her botanical sketches were well done but not the kind of art that a Nazi would consider amoral. I tried another approach to put Jeremiah's mother in the company of famous artists—as though offering him a bit of comfort in her absence.

"Mr. Abrams showed me some prints in a book he had brought with him when he left Poland. The artists were called *Les Fauves,* the wild beasts, because they broke the rules of painting with bright colors and distorted shapes. I didn't much like them, but Mr. Abrams said that it was art for our time."

I glanced out the window at a carpet of Indian paintbrush that Jeremiah told me is also called prairie fire. The brilliant coral sweeping low along the side of the road, under a sky of translucent blue, took my breath away.

Wanting to share what I was feeling with Jeremiah, I hesitated. He was too much like me. We both backed away from showing emotion. People with raw wounds repel a touch. So, I brought a friend to the conversation. "When Mr. Abrams saw a painting that he really liked, he'd always say the same thing: 'There is geometry in the humming of the strings.' Mr. Abrams quoted Pythagoras more often than Aunt Norma quotes Psalms."

Jeremiah gave me one of those blank looks that meant he wasn't much interested in my New York friends or a little lecture on art. He was interested in his mother's drawings, so I praised them again.

"This is the last book of drawings that Mom was working on before she left. I found it open on her desk. She and Pa had an argument just before she left for the grocery store. She didn't come back." Jeremiah handed me the sketchbook.

Her wild flowers were too perfect, their stalks upright, their blossoms absolutely balanced. They were the drawings of a jailed soul, of someone seeing the outside through the bars of a prison.

Jeremiah wanted admiration for his mother, not my analysis of her mental state. "Your mother's sketches of prairie flowers belong in the Metropolitan Museum," I said, with the widest smile I could muster.

That might have been overstating her skills, but her Indian paintbrush flowers stayed on the ground—they didn't fall off the edges of the page like Mr. Klee's subjects.

CHAPTER 19

An hour later, I feared that I might fall off the saddle and be sliced into slivers, thinner than Lucinda slices bacon, by those metal-clad hooves of Marguerite when she charged down the road behind Jeremiah on Skipper. A minute later, I knew that my teeth were dislodging themselves from my jaws when she broke into a trot.

"Lean back, Clio. You're humped over like a jockey. We ride western-style, upright. Brace your sandals in the stirrups. You should have kept my boots on. Those sandals are for show, not riding a horse. You and Mom are about the same height, so I didn't adjust the stirrups. I guess you haven't ever ridden a horse or you'd know not to hold the reins and the mane in both hands at the same time. Relax."

With an evil grin, Jeremiah popped Marguerite on the rump, and she tore down the road with me clinging on for dear life. But I wasn't afraid. This horse was rocking me with a great, rolling stride that was a comfort. Her trot had jarred me mercilessly. Her gallop set me free. I couldn't keep the smile off my face.

"You're a natural, Clio. If your aunts won't get you a horse, you can ride ours anytime. Pa won't care. He told me that he thinks you're a hoot. He said that you might live up to your mother's reputation."

I glared at him. My mother's reputation in Wolfe Flats had lingered long after she had left the place. When my aunts introduced me to people, they'd stare and mutter something like: "Delia's daughter? Really?" Then they'd launch into some memory of my mother that would stitch Aunt Norma's mouth into a line so tight that not a kind word would come out of it for the rest of the day.

In the distance, I could see the Wolfe Flats' water tower, with a ladder halfway up that always tempted me. Beyond that, the tornado-damaged cupola from the fire station hung at half-mast, reminding me of my brief visit with Lester Smith under the courthouse steps, while the storm roared above the town.

That investigation was unfinished business. I needed another session with Mr. Smith to see if I could bring to light the truth about what happened in Belleau Wood in France in World War I. Lester Smith must have been the radioman described by Lorenz Weber's wounded father when Aunt Norma's beau Larry was trying to help him.

When you grow up with a journalist mother—especially one who wants to be where the battle rages—you learn a great deal about how soldiers communicate. Radio sets in World War I were heavy and bulky. Operators needed aerials for wireless transmission. Wired systems were clumsy and easily damaged. Homing pigeons were used, just as they were in the Middle Ages, to carry messages. And dogs were sent back and forth from the front lines to the trenches.

It was highly unlikely that more than one radio operator would have been with those American doughboys in that same area of Belleau Wood when Lawrence Bresant came upon a German boy with half of his foot blown off.

Coincidences happen. But not one that involves two soldiers from a backwater place like Wolfe Flats—one of them mysteriously dead and the other one unable to remember what happened.

I was certain that Lester Smith recalled much more than he was willing to admit. He remembered well enough to edit the story that he told Larry Bresant's parents and Aunt Norma. Helping people remember what they'd like to forget is what I do best. I just needed more time to question the radioman, Mr. Smith. My questions can drive the sanest person up the wall. Just ask Aunt Norma. She'll tell you.

As Marguerite slowed down to a nice, steady walk, so that I could examine a blister on a thumb that had never released its grip on the saddle horn since we left the Whittaker farm, I saw an amazing sight.

The Brown twins stood on the corner of First and Main with their identical jaws locked into what might have been a gasp of surprise or supreme irritation.

Here I was, perched atop a feisty horse, wearing new sandals with exotic symbols tooled into the leather, riding side by side into town with Jeremiah Whittaker, the most popular boy in our class—at least, the most interesting one.

I couldn't have staged a finer entry into Wolfe Flats—or a less appreciative audience. The Brown twins had made it clear from my first day in class that no Yankee girl would ever fit into their inner circle. My little buck and wing dance in front of the class didn't break the ice with those two girls.

That suited me just fine. I had lots of friends: Jeremiah, Sally Tolliver at the newspaper, Manboy and his mother, Marek Neboja and his father, who owned the blacksmith shop. I rarely attract friends my own age. When I eavesdropped on their conversations at school, it appeared to me that the Brown twins and their girlfriends would be happiest in a harem in the Ottoman Empire.

Fingernail polish, lipstick, hair rollers, and the Hit Parade's top songs raced through their collective minds like whirligigs flapping in the wind. Twice, at the weekly assembly, the Brown twins sang "Amapola" with a harmony that would incite instantaneous beheading if we were lucky enough to have a guillotine on stage.

The Brown twins didn't like me, and I did everything in my power to stay miles away from them. However, my aunts were determined to put me dead center into their little clique. At dinner last night, Aunt Norma overcame her migraine just to let me know that I'd be attending MYF, Methodist Youth Fellowship, this very week.

Attending might be compulsory. Participating is quite another matter. I would decide. At this moment, I wished that I were wearing a medieval knight's armor. I could tip up my visor to those twins to assert myself, to show them I was in control. The Brown twins probably wouldn't get the gesture. They spent their dimes on *Movie Life*. I was saving my dimes for a train ticket back to New York City when Wolfe Flats became too oppressive.

"I thought you didn't like those Brown girls, Clio. Why did you wave at them? They didn't wave back."

"*Noblisse oblige.* Just acknowledging the peasants. Aunt Norma insists that I must be civil. She's putting me in the thick of it tomorrow afternoon—forcing me to go to MYF."

"The Baptists have better church camps at Turner Falls than the Methodists," Jeremiah said. "I hear that they sneak out at night and get up to no good. That's the camp I'd rather go to, but Mom's a Methodist." He shot me a rueful smile. "Maybe you and me will go to that camp. Pa needs me to help every day now. When the war is over, maybe we can go."

The cavalry had assembled on the porch when Jeremiah and I rode up together. Sliding down, I handed Marguerite's reins to Jeremiah and gave him a word to the wise: "Better get back to help your father. I can face the music here." Just as he turned his horse and headed down the street, I yelled after him: "I had the most stunningly amazing time at your farm. I don't remember a better day. Thank your father for me."

With those three sentences, I knew that I would get under Aunt Norma's skin like scabies. She didn't like Jeremiah's father; she hadn't given me permission to spend the day at his farm; and, she wouldn't like the fact that I had a better time looking at cows than I would have had at the Methodist Rummage Sale.

Actually, she said only one thing: "If I'd known you were going to ride a horse, Clio, I'd have looked for Delia's old boots. They're somewhere in the attic with the rest of her clothes."

After the day spent at Jeremiah's farm, I had begun to think of Wolfe Flats as offering a generous summer, full of free days, without the restrictions of school and church—and without piano scales and lists of books chosen by Aunt Norma.

I should know better than to think I could rest on my laurels. Crime never takes a vacation. Unsolved crimes linger for centuries. The mystery about Lawrence Bresant had been moldering in cold case files for two decades.

Unlike most of a detective's work, this mystery was personal. It had wrapped Aunt Norma into a cloud of sadness. That's what living with the unknown does to you. My own mother had wrapped me into that same cloud.

Aunt Harriet told me about the "cloud of unknowing." She said that Christian mystics in medieval times believed if they surrendered their mind and ego that they could glimpse the nature of God. "It's a selfless kind of meditation, Clio—I sometimes practice it when I'm not quite centered," Aunt Harriet added, as she left the room, leaning sideways, like a scalene triangle.

Being very possessive of my mind and ego, I'll let the mystics and the Methodists surrender. I prefer keeping my very secret self tucked away into a cloud of my own making, the sort of fog that keeps other people away from my private world.

CHAPTER 20

Needing a dose of reality to escape Aunt Harriet's "cloud of unknowing," I wandered into the kitchen, where a pig knuckle, with the warty skin still attached, decorated the chopping block. Lucinda reared back and swung a meat cleaver at it with the strength of a Viking warrior going after a helpless monk. "Some people leaves the knuckle whole to cook, but Claire Muller showed me how her grandma done it to get more stock for the cabbage. Germans is fond of hock and cabbage."

Holding the cleaver aloft for another whack, Lucinda paused and lowered her weapon. "I been thinkin' about Delia. You think them Japs bombing our boys in Pearl Harbor set her off about goin' to war?"

I shook my head solemnly. I knew exactly what set off my mother and when it happened. That pork hock and the mention of cabbage brought back a vivid memory. Our Polish refugee neighbors in New York, the Abrams, had invited us to dinner. We were knee-to-knee around their tiny kitchen table, watching Mrs. Abrams position a pinkish ham hock, afloat in a sea of cabbage, in the middle of the table.

I was only eight years old, but that memory is elephantine. The Germans had invaded Poland the day before. Mr. Abrams had turned up the crackle of the announcer's voice on the radio. In describing the invasion of Poland, the announcer used a German word. Mr. Abrams's face flushed the color of a brick as he shouted: "*Lebenstraum!*"

Startled by my mild-mannered friend, whose voice never reached 60 decibels, I had inched my chair back.

"That word *lebenstraum* means 'living space,' living space for Germans in Poland. That monster Hitler talks about the invasion as though the Germans just strolled across the border to claim a bit of Polish soil. The Germans are destroying Poland!"

"Saul. Saul." Mrs. Abrams patted his arm with one hand while she ladled pig fat and cabbage onto plates with her other hand. "You were smart to get us out in time. We are safe here. We have friends," she beamed at Mother and me, while easing a spoonful of gristle onto my plate.

To lower Mr. Abrams's temperature, I sliced a tiny shred of lean pork away from the gelatinous mass and pronounced it "delicious." I was shocked by his fury. The invasion of Poland had begun the day before. Maybe his pent-up fury had just reached the boiling point. Pig knuckle can do that to a person.

That mindreader, Mr. Abrams—who had introduced me to Gerardus Mercator and the world of mapmaking—answered me before I could ask the question. "It's the way that Hitler said it, Clio, that offends me more than his army of tanks and guns. It is the lie behind the smile. He speaks as though Germany is simply annexing Poland, taking it away from a willing and compliant population. The lie makes the deed more heinous."

He had reached over and touched my cheek. "You are too young, Clio, to understand how memory and regret merge into a kind of sorrow that becomes too heavy to bear. I want to make a difference, but I can't. I hope others will."

At that moment, a glint in Mother's eye seemed to absorb all the light in that small kitchen, with only one over-head bulb. She didn't say a word, as she struggled through too much cabbage with not enough pork. Something changed that night in the way that she thought about the war. It wasn't about the Poles. It wasn't about the threat to England. The words that Mr. Abrams said changed Mother—long before the Japanese smashed Pearl Harbor to smithereens.

After asking for a detailed report about what Jeremiah and I had done at his farm, Aunt Harriet launched into a running monologue during dinner, telling me about Jeremiah's mother. "Sonja came to Wolfe Flats when the Oklahoma Cooperative Extension Services set up an office in Ardmore. She was a widow with a little boy, Luke—and a Methodist. Then she married George and didn't attend church much that first year.

"Jeremiah come exactly ten months after that wedding, Harriet. That poor girl suffered nine months of the mornin' sickness. She had a five-year-old to look after, a farm to help run, and a new husband who was set in his ways. I think church was the last thing on Sonya's mind when she couldn't hardly get out of bed." Lucinda provided considerable history and a health report, as she plopped a steaming blackberry cobbler on the table.

"It's no surprise that she took off all secret like after puttin' up with George all those years. The final straw come when Luke joined the Navy without so much as a word. I give Clio permission to go to the farm with Jeremiah, because that boy needs a friend." Lucinda glowered at Aunt Norma, as though she were expecting the reprimand that was on the way.

"We don't gossip at the dinner table, Lucinda. I'm sure that Clio had a pleasant visit with Jeremiah on his father's farm. She could have discussed the invitation with us last night, but she didn't."

Sometimes I had the feeling that I was like that bronze bust of Mr. Beethoven in Felicity Langston's living room—cast in iron, frozen in time, guaranteed to be forever speechless as people talked past me.

Aunt Harriet soothed things over by heading down another track. "When I saw Clio coming up the street on that horse this afternoon, she looked exactly like Delia at that age. One of these days, we need to drive out to the ranch, Norma. We used to spend considerable time there when Delia was growing up."

"A girl needs her own horse. I'll grant you that. I'm sure that we can arrange something. I'll look into it. You do need to see our ranch, Clio. You and Delia will own it some day if she ever . . ." Aunt Norma stopped, flushed an odd shade of pink, and pinched the space between her eyes.

Just as I had begun to feel all warm and fuzzy with the thought of getting my own horse, Aunt Norma threw in a zinger. She didn't have to mention my mother with a voice that dropped down so flat and toneless that it sucked out every tiny bit of hope that I was feeling at that moment.

"I don't need a horse. I'm going out to the shed to check on my bicycle." With that edict and to express my anger, I pushed back from the table, reached across Aunt Harriet's plate to grab a handful of oozing cobbler, and dripped it all across the dining room and kitchen floors right out into the backyard.

The detached garage, sheltering Aunt Norma's Pierce Arrow, had once served as some kind of workshop and potting shed, with living quarters above. It intrigued me. You'd take your life in your hands if you climbed the stairs that led up to a second story, with big dormer windows that looked into the Mullers' backyard. I'd made it to the top of the stairs only once when I was exploring the property. Lucinda had caught me and screamed the house down.

"Don't you never go up them stairs. They's rotten to the core. Our last hired man stuck his leg through the landing halfway up. He didn't have no business goin' up there. No one has lived up there for twenty years. Nothin' but old boxes and cast-off furniture. And packrats."

The odors of damp sawdust and rusted tools hanging along the walls of the garage comforted me in an odd way. This old structure on my aunts' property was forsaken, left with only ghosts from the past.

Long ago, someone had actually lived upstairs and spent time in the workshop. The old bench vise that had held my Mary Janes in place, while I sawed off their tops, lured me like a magnet, with its big iron bar poised to move the jaws of the vise.

Never had I seen such an interesting collection of tools.

Mother kept a screwdriver and a small hammer in a kitchen drawer in our apartment. That was our tool supply.

In the corner of the workshop stood a big wooden chest with ornate metal handles on each end of it. I eased up the top and found an assortment of chisels and knives and wrenches and other things that I couldn't even name. Long, wooden boxes, with sleek, mitered ends that fit like a Chinese puzzle into the next layer, lifted out easily. Whoever made this chest was a master carpenter or a magician.

Edging past Aunt Norma's great, hulking car, I circled away from the workshop to stand at the foot of the stairs. The setting sun cast one long stream of dying light onto the dusty steps—and big shoe prints that led up and up. I froze.

You don't have to hear anything to know that something is there. Something breathing. Something waiting. Something that may or may not be human.

The packrats that Lucinda mentioned had not left those prints, which faced in one direction. Whoever or whatever had gone up those stairs had not come down.

I crept back to the big wooden chest, lifted the lid, and pulled out a foot-long chisel that might take out a carotid before the victim could scream for help. With that in my right hand, I grabbed the deadliest tool I could see hanging on the wall. An axe. Rusty, but with a big, sturdy handle.

Standing at the bottom of the stairs with one eye fixed on an escape route out the side door of the garage, I let loose a threat: "Show yourself. Come out of that room up there. I've caught you red-handed. I'll be calling the sheriff." *That was a lie. I'd gotten Wolfe Flats' sheriff fired when he defended Whitey Lewin and threatened me in my hospital room. Wolfe Flats hadn't found a replacement—only that poor excuse for a deputy was in charge.*

My voice sounded like someone speaking in a high falsetto, like one of those castratos, doomed to be a soprano for life. "Come out right now or I'll get the authorities." *There. That sounded as though I'd recovered my alto voice and just a smidgen of courage. I could be out the side door before anyone above the upper landing made it down the stairs.*

The head that appeared in the doorway just beyond the landing belonged to someone who couldn't have been much older than Jeremiah. Blonder but not much older.

"Please, miss. I am hiding. I am not hurting anyone. Do not tell the police. You will cause me much trouble. Is this not the Clower house? Mr. Muller told me he lived by it. So I found it."

Even in the twilight, I could see the faint stubble of light-colored whiskers on a face that seemed unnaturally pale. His clothes were odd, shapeless, wrinkled things— clearly clothes that had never been subject to Lucinda's sprinkler bottle and hot iron.

"Are you Miss Clower?" The voice sounded tentative. One foot extended toward the first step. "No. You are just a girl."

"Stay right where you are. Don't take another step. This girl is armed." I waved the chisel like a sword fighter, trying to demonstrate an expertise that I didn't feel. Then I answered his question.

"Yes. I'm Miss Clower. There are four of us, including my two aunts. My mother took back her maiden name and gave it to me." My nervousness made me babble like Aunt Harriet. I glared at the intruder, who opened his hands to show he wasn't armed.

"I came to meet with Norma Clower. It was the dying wish of my father to say what her friend did for him. In that other war." His heavily accented voice sounded sadder than Jeremiah's when he talked about his missing mother.

It didn't take a genius to figure out that I was talking to Manboy's POW—whatever excuses he might make for hiding in Aunt Norma's garage. Enemy prisoners could be dangerous. In different garb, this man might have stepped right out of one of those Storm Troop posters. I could almost see the flag with a swastika waving in his hands as he fixed his greedy eyes on a far-off country.

"You're a German prisoner. You're supposed to be behind bars in Camp Houze. How did you get here?" I kept my axe visible to the enemy.

He lifted one mud-caked shoe and leg. "I walked and swam across the river and walked more. Maybe thirty kilometers."

I lowered the chisel but kept a grip on the axe as I offered another threat. "They'll have military police looking for you. With dogs, I expect." Then, I remembered that he'd crossed the river. The dogs would have lost his scent. I inched the chisel forward.

"Why are you hiding in Aunt Norma's garage? Are you the one Manboy Muller told me about? The son of that man with the . . ." I paused. Saying "blown-off foot" sounded uncivil.

A broad smile lit up the man's face, as he eased his body forward but didn't take a step. "Yes. Mr. Muller. He is a nice man who let me tell him about my father and the American who saved his life. He's the one. He told me Norma Clower lives in his town, next to him."

"You're Lorenz Weber." I lowered the chisel but kept the escaped German on the staircase landing in my sights.

At that moment, a police siren blared down Choctaw Street with such a resounding wail that I whipped around to look through the garage window to see what it might be chasing and lived to regret my stupidity.

Two strong arms encircled me and yanked me backwards. One hand clamped over my open mouth. So, I did what came naturally. I savagely bit it.

The hand dropped instantly, followed by Lorenz Weber on his knees, prayerful one might say, like a sinner, with one hand aloft and a nice, deep circle where my teeth had been.

"Sorry, little girl. I don't scare you on purpose. The siren was loud, like the camp siren. I did not think clearly. I do not intend to cause trouble."

When you're looking down on the nape of a man's neck while armed with an axe in one hand and a chisel in the other, he doesn't seem so scary. It was a young neck, with strands of curly blond hair that needed a good wash.

"If you don't want to cause trouble, why did you escape from Camp Houze? Why did you break into Aunt Norma's garage? Why are you acting so creepy? Move back. You're making me nervous." I eased forward, positioning myself behind the workbench with the vise, in case I needed a barrier. Lorenz Weber stayed on his knees.

He needed a word of comfort. "That siren was just the deputy in the sheriff's car. He likes to chase teenage drivers. Aunt Norma says if he does that on her street one more time she'll have his badge."

"I do not understand." Lorenz Weber looked up at me with eyes bluer than Jeremiah's, bluer than Manboy's, probably identical to those ice-blue eyes of Hitler.

"It's a small-town thing. Aunt Norma doesn't like sirens going off, unless there's a real threat, like a tornado or a murderer on the loose." I checked out Lorenz's eyes to see if I could detect a deadly flicker. Nope.

Stone cold blue. No expression. I might be safe doing a little detecting of my own.

If Aunt Norma knew that an escaped Prisoner of War was hiding on the premises, she'd call out the National Guard. She did that once when Mother disappeared as a teenager. Mother was hiding out with George Whittaker, before he was Jeremiah's father. That's another story. I haven't gotten to the bottom of it yet. I will.

Lorenz Weber settled back on his haunches, looking a bit pale and shaky. Then he stretched out one long leg. Through his torn pants, I could see an oozing slash with missing pieces of skin extending the length of his tibia. It looked like he'd been in a fight with a shark.

"You're hurt." I pointed to the wound, not daring to get closer to examine it. "Who did that to you?"

"A pig. Three pigs. Maybe more. I tried to get away, but they caught me."

"At the camp? Are you talking about the camp guards?" I got a good grip on the chisel again.

"No. No, miss. In the woods near the river, I got into some big thickets of small trees. They were wild pigs, I think. A boar with big tusks got me. No trees to climb. Mud was so thick, I couldn't move. Then I got into the river and swam. I was not sure I could swim so far. I just kept going, until I got across the current. When I reached the shore, I walked north, and stayed on the back roads. I needed to get to Wolfe Flats. I promised my father."

"Clio, are you out there in the garage poutin'?" Lucinda's voice was louder than the Hallelujah Chorus. "It's bedtime. You get in this house, or I'm comin' after you. I'm done with the chores. I need to get on home."

Easing down to his hands and knees, my POW scuttled like a crab back to the safety of a dark corner of the garage and whispered weakly: "Do not give me away. I'll hide somewhere else."

Not on your life. I had lots of questions to ask Lorenz Weber. From the looks of that leg and his pale, sweating face, this POW wouldn't make it to the street. He wasn't exactly my prisoner, but I had to abide by the Geneva Convention rules. Mother would expect it. Aunt Norma might even approve.

"Stay here. I'll be back with medicine for your leg. We can't let anyone know you're here. I won't be long. Stay right where you are."

Shifting my voice into the register of a near-screech, I leaned toward the door and shouted: "I'm coming, Lucinda. Just airing up my bike tire. I'll be there in a minute. Hang onto your horses." That comment would put Lucinda into a snit. Now, she wouldn't insist on bringing me up a bedtime cup of chocolate before she cut through the backyard to her bungalow, just a street away.

CHAPTER 21

It took forever for Aunt Harriet to put out her reading light. Aunt Norma's migraine sent her to bed early. Leaving my new sandals at the side of my bed, I tiptoed barefooted down the hall and into the bathroom.

A box below the sink held more medical supplies than a Red Cross ambulance. I tucked it under my arm and walked quietly down the stairs.

Lucinda's flashlight was exactly where it was supposed to be, in the third drawer to the left of the kitchen sink. I had to work quickly without a single betraying gleam of the flashlight. At night, when I was trying to read past my nine o'clock curfew, Aunt Norma could spot my flashlight underneath three layers of quilts and through a closed bedroom door.

My German POW was wounded. He was probably starving. And, he might answer questions put to him by a benefactor. Me.

As I eased the Frigidaire door open, the small inside light cast a helpful glow. I grabbed a bottle of milk and a hunk of rat cheese. Lucinda had wrapped the leftover dinner rolls in waxed paper in the breadbox.

I couldn't carry all of the food and the first-aid box. Remembering how Lucinda tidied everything at the end of the day, I aimed the flashlight at the trash container. A brown paper sack had replaced the day's garbage. Snitching it, I shoved in the food, gripped the first-aid supplies in the other hand, and eased open the back door.

Getting through the backyard in the dark was no problem. Four steps down, then across the broken slab of concrete, up four more steps, and I was at the side door to the garage. Mapmakers do not need a flashlight to disturb nosy neighbors. They gauge and measure and know the exact lay of the land.

"Where are you, Mr. Weber?" I hissed softly, not daring to turn on the flashlight after I opened the door. "It's Clio. I brought you food and bandages."

The slight creaking at the top of the stairs caught my attention. One soft step. Then another. And another. "I'm up here. I've been watching out the window for police or soldiers. I put cloths over the windows. You can use your flashlight. Be careful. The stairs are not stable."

That was an understatement. They were as rickety as anything I've ever climbed. Aunt Norma really needed to do something about the state of her garage. Keeping one hand over the lens of the flashlight so that only a thin stream of light beamed around the room, I spotted my POW.

Like a rat in a nest, he had pulled old blankets and odds and ends of clothing into a pile in the corner of the room behind two big boxes, creating a sort of hidey-hole.

"I do not mean to be rude. I opened these boxes to get covers. I think I have fever. I am too cold. My leg pains me. I am sorry to complain, Miss Clio."

Anchoring my flashlight so that I could have free hands to help or hit, I moved closer to Mr. Weber. "You can drop the miss. Just Clio. My aunts are called miss. Not me. I'll call you Lorenz. I'm about to do something that will make you want to scream. Don't. Aunt Harriet can hear a mouse squeak."

I uncapped the bottle of alcohol and held it above his bloody, oozing, muddy leg and let it rip.

The groan came from me, not him. I could literally see the pale flesh of his leg shrink in horror as the alcohol washed and burned the germs out of that gash. While it was still quivering, I dribbled iodine all along the palpating wound. I didn't really know first aid, but I figured that the sting of alcohol and the brownish red iodine would cure anything.

Unwinding a big roll of sterile gauze, I wrapped that POW's leg as expertly as any medic could have done on the battlefield. The entire process took only minutes, and not a drop of blood leaked to the outside of the bandage.

If anything, Lorenz was shaking more after I'd treated his wound than before I started the process, so I handed him a quart of milk, broke off a piece of cheese and sandwiched it inside a dinner roll. "I just grabbed the food I could find without making any noise. You won't starve."

With one bite, the cheese sandwich disappeared, so I made another, while Lorenz gulped down half a quart of milk. "This is so good for you to help me, Clio. I did not have a choice. The time was near. I heard them talking about it."

The desperate expression on Lorenz's face almost convinced me. Almost, but not quite. "POWs generally don't have a choice. They stay put. In America, we treat prisoners well. You have a bed. You have decent food. You even have medical care." I pointed to his leg wound that had now begun to ooze pink sap through my carefully wrapped bandage. "Now, you got care."

Lorenz eased back onto his pile of blankets. "You are not understanding, Clio. I heard guards talk about it. Prisoners are going to be moved to a state called Tex Homa. I cannot meet with Miss Norma Clower if I am sent away. I cannot say what my father told me to say to her. I made a promise. This Tex Homa state must be far away."

I might have laughed had my POW's voice not seemed so disheartened. Tucking my legs into a lotus position, I settled down, situated the axe within grabbing distance, and stuck the chisel with a loud pong into the wooden floor. "There is no state in America called Tex Homa, Lorenz. The guards were talking about a new project called Lake Texhoma, not a state."

"I heard them clearly. They talk in front of us, because most of the prisoners do not understand English. I understand everything. They said we will be moved from this camp to another camp."

"Yes. A work camp, not a prison. You met Mr. Muller. He's my good friend and neighbor." I pointed vaguely in the wrong direction in case Lorenz decided to vamoose toward the Muller house. "Mr. Muller told me that the prisoners would be digging the new lake. They'll have a bed, food, and be paid eighty cents a day. You wouldn't get that in a German or Japanese prison." *I wanted to put the idea of digging a hole halfway to China into perspective. It wasn't exactly slave labor. It wouldn't be a Sunday school picnic either.*

"They didn't tell us where we would go, Clio. They said we would be moved, and I misunderstood the name. It sounded far away. When I told Mr. Muller that I have things to say to Miss Norma Clower, he acted uneasy. He said he would think about it. When I heard we would be moved soon, I had to escape so I could say some things to Miss Norma Clower, as I promised."

Lorenz stretched out his good leg, pulled a blanket over himself, and let out a long, low sigh. "I am so very tired. Do you mind if I . . ." Not another sound came from him.

When you're just about to get the information you need to sort out a really puzzling situation and your source dies, you want to scream down the house. Given the fact that Aunt Harriet wakes when an owl hoots, I decided to keep mum and dispose of the body when no one was around.

I crawled over by where Lorenz was lying, his face pale and gleaming in the faint moonlight, through a slit in his makeshift curtain that didn't quite cover the window. Touching his damp forehead with the back of my hand, I jerked back. His skin was warm. His ragged breaths meant that my dead POW was simply my exhausted, feverish POW.

Ripping open a box, I found it full of pots and pans. Using my chisel to rip open a second box, I struck the mother lode. Pulling out two thick Hudson Bay blankets, I sniffed them cautiously and shook them vigorously to get rid of Brown Recluse spiders. According to Lucinda, who had turned me into a first-class shaker of clothes and shoes, a bite from one of those innocuous looking creatures can peel flesh right down to the bare bone.

Before piling the blankets on top of Lorenz, I put my head close to his chest to check the old thumper. It was pinging right along. The faint odor of river mud hung about him. Lucinda used her homemade lye soap to do our laundry. She claimed that store-bought soap was in short supply, but I think she just preferred her own. I'd bring some of it to Lorenz once he had the energy to think about hygiene.

Reaching into the pocket of the playsuit I'd had on all day, I pulled out my little notebook and a stub of a pencil. A mapmaker and detective never goes anywhere without those tools. Tearing out a page from my notebook, I wrote in block capitals so my POW could read it easily in his weakened state: STAY HIDDEN! DO NOT LEAVE OR YOU WILL BE CAUGHT. I WILL HELP YOU KEEP YOUR PROMISE TO YOUR FATHER. CLIO CLOWER

I started to write down other promises, such as helping him find a bathtub, better food, a comfortable bed, and an interview with Aunt Norma. I wasn't sure that I could keep any of those promises. We were at war. Lorenz was the enemy. Except for constantly worrying about my mother, I had mixed emotions about what I should be doing to aid the war effort.

Lucinda took all of our leftover grease to the Methodist Church to send to the bomb makers. Aunt Harriet read about German and Japanese atrocities in the morning paper and wept at the breakfast table. Aunt Norma didn't discuss the war at all. She said she "couldn't." Claiming "wars ruin lives in more ways than we can imagine," Aunt Norma put the kibosh on that topic as a mealtime discussion, but she continued to knit socks for the troops.

It would be best if I could keep my POW in hiding until I learned exactly what he intended to tell Aunt Norma. I could edit his story, so to speak, not the way that those editors clip Mother's news stories at the end, but just enough to make his information palatable to Aunt Norma.

As stern as she was to me, my no-nonsense Aunt Norma lived with a pain that turned her into a sad and sobbing woman. That weakness only surfaced at night when she read that old journal from the drawer in her bedside table. Just observing her in that state through the crack of her door set me on edge.

When a normal person like Aunt Norma steps outside of her every-day persona, I get jittery. It's as though a principle of geometry has been violated and something stable has shifted on its axis. Aunt Norma rarely shifts on her axis. For instance, when the collection plate is passed at church, Aunt Norma puts her envelope face down with her eyes averted—like a duchess giving to a charitable cause while trying not to attract unseemly notice.

As for cloaking his true nature, I wasn't surprised that a criminal such as Whitey Lewin wore a façade—that how-can-I-help-you-dear public face he put on around old ladies in the Methodist Church. That's how serial killers avoid detection: they never let their public mask slip.

The raspy grunts traveling from beneath the thick, woolen blankets covering my POW gave me no cause for concern. A German's snores, I figured, would be more guttural. He was simply in a dreamless sleep.

Easing past him, down the rickety stairs, walking carefully through the garage, and across the yard with no flashlight beam, I approached the back door leading into the kitchen and paused. Nothing stirred. Then, I tiptoed up the stairs and halted outside Aunt Norma's door. Her faint snores comforted me. My POW might cause her even more grief with what he had to say, especially if Lester Smith, her former high school friend, was somehow complicit in Larry Bresant's death.

CHAPTER 22

"Does anybody know what happened to that quart of milk I left in the icebox?" Lucinda looked accusingly at me as I plopped onto my chair at the breakfast table. I needed a reasonable lie quickly.

"I couldn't sleep. I came down to get a glass of milk and dropped the blasted bottle right onto the kitchen floor. Broke to smithereens. But, I cleaned it up and put the glass in the trash in the alley." Smiling apologetically, I speared two of Lucinda's buckwheat pancakes. "I need to work on my bicycle today. The chain is wonky. I expect it will take me most of the day to fix it." I flashed one of my friendlier smirks at my aunts.

"We don't say blasted, dear. It's uncouth." Aunt Harriet reprimanded me softly, but Aunt Norma sent me a fierce, questioning glance. She was a regular Sherlock when a lie popped out of my mouth.

"You spent the entire day yesterday at Jeremiah's farm. You neglected your piano practice and your summer enrichment reading." Aunt Norma's expression was unreadable, but her words pointed a finger directly at my character flaws. I needed to cover my tracks carefully.

"I'll practice scales this afternoon and tick off one of those books on your list. I really need to work on my bike chain, or I'll be afoot." Smiling sweetly at Aunt Norma, I reached for two sausage links and made a devious flip of my napkin to slide them inside. My POW would be hungry.

"Far be it from me to dictate your schedule, Clio. This is summer vacation. But idleness does not build character. One hour on the piano and one hour reading one of the classics on your list. It's a good idea to get your bicycle fixed. You'll be riding it to the Methodist Church at four o'clock."

With my chair half-scooted away from the table and my eye on the rest of those pancakes for my German, I stared at Aunt Norma. "Why would I want to go there on Wednesday? I'm too old for summer Bible School."

I had considerably more to say on the topic of church going, even on Sundays. Needing to stay on the wind-ward side of Aunt Norma, I tried to pull a blank look across my face, but my mouth kept going, in spite of my good intentions.

"It's like this, Aunt Norma. I'm an independent kind of person. I used to visit St. Patrick's Cathedral in New York City to admire the architecture. And, to meditate," I added brightly. "Freethinkers find it hard to listen to sermons."

"I told you the day before yesterday, Miss Freethinker, Methodist Youth Fellowship, MYF, meets every Wednesday at four o'clock in Fellowship Hall at the church. It's not Bible School. Young people from our church socialize under adult supervision. Games or quizzes or plans for an outing may be discussed. Treats are provided. I suspect someone will have ideas for how you young people can help with the war effort. Collect metal, or something like that."

Something like that sounded deadly dull. I'd seen five-year-olds hauling their wagons full of rusting metal down to the junkyard.

A town hero, like me, wouldn't be caught dead pulling a wagon anywhere.

At that moment, it hit me like a bucket of clear, cold water. Aunt Norma had just given me an excuse to bring her archenemy into our backyard. This morning's ad on the back page of the weekly newspaper touted Lester Smith's Victory Chickens. "In Every Yard for the War Effort."

Grinning broadly at Aunt Norma, I dropped the first hint. "I have an idea for how we can help with the war effort, Aunt Norma, but I need to do some measurements first." Then, I needed to explain why MYF didn't make me salivate. "I don't know those kids at church, except for the Brown twins. I don't like them. They don't like me. I'd rather weed Aunt Harriet's flowerbed," I added, dismissively.

"You can certainly do that, but at four o'clock this afternoon, you will be at the Methodist Church. I've told Pastor Wyndom's wife that you'll be coming. She'll introduce you. We are part of a religious family; we welcome newcomers. It's the Methodist way."

I could have interjected: "It's also the Methodist way to harbor a serial killer like Whitey Lewin." But I didn't. There was no point in setting Aunt Norma on edge with me. She stayed there most of the time anyhow. I just nodded soberly, as though alien Methodist bacteria had already invaded my bloodstream and were heading up to take over my brain.

Aunt Harriet reached across the table and patted my greasy hand, holding a napkin full of sausages. "Norma and I are concerned that you haven't made any friends with girls your own age. We like Jeremiah, but you need to make friends with girls."

"When Aunt Norma was growing up, her best friend was Lawrence Bresant. Is there a difference in being friends with a banker's son rather than a farmer's?" I'm known for my clever repartee, although my timing needs improvement. As I watched Aunt Norma's face fade from irritated to ashen, I knew I'd crossed the line. Without a word, she ducked her head, pushed her chair back, and stalked out of the kitchen.

"Well. You done it this time, Miss Motor Mouth," Lucinda shoved her skillet against the back of the stove with a loud bang and turned toward me.

"Clio, I tole your mama more times than I can count that you draw more flies with honey. Openin' old wounds never does any good. Some thins we just don't talk about around here. Larry Bresant is one of them."

From the music room at the back of the house, I could hear Aunt Harriet's fingers running up and down scales, as though she might cascade herself into some wild blue yonder where no one would ever trouble her.

I hadn't seen her leave the table. My snide comment about Larry Bresant had cleared the kitchen of both of my aunts.

Pouring more than my share of syrup over my pancakes, I tried to think of how Aunt Norma felt when she closed her bedroom door at night. She might experience a gnawing sadness that comes on at the end of a day, just like I do, no matter how many activities fill up the space. The thought of Aunt Norma's committee work boggled my mind—from the Women's Christian Temperance Union's battle against booze to encouraging an army of local children to dig up scrap metal for the war effort.

Thinking of Aunt Norma behind her bedroom door took on a deeply ambiguous meaning, as though I had somehow sliced into the past to a place where I didn't belong. Jabbing another sausage, I reflected sagely that Aunt Norma might be filling her days with busyness as a way to keep sadness at bay. Maybe those hours that she spent reading from her old friend's journal were the truest hours she had spent since Larry left.

Lucinda was keeping her back to me as she scrubbed pans in the kitchen sink, letting me know that I was in disfavor because of my comment to Aunt Norma about her friend Larry. So, I tried to think of my ancient aunt as that eighteen-year-old girl in the photo album. Her well-controlled curls, her perfectly oval face, her posed-for-the-camera stiffness suggested an obliging subject. A certain quickness in her eyes, almost sparking in defiance, hinted at another Norma.

I began to wonder if I should have alerted Aunt Norma to my presence outside her bedroom door. Given what I knew or had guessed about Larry, I could have said sorry to her. I don't think that would have been a good idea.

Somehow, I understood that Aunt Norma's reading routine was a private and solitary activity. People spying on her should hold their breath, tiptoe down the hall, and think about their own sad situations. Think about missing mothers. Think about how aloneness puts us adrift, like someone lost at sea.

I'm the kind of person who likes tossing out lifelines. Time to try one on Lucinda. "I know a few things, Lucinda. Things that might help Aunt Norma with the sadness about her friend Larry. My investigation is in the early stages, but I'm that close to . . ."

"Yer that close to getting grounded for the entire summer if you don't stop meddlin' in what don't concern you, Clio," Lucinda muttered between tight lips. "You don't know the pain that Norma went through when Larry didn't come back. Then all the gossip. There are thins worse than death. To some people. Your Aunt Norma bein' one of them people."

With a poker face, I tried not to show any emotion, such as my hurt feelings. All I am trying to do is to set the record straight. Clear Lawrence Bresant's name. Put it on that Courthouse Memorial plaque for WWI soldiers, if that would comfort Aunt Norma.

At this very moment, the man who could tell Aunt Norma what really happened to her friend Larry in Belleau Wood might be stone cold dead or bleeding out in her garage loft. At the very least, he would be starving.

I sat hunched over my soggy pancakes, trying not to feel as misunderstood as I usually did in this house, waiting for the moment when I could raid the kitchen larder for my POW, in case he hadn't expired in the night.

"I'm runnin' down to the grocery store for a quart of buttermilk to make them chocolate cupcakes you like, Clio. You can take some to MYF. Them girls will roll out the red carpet for you." Lucinda retied the bow on one of my pigtails. "I'll get you new hair ribbons at Lewin's. Hedy Lewin don't blame me for stoppin' the crime wave in Wolfe Flats."

Lucinda was almost as expert as I was at backhanded compliments. I grinned at her and pushed the pancakes around in more syrup until I heard the screen door slam behind her.

CHAPTER 23

Rummaging around in the upstairs bathroom, I found an old gold-colored safety razor, a spare comb, and a toothbrush. I grabbed a bar of lye soap and a box of soda in the kitchen. With those, my breakfast sausages, a box of saltines, and slices off the shank end of a ham that Lucinda was saving for a pot of pinto beans, I slipped out the door, checking first to be sure that Manboy wasn't in his back yard.

As a lawyer, Manboy was a stickler for following the letter of the law. He'd turn my POW over to the Camp Houze guards without letting me get a word out of him. That wasn't going to happen if there was a word left in Lorenz Weber.

"Lorenz? Lorenz? You up there?"

The faintest groan came from the top of the ramshackle stairs. I hop-scotched from one broken step to the next. The pile of blankets had been moved away from the stacked boxes next to the door of a small half-bathroom, tucked into an alcove of the loft.

"Water, Clio. I needed water. For the fever. The spigot works in the sink." Lorenz's lips appeared to be in need of a chap stick, but his face wasn't flushed, just covered with messy stubble.

"I brought you things if you feel like getting clean, Lorenz. This old razor might be rusty."

"Or gold, Clio. That's an old one. Maybe I shouldn't use it." He held it up toward a ray of sun streaming past the blanket he'd draped over the window, and then dropped it into my open palm.

"No reason not to. My aunts keep lots of old stuff that belonged to their father. He was my grandfather. I've seen photos of him. His beard was a sight to behold, would put Moses to shame. He probably never used this razor. Be my guest. Never let it be said we don't give our POWs first-class treatment."

With just the smallest twitch of a grin, Lorenz reached for the sausages and ham that I'd spread on top of waxed paper. "You spoil me, Clio. In my home in Germany, we had sausage often. Not just for breakfast. Different kinds of sausage. It makes me homesick."

I didn't want to rush Lorenz through his breakfast or let him know I wasn't much concerned about a POW's homesickness, but Lucinda would be back from the store soon. If she didn't see me working on my bicycle in the backyard, she'd be inside the garage in a heartbeat. I needed to set some ground rules for my prisoner.

"Here's the thing, Lorenz. When you feel like talking, I need to get some facts from you. My aunts are home today, and Lucinda. They can't know you are here. I have to go out this afternoon. I'll come back at night so we can have a good chinwag."

"A what?"

"A talk. You tell me about your father and Lawrence Bresant in Belleau Wood. Every single thing he told you. If I think Aunt Norma is strong enough to hear it, I'll figure out a way for you to meet with her."

Despite his cast-down eyes, my prisoner spoke with determination: "What I have to say is to Miss Norma, not anyone else. It is a promise I made my father. When I was a boy, he told me we would go to America on a big ship and take a train to Wolfe Flats so that he could tell Norma Clower how Lawrence saved his life and paid with his own."

My POW paused and looked past me at the moldy wallpaper. I followed his gaze toward bilious green ivy fronds that appeared to be melting down the wall. It struck me that the wallpaper might have been from the Victorian era when color pigments with arsenic were all the rage—and toxic killers.

"Then the influenza killed Papa when I was only fourteen. Before he died, I promised. Just her. I must tell her. I cannot tell you." Lorenz sank back onto his pile of blankets with an expression that might have been fatigue and pain or just bloody-minded stubbornness.

Eying my POW, lying limp as a rag, but with his jaw set in silence, I thought that the wallpaper poison might be zapping him before I could get the information I needed.

It was time to ramp up the fear factor. "Guards from Camp Houze are probably looking for you right now. An escaped German prisoner scares the locals. These are rural people. Every one of them carries a gun. They don't know much about foreigners. No telling what they might do to one," I added darkly.

Blood had seeped through the gauze bandages on Lorenz's leg. It was probably infected. Doc Lontry might have to chop it off. He'd use ether, of course. No Civil War surgical butchery. I moved closer to Lorenz and plastered on my sympathetic face. Frightening a wounded escapee might not be the best strategy. Time for another approach. Lorenz was my prisoner, as long as I could keep him hidden.

"I understand deathbed promises to your father, Lorenz, but Aunt Norma gets terrible headaches when anyone mentions Lawrence Bresant. *I didn't tell him that I'd managed to bring on one of her migraines this very morning with a snide comment about her old boyfriend, a remark that brought me considerable guilt.*

"When you're feeling better, I'll find some clothes for you. Make you presentable. Then, I'll help you decide what Aunt Norma can bear to hear. You have to trust me. I'm all that's standing between you and prison."

Threatening prisoners is probably against the Geneva Convention, but this close-mouthed German had let something slip about radio *mit ihm* when I was dumping alcohol into the gaping wound on his leg. Lester Smith, the WWI radioman, the so-called friend of Larry's, remained a fly in the ointment. Just like Agatha Christie's Poiroit, I needed to question suspects in the same room with the innocents.

I remembered the clever idea I had this morning about one suspect in particular when Aunt Norma had mentioned that I should help with the war effort. Actually, at exactly the same time she mentioned collecting scrap metal with the Methodist youth, I had spotted the weekly *Wolfe Flats Messenger* on the breakfast table with Lester Smith's Feed and Seed Store's back page ad: "Coops for Victory Chickens—Eggs and Pullets in Every Backyard Will Help the War Effort."

When I first met Lester Smith on the day of the tornado, he had been bullying my reporter friend, Sally, to get a new ad in the newspaper, even though the ad pages had been set in stone for that week. Sally must have capitulated. Maybe Aunt Norma would too, and I could lure Lester and his chicken coop into our back yard.

Time was wasting, and Lorenz wasn't saying another word. With a brisk raised arm palm-up salute to my POW, just to remind him which side of the war I was on, I headed toward the stairs. "Later, I'll bring clean gauze and a big bottle of alcohol for that." I pointed toward his seeping wound and watched him flinch.

Downstairs in the shop area, I spotted a big metal measuring tape on the workbench. Grabbing it, I trotted into the backyard and checked out the grassy space between Aunt Harriet's beds of floppy dahlias, lined with rows of those bitter-smelling marigolds. Edging my way along the fence that separated the far end of the Mullers' back yard from ours, I peeped through a gap in the vertical board fence to take a gander at Martha's grave.

When I first arrived in Wolfe Flats—before I had become friends with Manboy Muller and his mother Claire—I was hot on the trail of three missing girls that no one in this boring town had bothered to mention. Maybe I let my imagination goad me into an imprudent act, but the mound of dirt in the far corner of the Mullers' yard was the length and width of a human grave.

I had been compelled to dig, determined to find a body. You can imagine my state of shock when the first strands of blondish hair appeared atop a skull—and then sprouted in hairy masses along the length of a putrefying yellow Labrador.

Manboy was downright civil when he caught me in the act of exhuming his family dog, Martha. He exhibited what Mother calls "good form," helping me shovel dirt back onto Martha while he made polite small talk about her virtues as a beloved family pet. I made an important observation at that time, as we reburied Martha. Etiquette, or what Aunt Norma would describe as "observing niceties," takes precedence over the ruthless fact-finding required to root out serial killers.

After risking life and limb down in the well where Whitey Lewin tossed me with his other victims, I had experienced a short-lived spell of local fame for solving a decades-old mystery of disappearing girls. Now, a month after making headlines, I was of no more consequence than the neighbor's dead dog.

A sly smile edged along my pursed lips. Solving the mystery of what happened to Aunt Norma's beau in Belleau Wood in the First World War couldn't hold a candle to nailing a serial killer like Whitey. But it was just possible that high-profile crimes such as multiple murders were too rich a dish for Wolfe Flats' rural palate. Perhaps, finding out the truth, almost a quarter of a century later, about a popular local boy like Lawrence Bresant would suit the tastes of the locals better than my major criminal investigations.

If I managed no more than a factual account of what actually happened to Lawrence on the battlefield in France, I might make headlines again—especially with my POW angle.

"Angle is everything in a news story. Getting a certain slant, that clever twist on a story, separates a journalist from a hack." Mother drummed that into my head often enough as she pedaled her human-interest stories to New York City newspapers. I had no doubt that wherever she hunkered down in Europe, my mother was finding more angles than my idol Pythagoras, with all of his triangles.

Stretching out the tape measure and stepping off a sizeable angle from the back fence to the side of the garage, I determined that we had plenty of room for chickens, without infringing on Aunt Harriet's flowerbeds. That old radioman Lester Smith would surely be willing to advise me on the best location—if and when Aunt Norma let him set foot on her property for the first time since WWI ended, when he brought her Larry's journal.

CHAPTER 24

After fiddling around with my bicycle chain in the back yard, putting air in the tires, releasing it, and putting air in again, I couldn't seem to escape Lucinda's watchful eye. She hung laundry on the line, carefully slipping underwear inside of pillowcases, so the neighbors wouldn't be offended, taking forever—just so she could check on any suspicious behavior from me.

I didn't dare slip into the garage again to check on my POW. So I turned my bicycle upside down and spun the wheels in endless rotations, imagining just how far I could travel if those spinning wheels were touching the ground. I sauntered past Lucinda and headed into the house to chain myself to the piano and check out that reading list Aunt Norma had given me.

The clock speeds up in summer. Ask any levelheaded person who's just been let out of solitary in Wolfe Flats' public school. With only a week into my summer vacation, one hour of this precious day had been spent trying every innovation possible in that dull piano book of scales that Felicity Langston gave me; another hour was spent trying to speed read *Silas Marner*.

I particularly liked the part where the child Eppie wanders into his house and transforms the old gold-hoarder Silas into a kind man. Maybe Aunt Norma should reread the novel. I didn't exactly wander into her house. Dumped there is a better description. I don't think I've transformed my aunts at all.

"About this morning." Startled by Aunt Harriet's soft voice, I glanced up from *Silas* and moved my feet off the couch. She sat uncomfortably close to me. "Don't you think that your curiosity is an invasion of your Aunt Norma's sanctity?"

"Sanctity"? I asked. "You mean she's in some holy place where I shouldn't go?" I was intending to be sarcastic, but Aunt Harriet's naïveté stopped me short when I remembered that Mother said sarcasm was a nasty form of word play. "It comes from the Greek, Clio, meaning to 'tear flesh.'"

Aunt Harriet wrapped her arm around my shoulders. "Exactly. A holy place. That's what I mean, Clio. I think of our secret thoughts as belonging to a private place. Maybe holy is the best description. When you were sitting on the back door step this morning, staring into the distance for the longest time, I was careful not to disturb you. I thought that bulky sweater you were wearing could cause a heat stroke, but I know that we all need private moments."

Aunt Harriet's conciliatory tone nettled me. I had been sitting on the back step in an over-sized sweater for a reason. Under it was a bottle of alcohol, a new roll of gauze, and her recently purloined embroidery scissors. My

POW needed supplies to change his bloody bandages. I wasn't about to give him kitchen shears so he could stab me if he suddenly remembered that I was on the side of the Allies, not the Axis, in this war. The tiny blades on Aunt Harriet's scissors could hardly slice a piece of gauze. They'd never make it into a struggling victim's carotid.

For some reason, I recalled Aunt Norma's tiresome Biblical lecture about the letter that old chatterbox Saint Paul wrote to the Colossians on forgiveness, and I smiled benignly at Aunt Harriet. She'd surely forgive the theft of her small scissors for a good cause. Inspired by my own beneficence, I took a stab at twisting Aunt Harriet's "private moments" theme to my advantage. The threat of the MYF meeting at 4 o'clock hung over my head.

"You understand what other people don't, Aunt Harriet. I need time alone. When I lived in New York, I was by myself for days on end while Mother tracked down news stories."

Observing Aunt Harriet's eyebrows soaring up into her hairline, I back peddled. "Our nice neighbors, the Abrams, checked to be sure I was always OK. But I didn't have to do group things. I'm not into camaraderie."

Aunt Harriet's hesitant smile suggested that she wasn't getting my message. Time for a poleaxe aside the head. "It's those Methodist kids, Aunt Harriet. They don't like me. Those Brown twins are a couple of Janus-faced bookends."

"Those Brown twins were such a surprise to their mother. Their parents had been married for over twenty years with no children and no notion that they'd ever be parents. When she began to extend, Mrs. Brown feared she had a tumor. Doctor Lontry had such a time convincing her otherwise."

Biting my lip to keep from muttering "two tumors," my eyes fell on the open page of George Eliot's *Silas Marner*. *"All cleverness, whether in the rapid use of that difficult instrument the tongue, or in some other art unfamiliar to villagers, was in itself suspicious."*

George Eliot and I had something in common. We could both size up a small town. Hers was in rural England; mine is in rural Oklahoma. I'd best curb my cleverness around the "villagers," even my blood kin.

Aunt Harriet is a bit dotty, so I have to cut her some slack. Aunt Norma's stiff upper lip gives a new meaning to self-restraint. The fact is that I miss Mother and prefer thinking about her alone. An odd thought popped into my mind just as I mentioned the MYF meeting that I was trying desperately not to attend this afternoon.

Through my superior sleuthing, I did learn that when Whitey Lewin conked Mother on the head, he did something unspeakable to her at a MYF picnic at Lake Murray. The "unspeakable" thing is what got my mother crosswise with Aunt Norma and Aunt Harriet—she left Wolfe Flats for all those years just because they wouldn't report the crime. You'd think my aunts would keep me at arm's length from MYF.

With both my arms locked at a firm angle, I rode my bicycle full speed ahead, balancing a box with a dozen chocolate cupcakes so that those fancy little twirls Lucinda put atop every one of them stayed kinked up until I could put them in pride of place on the treat table in the Methodist Church Community Room.

When I whipped my bicycle down the alley so that I could come up to the backside of the church unobserved, I saw the preacher's wife looking up and down the street, like a one-person welcoming committee.

"Clio! Clio! Through this door. The other kids are already here. Games are starting."

Clutching Lucinda's box of cupcakes until I could determine if something else looked tastier, I spotted the Brown twins sitting in a circle of fold-up chairs in their nifty playsuits with red, white and blue bibs. I was tempted to make a snide comment about Betsy Ross but restrained myself. Flexing my toes in my special, imported sandals, I moved a best foot forward and pushed a folding chair between those two patriotic bookends. Divide and conquer.

Matched expressions of irritation met my broad grin. The Brown twins' *hippocampi* function like wireless radio waves—no connection is visible, only identical reactions. I could almost trace the wave they sent to travel around the group of ten girls and four nerdy boys; the unheard sound crackled like electricity: *she's not one of us.*

That was true. I've never been properly socialized. Mother's fault. None of my classmates could be invited over to our apartment because of my mother's erratic work schedule. She had to be ready to go when the news desk called. "If you had company, Clio, we'd have to impose on the Abrams to take two children. They're accustomed to you."

I was accustomed to the Abrams. They talked about real things, directly to me—not *at me* like Aunt Norma does. They loved museums, art galleries, and libraries. They called me their adopted child and took me to see a thousand things. Mr. Abrams honed my map-making skills by tutoring me in geometry. Mrs. Abrams baked isosceles-shaped cookies and made me a bumblebee-striped dress.

The buzzing sound of the preacher's wife brought my attention sharply to the present as she commended something called the Girls Auxilliary for "making up a nice box of property bags and wristlets for our troops."

She gestured toward me with a put-upon smile. "Clio Clower is new to our group today. I'm sure some of you know her from her few weeks in school and at our church. She came from New York City to live with her aunts while her mother is in Europe, writing for newspapers about the war," Mrs. Wyndom paused. "That's a very brave thing for a mother to do."

Not as brave as entering a den of hostile MYFers. Looking around the circle of faces, I saw boredom, amusement, and skepticism—and heard nothing but the noise of shuffling feet.

"Clio might be interested in the Girls' Auxiliary projects—our Methodist girls are knitting more wristlets than the Baptist girls," she pronounced proudly. I stood like a dumb Dora, like that dimwitted cartoon character.

I couldn't imagine spending my time knitting fingerless gloves—even if I could knit.

"Let's get some snacks, then we'll have the first contest," the preacher's wife said. "Since this is Clio's first MYF meeting, we won't ask her to participate in the Bible verse challenge. We don't want to make her feel uncomfortable here. I don't suppose Wolfe Flats is a bit like New York City," she patted my head, looking down at me as though I were someone's stray dog left tied outside the church with no bowl of water. "Let Clio go first to get a treat. It's the Methodist way."

I was pleased to observe that sugar rationing hadn't imposed its stingy rules on Methodists. Molasses cookies and odd, dark, crumbly things that might have passed for brownies filled two platters. A luscious, three-layer, chocolate cake with icing that must be an inch thick held center place. I eased my hand around a knife handle and eyed the line behind me.

The look-alike jaws of the Brown twins clamped tighter than a wounded soldier about to have his leg surgically removed without a whiff of ether. One of the boys snorted. So I lifted the knife to take a sizeable cut of cake when Mrs. Wyndom screeched. "Not the cake, Clio. That's for the winner. A cookie. We each take a cookie."

Humiliation can descend in many forms. Like wearing mismatched socks to school because none of your socks match. Or having your mother forget that you were with her on Coney Island when she boarded an ambulance to interview a pier jumper and left you behind without so much as a friendly wave.

Humiliation digs its claws right into your gut when the preacher's wife tries to make things better by encircling your hand with pudgy fingers. "The cake is the prize, Clio. We have a Bible verse contest. The MYF member who recites the most lines gets to take the cake home. Your Aunt Norma told me you're new to Methodism, so you can just listen. Have a cookie."

I'd rather have a Heretic's Fork put under my chin and propped against my sternum—a favorite medieval torture technique—than eat a Methodist molasses cookie. Lucinda's cupcakes were still inside the box by my chair. None of these believers would get to taste one.

"I want to be in the contest. I know lots of verses from the Bible," I announced, as scornfully as possible. I did. Aunt Norma was a fiend for forcing me to memorize Psalms.

An hour later with my big chocolate cake carefully housed in a borrowed cake carrier with red cherries painted on the side, I pushed my bicycle home. I'd take Lucinda's cupcakes to my POW so she wouldn't ask any questions about sharing. The cake would go on the dining room table as my triumph of the day. Five entire psalms from memory without a prompt managed to trump the Brown twins who prompted each other constantly.

"Cheater, cheater, pumpkin eater," I whispered as they sat back down, flushed with defeat.

CHAPTER 25

It was after five o'clock when I propped my bicycle against the side of the house and tromped through the back door, holding my prize aloft. Aunt Harriet was stirring a pot of beans and ham. "Where did you get that nice cake carrier, Clio?"

"MYF. The carrier belongs to the preacher's wife. I won the prize cake. Quoted more from the Bible than Billy Sunday on a good day. Wowed those Methodists. They probably all want to make friends with me now, but are too gobsmacked to say so."

"Humility goes a long way toward making friends, Clio. I doubt that showing off your considerable memory is paving the road to friendship," Aunt Harriet said. "Norma is feeling much better. She'll be pleased that you won. She used to win spelling bees, dance contests, barrel races—all kinds of events when she was a girl."

The idea of Aunt Norma charging along in a barrel startled me. "How does a barrel race work?"

"On a horse. The rider is timed riding around barrels in an arena at our rodeo. Norma was good. Your mother was better. Delia had such a good horse. Its ancestry went back to Dan Tucker. Didn't she ever tell you about barrel racing?"

"Before I rode Marguerite home from Jeremiah's farm, the closest I'd ever been to a horse was in Central Park. Tourists ride in buggies around the Park. I touched a horse's nose once. After riding Mrs. Whittaker's horse, I think I'm a natural. I wouldn't mind having a horse of my own." Might as well throw a wish at Aunt Harriet. She might carry it upstairs to Aunt Norma. Or not. Me with my own horse would really push those Brown girls' jealousy buttons.

Lucinda waved a cuptowel at Aunt Harriet and me, as though she were dislodging setting hens. "Cornbread's almost done. The table is set. That was your job, Clio. I done it for you. Don't make it a habit. Now, you need to wash your hands and scrub the grease from the bicycle chain off your leg. I'll go upstairs to see if Norma's headache will let her have a bite to eat." Lucinda didn't stop talking as she flipped down the latches on the cake carrier and lifted the lid. "That cake's a beauty, Clio. We're right proud of you winnin' a nice cake like this. Makes my cupcakes look plumb ordinary, but I'm sure the kids enjoyed them."

I looked dead straight ahead without answering. I'd be flying in the face of Fate if I confessed that I hadn't shared the cupcakes. Having just won a cake by reciting more Bible verses than any of those Methodists, I'd best keep my little falsehoods in line. I intended to give the cupcakes to my POW when I could sneak out to the loft.

Aunt Norma's warm hand settled on the nape of my neck. "We are proud of you, Clio. I do hope you enjoyed being with the young people at the church. I was sharp with you this morning. I've been giving it some thought. I know that you are curious about our family and friends. You shouldn't have to ask other people. After dinner, I thought we might look through an old photograph album. My headache is so much better."

Even with the dark circles under her eyes, Aunt Norma seemed almost tranquil as she walked around the dining room table and adjusted knife handles to exactly one inch from the edge of the table.

"Trepanning," I whispered to Aunt Harriet. "For the migraines." I had considered telling Aunt Norma that ancient physicians drilled holes in the skull to alleviate headaches. That information alone should keep a migraine at bay.

"Heavens to Betsy, Clio," Aunt Harriet hissed at me. "This is the Twentieth Century, not ancient Egypt. Stress brings on Norma's migraines—not fluid on the brain. Sit down. You can offer grace."

With the second-best floral porcelain soup tureen held aloft, Lucinda pushed through the swinging kitchen door with the most restorative of medicines—ham and pinto beans. I offered a seemly prayer, thanking God right out loud that Lucinda had used nice brown pinto beans instead of those squashy pale navy beans. I didn't add the words about "gifts from thy Bounty." Beans can hardly be considered bounty. The silence around the table did not encourage me to say another word.

The words from the radio in the parlor where we sat after dinner startled us. Just as Aunt Harriet flipped on the massive curved Zenith that was shoved discretely into a corner of the room, the announcer said something about Corregidor. I knew that the tunnels and bay of that Philippine Island had been a deterrent to a Japanese invasion until Corregidor fell, and General MacArthur hightailed it to Australia.

Bursting in from the kitchen, Lucinda stood in the door of the parlor with a pained expression on her face. "I heard that newsman say 'Corregidor,' that island where all them Japs landed in March and took all our boys off to God knows where. Turn it up so we can hear!" Lucinda's voice was unnaturally sharp, troubled. "That's where Amaday Terrill's daughter Opal wuz nursin' last she heard from her."

Scrunching down beside me on a chair that wouldn't accommodate her considerable dimensions, Lucinda strained to hear the evening news.

Our source was the radio, newspapers, and newsreels at our local theater. The underlying theme of every news story was the same: all of our soldiers are brave; all the commanders are brilliant; and, the Allies are winning even when they lose.

"I got nothin' bad to say about General MacArthur. I know he had to git away from the enemy on that sub, but I jest cain't figure out why he couldn't of took Opal with him to Australia. He took some of them nurses. Why not our Opal? It don't seem right to leave young gals behind in that kind of situation. He shoulda gone back fer them." Lucinda's pronouncement was as sonorous as General MacArthur's speech when he landed in Australia: "I came through and I shall return."

News about the British Eighth Army's counterattack against Rommel somewhere in Egypt blared out of the Zenith, but Lucinda's mind was fixated on a Philippine Island more than five thousand miles away from the pyramids. "I don't reckon that Amaday holds ill feelings against the General fer not gettin' her daughter off that island, but she's worried sick about Opal. The newsmen don't say much when things goes against us. Our bad news comes by telegram." It didn't seem to be the right moment for me to explain to Lucinda the Code of Wartime Practices for the American Press.

Mother had told me that news correspondents stay close to the troops to bring the war into living rooms. "We're all part of the war effort," she reminded me. "We ac-cen-tu-ate the positive," Mother sang a phrase from that popular song before adding "even though it may be far from the truth."

Compressing myself into a squiggle of arms and legs, I wound tightly around Lucinda, a woman who really didn't want to know the truth about what might have happened to her friend's daughter when the Japanese invaded a distant island in the Philippines.

Just at that moment, the voice of Kate Smith flowed from the radio like liquid gold as she sang "God Bless America." Lucinda's spine stiffened; she unwound herself from my embrace and stepped toward the front door like a duty-bound soldier. "My Fat Salvage Committee meets in the mornin' at the church. The two billion pounds of grease this country used to throw away can build ten billion cannon shells. I reckon we can help dislodge them Japs."

When the front door closed behind Lucinda, Aunt Norma walked over to a large walnut cabinet with wide curved drawers and tugged the top one open. Pulling out a leather album with Clower embossed into the cover, Aunt Norma beckoned me over to the sofa, the one with little legs splayed outward, as though the agony of holding up rear ends might be insupportable. I scrunched over to the far end where a small pillow blocked me from flinging my legs over the armrest.

Patting the space next to her, Aunt Norma said: "We'll start in the middle of the album, Clio, when your Aunt Harriet and I were girls." She flipped the page to a large group photograph. "This is my graduating class." The girls were all in white dresses; the boys posed awkwardly in their coats and ties.

"This pretty girl on the left is Felicity Langston, your piano teacher. "There on the top row is Luther, who became her husband."

I touched the faintly familiar face of a boy standing next to Luther. He was the only boy with a scarf around his neck, rather than a tie. "Him. I think I may have seen him." *I know I have seen him, but I wanted to keep the conversation light.*

"Perhaps. Lester Smith. You might have seen him at the Methodist Church," Aunt Norma answered, with a curtness that suggested we move right along. It wasn't the time to tell my aunt that I had interviewed Lester Smith on a bench after spending time with him under the courthouse steps during the tornado. An idea began flickering in my frontal lobe about victory chickens and a way to nail down a WWI suspect.

I could come back to those chickens when the timing was right. At the moment, I was looking at the King of Hollywood. Clark Gable's toothy smile flashed at me from the back row. His arm reached forward to caress the sleeve of the girl in front of him. Someone with the same perfectly oval face was beside me.

"That's you, Aunt Norma." I touched the photograph of her and let my forefinger trace the face above her. "This boy is so handsome. He must be . . ."

"Larry. Lawrence Bresant. You mentioned his name this morning. It shouldn't upset me to think about him. We were best friends. Ever since I can remember. Then he went away. To war. War is so terrible, Clio. I pray every single day for your mother to be safe. As do your Aunt Harriet and Lucinda."

Not to interrupt the prayer chain, but I wanted to get back to Clark Gable's look-alike. Until I could get Aunt Norma's take on what was in that journal of Larry's that caused her such grief at night, I couldn't fit all the pieces together—even if I could get my POW to talk.

"He was really handsome, Aunt Norma. And you're beautiful. You look like Vivian Leigh. Scarlett O'Hara and Rhett Butler right here in Wolfe Flats." *A little flattery never hurts a good investigative cause.*

"That movie was twenty years later, Clio. It did make the point that there is no glamour in war—despite what those recruitment posters try to make young people believe. Now, this fellow on the end. Who do you think that is?"

A handsome face topped by a thatch of light hair seemed familiar, but I couldn't place him.

"It's Manford's father. He was Manford Muller the second. Our neighbor, Manford, is the third."

"But he doesn't have . . ." I dropped the thought. I wanted to say: short arms and legs.

As though she heard the comment that I didn't make, Aunt Norma continued. "His father was of normal size. The condition is called *Phocomelia*, probably genetic. The first Manford had one short arm—Manford's mother told me that it was noted in the family Bible when the first Manford was born in 1870. She had no idea it might surface again. Then our dear Manford was born with both arms and legs affected."

She flipped the pages of the photograph album. There was Mother beaming down at me from atop a stocky horse, holding a rosette with ribbons in her hand. "Second place in teenage calf roping at our annual rodeo. She was only fourteen and not supposed to compete. Boys only, but that night Delia talked the cowboys behind the chutes into letting her try. One of them loaned her a pigging string. She wasn't close to a seven-minute tie, but she took second place."

"We never suspected a thing. Our ranch manager brought Delia's horse into town for the parade and the grand entry at the rodeo. We had no idea that she'd been practicing roping a dummy on a bale of hay. Calf roping was not considered a sport for girls," Aunt Harriet said. "Those rodeo cowboys were simply not the kind of . . ."

"That's why we are so pleased to see how well you fit into the group of Methodist young people this afternoon," Aunt Norma interrupted her sister.

Rudely interrupted her, I thought, just as I was hankering to hear more about what might have been going on with my mother and those cowboys behind the chutes.

Noting my sulky expression, Aunt Norma continued: "You recited more Bible verses from memory than those girls and boys who have been raised as Methodists. You are acclimating so well, Clio, channeling that competitive spirit you inherited from Delia into an encouraging activity."

Actually, I inherited her investigative spirit, and I needed to set a trap for that elusive WWI radioman, Lester Smith.

The muffled sound of lead weights striking a brass bell caused Aunt Norma to close the photograph album with a decided thump. "George is telling us that it's bedtime."

I had a bone to pick with George. Given an opportunity, I'd unbalance his weights. The George III grandfather long case clock in the front foyer attracted me the moment I set foot in my aunts' house. Opening the bottom compartment, I'd found an interesting set of what appeared to be lead weights, balanced to strike a brass bell. Curious about what triggered it, I'd stuck my arm up into the innards when Aunt Harriet caught me.

"That's an Eighteenth Century English clock made when George the Third was king of England. It's temperamental. An horologist from Ardmore has to adjust it occasionally," Aunt Harriet had slowly moved my hand out of its inner workings. "My father bought it in London. He's your Great-Grandfather Clower, Clio. Up there."

Aunt Harriet had pointed to a large, sepia-toned photograph of a man who looked like a Biblical patriarch, with a great froth of beard swooping from ear to ear and eyes so piercing that I felt guilty about touching his clock.

Reluctant to be hustled off to bed, I turned to the aunt who was the softer touch. "I'd really like to see more photographs, Aunt Harriet, of you and Aunt Norma and your friends when you were young." I wanted to get back to Lester Smith but needed to go in a circuitous way since Lester was *persona non grata* in this house.

Aunt Harriet lifted her eyebrows to a startling height. I backtracked. "I mean when you and Aunt Norma were in high school. When you had boyfriends. I guess Aunt Norma might have been in love when she was young. Maybe you were."

"Young? Really, Clio, we're not prehistoric fossils. We didn't arrive at this point in our lives without experiencing the same feelings, the same emotions you'll have in the future. Betrayal, passion, pain are all part of the human condition. Most of us don't reach old age without that kind of drama in our lives."

I tried to mask the astonished expression that I could feel lifting my own eyebrows. It was no time to tally a defense for my careless words. Behind those tear-rimmed eyes of Aunt Harriet lay a sense of disturbance, an immediate friction that had nothing to do with old age. "They were soul mates, Norma and Larry. When they were in a room together, the air felt different, the way it does before a summer storm."

Ignoring our muted conversation, Aunt Norma was straightening the antimacassars, those little crocheted things on the backs of all the chairs—the time-to-go-to-bed sign. It was time for my own diversion.

"Seeing that old photograph of the man who owns Smith's Feed and Seed Store reminds me of something very important that we need to discuss—our way to help in the war effort. Lester Smith is the man to help us," I blurted out.

Both of my aunts froze in their tracks. Before either of them could say a word, I gave them my speech: "You said this very morning that I needed to do something to help with the war effort. I saw Mr. Smith's advertisement in today's *Wolfe Flats Messenger.* Chickens in every backyard. Feed ourselves so that the farmers can feed our troops."

Looking into two disbelieving faces, I struck home. "I've measured places in the backyard for a small, unobtrusive coop with a patch of grass. I'll take care of the chickens and keep the area clean and tidy. We'll have fresh eggs every day. I'll be responsible. It's the least I can do for our troops."

Other than Aunt Norma's single response of "No roosters!" neither of my aunts protested. Amazing. Now, I just had to prime my POW for more information about the radioman with the soldiers who had come upon his footless father and Larry Bresant in Belleau Wood. Then, I could set a snare for Lester Smith who knew more about what happened all those years ago than he would yet admit.

CHAPTER 26

Before old George's clock struck ten that night, I was out the back door and into the garage with Lucinda's cupcakes, half a pan of leftover cornbread, and Mark Twain's *Huckleberry Finn*. I figured my POW might be amused by the adventures of Huck and Jim, since he was on the lam like they were.

I crept up the stairs to the loft and nudged the pile of blankets with my foot. In the beam of my flashlight, Lorenz's head moved turtle-like from under the pile of blankets. Then, the turtle croaked out: "This waiting fears me that I will never get give my father's message to your aunt."

My POW's verbs rattled around in his sentences like loose marbles. "You don't need to worry, Lorenz. I have a strategy. My Aunt Norma needs to know exactly why her friend didn't come home from the war."

"His own soldiers, the Americans, took him. One of them said he deserted. It was capital offense. That's what my father told me."

"Which one said that?"

"I don't know. My father was in great pain. Half of his foot gone. Most of all, he remembered the kindness of Lawrence Bresant. He bound up the foot and talked good to him for hours."

"I think I do know who said it," I spoke, more confidently than I believed. "I think it was the radioman, Mr. Smith."

"I never heard that name Smith. Papa said Lawrence begged the soldiers to take him to the Evacuation Hospital at Juilly. They left him. Our own soldiers found him."

"When you were feverish with your leg, Lorenz, you said Lawrence recognized one of the men."

"I do not remember all things my father said, Clio. The men were all Americans. Lawrence probably knew them. My father did not say. He said he must tell the woman Lawrence loved about a kindness. A kindness that took his life. My father wanted me to say the words to her. Only me. I must say his words to Miss Norma."

Lorenz's one-track mind needed to be rerouted by a slight change of subject. "I want to know if the radioman, who was supposed to be one of Lawrence's best friends, accused him. When the war was over, that radioman brought my Aunt Norma a journal that Lawrence was keeping. Something he told her or something in that journal made her never speak to Mr. Smith again. And they go to the same church."

"That was over two decades ago, Clio. How can you get truth about what happened years ago? It is impossible."

"Not if I get Mr. Smith to put a chicken coop in our backyard."

Heaving a great sigh, Lorenz burrowed down into the blankets. "Sometimes I don't understand American English, Clio. This is one of the times. A chicken coop? You make dizzy my head."

The flash of the kitchen light above the sink sent a warning signal out the window. "Whoops. One of my aunts is up. I need to sneak back through the side door of the porch without being seen. I'll try to speak the King's English tomorrow, Lorenz." If I sounded a bit snarky, it was purposeful. For a POW, Lorenz wasn't the least bit submissive.

I should have checked the garage loft early the next morning, but the odor of cinnamon overwhelmed me as I watched Lucinda knifing through mounds of sticky buns bursting with honey-coated pecans. She gave me an accusatory look as I sauntered into the kitchen.

"Would you like to explain why the left-over cornbread is missin'?" Lucinda pointed to a plump chicken on the drain board next to the sink. "Baked chicken and cornbread dressin' was planned for dinner. Now I gotta rethink." She eyed me again. "Seems that quite a bit of food goes missin' these days."

Rather than stack on another falsehood to a steadily growing pile, I changed the subject. "Aunt Norma didn't say that we couldn't have a few chickens in the backyard, so I'm taking that as a yes. I'm off to see what kind of coop and chickens Mr. Smith recommends."

"Whoa. Whoa. Clio, it don't set well for you to be palling around with Lester Smith. Norma won't pass the time of day with him. Don't even speak to him at church. Afore you make any plans for chickens, you need to talk to your Aunt Norma."

"Already have, Lucinda. Last night. She just said no roosters. I'm off to Mr. Smith's Feed and Seed Store."

With a brief detour around the table to snatch up a cinnamon roll, I scooted out the back door, grabbed my bicycle, and pedaled down the street so fast that Lucinda's voice couldn't possibly reach me.

"A chicken coop in Norma Clower's backyard? Even if Alexander's army was on the march through Wolfe Flats, and he sent out the order, Norma wouldn't allow chickens in her yard. Her father thought he was the Capability Brown of landscaping in this part of the country. Everything had a place. We had to put the croquet set in the Mullers' yard."

Mr. Smith might as well be speaking Greek. I never heard of a person named Capability. Interesting name though. New York City had concrete yards—there was not a croquet set in city limits. "It's the war effort, Mr. Smith. Aunt Norma wants me to do my part. Raise chickens. Collect eggs."

If an ashen face could take on a tinge of hopeful color, the little spider veins in his cheeks were working over-time—maybe charging themselves up for a stroke. "Mr. Smith, I really need for you to come to the house after you close the store this evening. I've staked out a couple of places where a coop might go, but we need your expert advice."

"Why would a woman who has ignored me for almost twenty-five years want to consult with me about a chicken coop?"

I was forearmed for that kind of question. "It's because of my mother, the niece that Aunt Norma raised like her own child. My mother is in Europe at this very minute interviewing our soldiers." *I let just the tiniest tear ease out of my eye.* "Mother is doing her part for the war. We have to do ours. That's the way we see it. Lucinda, Aunt Harriet, me, and Aunt Norma."

I thought about tossing the word "sacrifice" into the mix. It was a word I'd supplied to Lester Smith when I was interviewing him on the courthouse bench about what happened to his used-to-be friend Larry Bresant.

"We could really use your help, Mr. Smith. Just a small sacrifice—your time and expertise." There. I inserted the word and watched that little cravat pooch out from his neck like one of those little scarves that dog lovers in New York City tie on their pets. Wolfe Flats dogs wear leather collars or nothing at all.

Mr. Smith checked his watch. "I don't close here until six o'clock tonight. We'll have enough light for me to see where the chickens can get enough sun in that yard. Without enough Vitamin D, the eggshells are brittle. I suspect your aunts will be grateful for that advice. I'll load a couple of crates on my pickup. See what works best."

He turned and shouted: "No! No! Jakeleg. Put the matching chicken feed sacks together. Ladies need at least three or four matching for a dress of any size."

The shifty-eyed, stiff-legged fellow that I had seen in Sally's newspaper office flashed me a wicked smile, as though he'd been eavesdropping again and knew exactly what I was doing. "I'm putting these purty sunflower sacks on the bottom here, Clio. Real fashionable for a New York City gal."

I flounced out of the Feed and Seed Store without a backward look.

Jakeleg Simmons made me nervous, so I charged down the street as though the Greek Furies were after me, stinging my conscience. It was time to get up to the loft and sting the conscience of my POW. Lorenz needed to follow my script when I introduced him as a witness this evening, along with Lester Smith.

An uncanny silence stopped me before I made it up to the first landing of the loft. Maybe my POW was caught up in the adventures of Huckleberry and Jim. Nope. Not a single sign of habitation remained. Blankets were neatly folded and stacked on cardboard boxes. A gold razor and a well-used tablet of soap sat on the edge of the bathroom sink. *The Adventures of Huckleberry Finn* was nowhere to be seen.

How could I search publically for a POW when it was probably treason to hide a prisoner? Disheartened, I poked around in the shed, looked under Aunt Norma's

Pierce Arrow, moved rusty tools, and walked up and down the back alley until I was out of breath. Not so much as a note from that ungrateful Lorenz Weber after all the thieving of food and the wound care I'd provided.

"Something about that old garage attractin' you these last few days, Clio?" Lucinda circled around behind me with a basket full of soggy laundry. "You can help me hang up the sheets on the line behind the back fence. Norma don't like seeing laundry flappin' in her papa's nice yard."

"She surely wouldn't mind a few chickens if the pen was behind that big magnolia?" I pointed to a far corner of the yard, before confessing. "Mr. Smith is bringing over a chicken coop this evening after he closes the store. For the war effort."

Just like the sorrowful Niobe in Greek mythology who lost her children, Lucinda stood with a damp sheet draped across her shoulder and managed to speak with two clothespins in her mouth. "You are courtin' trouble, Clio. Norma won't let Lester Smith step one foot into her yard. She shut that door years ago."

CHAPTER 27

My POW was on the lam. Lucinda was in a state of shock that I'd invited Mr. Smith or she'd be saying a lot more, as she flapped wet towels and hung them with rectangular precision that would have made Euclid proud. Moving along the clothesline, she mumbled the words of that hymn "Truth divine by angels spoken," in a singsong voice, over and over.

Without my POW to describe what his father had witnessed, I had to make the most of this mishmash of an investigation into what really happened in Belleau Wood. Mr. Smith, the radioman, was now my only viable source.

In spite of the fact that Lucinda's hymnody vexed me—to use one of Aunt Norma's favorite words, I shot her a dazzling smile and, helpfully, moved her laundry basket. That hymn about "truth divine" reminded me that I might need Methodism as a trump card. Maybe I could persuade Lucinda to put in a good word for victory chickens if the discussion with my aunts got sticky.

"I promised Mr. Smith a slice of the chocolate cake that I won at the Methodist Church today if he would deliver the chicken coop and find the right spot for it.

He said the eggs shatter all over the place if the chickens don't get enough sunlight. I know that Aunt Norma will be cordial to him. She just needs to be reminded that Methodists are always civil to guests. That's what she told me. I'm trying to follow the Golden Rule."

"Whatever yer followin', Clio, don't have a thin' to do with rules. Yer up to somethin'. I've known it for two days." Lucinda whipped up the laundry basket and whirled on me like a dervish. "When your mama was up to no good, I knew it. I got the same feelin' about you. Right now. I smell trouble."

At this moment, I needed an escape. I wanted time to think and plan a strategy for getting Aunt Norma and Lester Smith around the same table tonight, with me as the chief interrogator.

In the distance, Aunt Harriet's piano keys gave me an idea. Without a second look at Lucinda, I headed toward the back door and shouted: "Practice time." If I could manage that lowdown, thumping sound of Jimmy Yancey on the keys, I'd clear the house. At best, I could search out the melody of "Five O'Clock Blues" and manage to keep Aunt Norma upstairs until the witching hour arrived.

I moved my fingers up and down the black keys and thought about Sherlock's "Blue Carbunkle." Thinking about victory chickens had brought that story to mind. The criminal stuffed the blue diamond into a dead goose. The brilliance in that story is what Sherlock had to say about making inferences as he investigated the crime.

Continuing to mindlessly pound the piano keys, I thought about my own inferences: one) Lester Smith was a radioman with Larry Bresant's battalion in Belleau Wood; two) the American soldiers who found Larry trying to save a German boy included a radioman; three) one of the soldiers said that Larry had deserted his battalion to aid the enemy; and, four) I knew that Mr. Smith was jealous of Larry.

That last one might have been an inferential leap. How did I know that Mr. Smith resented Larry Bresant? Simple. He said it himself when we talked on the courthouse bench. Larry was handsome, rich, popular, and loved by Aunt Norma. It didn't take any amount of reasoning to reach that conclusion. A woman who keeps her dead boyfriend's journal and cries over it every night for decades is besotted.

Any good detective knows that inference requires both reasoning *and* evidence. I thought about that photograph Aunt Norma had shown me of her high school graduation class. Larry Bresant's hand lightly caressed the sleeve of Aunt Norma's dress. Standing stiffly by Larry, Lester Smith appeared to be strangling—either by his cravat or his jeolousy.

Just thinking about Aunt Norma's grief made me realize why certain stories are better than others. It has to do with the beginning, the middle, and the end. This story had a happy beginning. A girl and a boy grew up together and loved each other. This story had a sad ending. Aunt Norma's life unraveled when Larry Bresant died—she had nothing left but an old journal and midnight tears.

What we don't know about this story is the middle. That's the mystery. It's the mystery that keeps a good story going long after it happened—the mystery holds the memory of the story. Unless I can find some answers, Aunt Norma's story won't ever be complete.

I hit about a dozen sour notes, closed the lid on the piano, and wandered into the kitchen to aggravate Lucinda while she cooked dinner.

The whack of the front door knocker hit at a timely moment, just as Aunt Norma finished blessing dinner—calf liver with onions; the likes of it was just about to send me into projectile vomiting.

"Who in the world comes calling at dinner time?" Aunt Harriet's question was a little morality lesson about rules in Wolfe Flats. Phones didn't ring nor people visit at mealtime.

Lucinda picked right up on it: "Must be them Jehovah Witnesses with their pamphlets. Ever since we was trapped by the tornado in the McNair's storm cellar, we've had regular visitations. And this liver from Oscar McNair." She pointed toward a mutinous pile of reddish meat in dark gravy. "Right nice of him."

I could shoot out of the room and answer the door, but I knew it was probably Mr. Smith with his chicken coop walking right into the trap I'd set for him. Better let matters follow their own course. Aunt Harriet pushed back from the table and walked down the hall toward the front door.

Undercutting Aunt Harriet's faint, querulous voice was a series of emphatic statements: "Your niece asked me. That's who. She said you want advice on where to put it. I'm here to tell you."

The same voice shouted: "Jakeleg, haul that big coop on around to the back yard. Bring those stakes so we can figure out how big to make the pen." Mr. Smith's take-charge approach made me want to admire the man, even when I didn't.

In the foyer, Aunt Harriet had gone as silent as the grave; Aunt Norma no longer cocked her head to listen. With one smooth move, she pushed back her chair, rose, and headed out of the room. I trotted behind her.

"To what do we owe this visit, Lester? Why is the Simmons boy taking that wooden contraption around the side of our house?"

"For the victory chickens, Aunt Norma. Hens for our own eggs. You said no roosters. Just a little hen party in the backyard." From the expression on Aunt Norma's face, my attempt at levity had dropped like a bomb. "I'll be totally responsible. I'll feed and water and collect eggs."

"Yes, you will, Clio. And you will clean the pen every day so that I neither see nor smell anything that remotely reminds me why I don't like yard fowl. Can we offer you a glass of iced tea for your trouble, Lester?"

Noting that Aunt Norma was leading Lester toward the second-best parlor, I felt a shiver of pure delight. Just like characters in an Agatha Christie novel, mine were assembling for a little investigative chat. I would do my best to channel her detective Poirot, although my prospects were grim. Two great aunts, Lucinda, and a reluctant Lester Smith were hardly a gaggle of suspects.

Mr. Smith settled into a high-backed chair with an air of good-natured complacency, as though he were a long-awaited guest in this house. "You haven't changed this room at all, Norma. I remember sitting in here when we were in high school. These old spindly chairs are as uncomfortable as ever. I got rid of my folks' Victorian furniture like this for something more solid. We need to move on, not hold on to useless things."

I felt an immediate distaste for this man, uttering banalities about furniture. He had harbored a bad secret for too many years and should be feeling edgy.

"Those are Gustav Stickley chairs, Lester. Not Victorian. Arts and Crafts period. Papa bought them when they first came on the market around the turn of the century. They are very simple, sturdy chairs—not at all Victorian," Aunt Harriet leaned toward Mr. Smith and added softly, "Mr. Stickley just died last month."

CHAPTER 28

As though preparing for an interment, funereal voices came from the back of the house.

"Lucinda, is Norma here?" Manboy's voice at the back door usually meant that something was afoot—a new movie had come to King Theater or bananas that made it through the tropical blockade were at the grocery. His voice tonight was oddly stressed, down at the mouth. Just as I was getting ready to tell him that we were busy at the moment, I saw a tall, grayish shadow behind him.

Clean-shaven cheeks, shampooed hair, and civilian clothes did wonders for my POW. Lorenz Weber looked downright respectable, in spite of a slight limp.

No one moved from the circle of chairs, and then Aunt Norma rose and gestured toward the frail settee. "You brought a guest, Manford. Won't you sit? It's such a hot day that we're having a glass of iced tea. Mr. Smith here has been kind enough to deliver a chicken coop for Clio's war effort."

"What a coincidence." Manboy gave me that witness-in-a-box stare. "Our visit is about a war, Norma. Not this one. The last one." He shot a quizzical glance toward Mr. Smith. "I'm surprised to see you here, Mr. Smith."

Manboy pulled my POW into the room and stood next to Aunt Norma. "Norma, I'd like for you to meet Lorenz Weber. He's been a guest in your garage loft for a couple of days. Right, Clio?"

Talk about pinning down a hapless butterfly, Manboy had an entomologist's gleam in his eye, but I knew the lawyer inside him was just about to surface. I wasn't the one who was supposed to be in the witness box. My defense needed to be better than the prosecutor's.

"Lorenz was bleeding all over the place. He wasn't just a POW from Camp Houze. He came to deliver a very important message to Aunt Norma. I was just helping him so that he could do that very thing. A Christian act." Smiling at Lorenz, I gave him an affirmative nod. Might as well let my POW talk. Manboy could out-question me any day of the week.

Hopping up from my chair next to Aunt Norma, who seemed frozen in her tracks, I shoved it toward Lorenz. "Here. Sit here, Lorenz, next to Aunt Norma so she can hear what you came to tell her."

Bowing from the waist over his partner's hand, like an Eighteenth Century dancer, Lorenz Weber lifted Aunt Norma's fingers, touched them to his lips, and said ever so softly in perfect English: "I'm alive today because your dear friend, Lawrence Bresant, saved a fifteen-year-old boy's life—that of my father, Dieter Weber, in Belleau Wood, in the first war."

With a disgusted snort, Mr. Smith pushed himself up and screeched: "He's a German, the one they've been looking for who escaped from Camp Houze! This POW needs to go back across Red River to prison. He's the enemy. We've fought the Germans in two wars now. He's got nothing to say to anyone about Belleau Wood. I fought his people there. I'm calling the deputy sheriff."

"You will not, Lester." Aunt Norma's voice was decisive. "We will hear what Mr. Weber has to say. All of us. We will all listen. Sit down, Lester."

At Aunt Norma's sharp command to Lester Smith, my POW's head snapped around. His mouth dropped open but no sound came. He simply stared at Mr. Smith as though the cogs were turning in his head, but he had forgotten the English language. Mr. Smith's threats must have set him on edge.

Just to show Mr. Smith that my POW was harmless, I stepped close to Lorenz and grabbed his hand. I didn't want to lose this opportunity to keep my prime suspect in the inner circle. "You're OK here, Lorenz. Mr. Smith was a friend of Lawrence Bresant. They were in the same unit in Belleau Wood." I tapped Lorenz's arm. "Go ahead. Tell Aunt Norma what your father wanted you to say."

My POW stood gaping—not at me but at Mr. Smith—as though bile traveling up his throat had stopped the sound. Then, the magic words came in a torrent: "He said this man's name, Lester. It didn't make sense. My father said that Lawrence Bresant shouted out the word "laster . . .laster" to the radioman when the other two soldiers were dragging Lawrence away."

Lorenz lowered his voice to a near whisper: "Laster is the German word for vice, for something very bad. My father thought Lawrence was shouting out the word for vice, over and over. He did not. He was calling this man's name." Lorenz pointed an accusing finger at Lester Smith.

I never thought that silence has a sound, but it did in that space at that moment—a noiseless hum as though all of the oxygen were being sucked out of the room. One of Lester Smith's hands was working his cravat into what I thought would be a perfect hangman's knot. I had practiced tying the hangman's noose until I had it down pat. With a good jerk of a thick rope, the knot pops the neck vertebrae apart. Mr. Smith might choke himself to death with his silk cravat, but it would be a long and painful process.

Considering the color of his face, I braced myself for a cerebral hemorrhage of the first order. Then, he inhaled a deep breath and exhaled a single, long, drawn-out phrase. "Lying Kraut," and stepped briskly toward the parlor doorway.

Not briskly enough. Manboy is short but fills a door-frame with authority. Those stumpy arms had hauled me practically lifeless out of Whitey Lewin's deep well. "I suggest that you sit down, Mr. Smith, so we can hear what Mr. Weber has to say. Or, rather, what his father wished him to say."

Lester Smith dropped back into Aunt Norma's Stick-ley chair with a thump that made its sturdy legs quiver. He glowered in my direction as I turned to face to him, wishing that I had a nice, waxed mustache like Poirot. Twisting the ends would have been pleasurable at that moment.

As my POW knelt beside Aunt Norma's chair, he touched my arm gently and said "*Keine angst*, Clio. No fear." He moved so close to Aunt Norma that I was tempted to pull him back, to give her the space she always seemed to require. She actually leaned toward him.

"Miss Norma, I am the poor substitute for my father. Always, his dream was to come to America to say what your friend Lawrence did for him in the war. Papa wanted me to be here, because he named me Lorenz after your Lawrence. When the war started in Poland, we could not travel. My father's lungs were bad. He died two years ago. He made me promise to tell you what your brave friend did for him."

I glanced over at Mr. Smith, who sat there in craven silence, his mouth dropping and closing, like a fish long-ing for the hook to put him out of his misery.

"This is very personal, Miss Norma, a debt I must pay. When I was sent to Camp Houze, I had an opportu-nity to see you. I had to take it. I escaped from the camp for this important reason."

I watched the pinkish hue traveling up my POW's neck into the roots of pale, newly trimmed hair. "Your Lawrence found my father, just a boy, with his foot blown away. Lawrence stopped the bleeding and talked to him all that night. He told Papa about his life in Wolfe Flats. I think that he was trying to help Papa forget his pain."

Aunt Norma's body flinched, but her face remained impassive, as though she had met and mastered worse pain.

"Papa said three soldiers came, but they wouldn't listen. Lawrence told them to help him take Papa to a nearby field hospital. He told the soldiers he would go back with them and explain to the officer in charge."

Lorenz rose to his feet and sent a coldly determined glance at Lester Smith, shifting in the Stickley. "My father said the radioman shouted 'Lawrence deserted.' The two soldiers took Lawrence away—not back toward their own lines."

Lorenz knelt down beside Aunt Norma again, lifted her hand, and stared at it with admiration—as though he might have discovered a missing limb from the Venus de Milo. "There were some words that your Lawrence asked Papa to tell you. It's something from Shakespeare. He said you would remember, because the lines were very personal."

Well, pooh. I was so miffed by this namby-pamby scene playing out in the parlor that I was speechless. Shakespeare is just the best-known writer in the world. There's no big secret about the Bard. Unless it's the secret about whom he really is rather than who he's supposed to be. I was just getting wound up to puncture that little secrecy balloon when Manboy sent me that zip-your-lip expression.

Lester Smith leaped to his feet and beat me to the punch. "I never heard such blither-blather. Shakespeare, my foot. The Germans were attacking us from every direction. I was breathing in mustard gas, fighting to stay alive. Mortars going off like fireworks. Our own men dying everywhere around me." He paused, for emphasis, like an amateur actor. "There was Larry cuddling an enemy soldier for hours, deserting his own men to help a dirty Boche."

It wasn't Lester Smith's lies that chilled me to the bone; it was his mockery of his dead comrade. I was having a devilish time getting a word in edgewise, when Lorenz responded.

"My father was only fifteen. He had no gun. Only supplies. He was not a soldier, just a boy helped by a kind stranger. You were there. You know exactly what happened." Lorenz turned a stern face upward, toward Mr. Smith.

"No, you lying Kraut. I was back in the trenches, trying to find a frequency to send information. That was my job. Staying back of our troops with my equipment, so we wouldn't lose contact. I wasn't anywhere near those guys who found Larry. I was told about it later. That's how I knew. After we pushed the Germans back. After we took Belleau Wood."

"He's a contortionist," Aunt Harriet whispered in my ear. "A boneless wonder. He claims he was breathing mustard gas, but Lester Smith never wheezes. He sings in the Methodist choir. Too loudly. Baritone."

I whirled around to face Aunt Harriet, but my dotty aunt appeared to be paralyzed by her own observation. *Very clever, I thought. Maybe more than one Poirot lives under this roof.*

"Don't anyone move!" No one would have dared. Even Mr. Smith dropped back down into his chair. When Aunt Norma barks orders in that tone of voice, she could halt an invading army in its tracks.

I have never seen Aunt Norma move faster than her usual leisurely pace to the Methodist Church on Sundays when it doesn't rain. At that moment, she actually dashed. Out of the room and up the great, curving staircase. As commanded, we all stayed put in silence.

Like a Regency dandy from another century, Mr. Smith lifted one leg across the other to expose bright yellow socks. They matched his cravat perfectly. Yellow was not a good color against the reddish hue of his face.

When Aunt Norma re-entered the room, she waved the old buckram journal right in front of Mr. Smith's nose. "The missing pages. Did you tear them out, Lester? Did you?"

Hardly anyone would dare to counter Aunt Norma when her blood was boiling. I have to give it to Lester Smith. He tried.

"I knew that Larry was keeping a kind of diary, a journal. He was always writing in it. That's why I went through his haversack to find it. I thought it might be a comfort to you, Norma, considering . . ." His voice trailed off.

"Considering what, Lester?" Aunt Norma's voice was at a minus 273 degrees centigrade. Kelvin's scale for absolute zero. She held the buckram-sided journal open just past the middle stitched seam. "Three pages have been ripped out. See the ragged edges. The last entry is June

20, 1918. You told me that you never saw Larry after he went off with his unit on June 21st. So, where did you get his journal?"

Lorenz interrupted: "From the ground, where Lawrence dropped it, next to Papa. He said Lawrence wrote in it that night. There was almost a full moon. Papa said he was writing something for you, Miss Norma. No. Something to you. Something about *Romeo and Juliet.* He told Papa that you both were in that play here in Wolfe Flats." Lorenz's words might have broken the tension in the room had his voice not been so sad. I clutched Aunt Harriet's hand. Much as I admired Agatha Christie's detective, I didn't like the way this interrogation was going.

"Two soldiers took Lawrence away. Papa remembered that very well. Papa thought the third soldier, the radioman, was going to shoot him. But he didn't. He just picked up Lawrence's *brotbeutel* and left."

"Haversack," Manboy inserted softly.

"Why would you tear out pages of your friend's last words, Mr. Smith?" Lorenz's question was an accusation.

"Since you seem to know so much about a war that took place before you were even born, you German convict, maybe you have the answers." While he shouted at my POW, Mr. Smith kept Aunt Norma's chair between him and Lorenz.

"I have no answers. I'm not the kind of man to betray my friends," Lorenz's voice was low and lethal.

"We never got any answers," Aunt Norma interrupted in a hesitant voice. "Larry's parents sent letters to the War Department, trying to find out what happened.

So did I. The war was on French soil. We were supporting the British troops, so the administrative structure was confusing or nonexistent. The Bresants finally had a response. The letter simply said that Larry was presumed dead, and his file was closed related to findings of dishonorable behavior."

"That's exactly why I didn't want you to see those pages in Larry's journal, Norma. He had written notes about *Romeo and Juliet*. His big moment on a stage," he sneered. Getting no response, he added. "He scribbled all kinds of excuses for deserting his men, for aiding and comforting the enemy. It was a treasonous act in the middle of a battle. I was just trying to save you from finding out what Larry was really like. You were always blind to his faults," Lester added, like a wheedling Uriah Heep.

CHAPTER 29

Before I could tell Mr. Smith how much he reminded me of Uriah Heep, that weasely Dickens's character, who says he has to "get on umbly," meaning by deceit and scheming, the lawyer interrupted.

"You need to read the Constitution, Article II, Section 3, Mr. Smith. It does not define 'aid and comfort to the enemy' as providing emergency medical care to a wounded boy, regardless of his nationality." Manboy's voice rang out with the assurance of someone who actually read those yards of books with bills, resolutions, and briefs.

Manboy might be a master of legal jargon, but I sensed that we were losing focus here. From the bright hue of Mr. Smith's face, I deduced that a full confession or a major myocardial infarction was on the agenda. I needed to reshape this interrogation to reveal exactly what role Mr. Smith played in Lawrence Bresant's last hours in Belleau Wood. I'd throw up a smokescreen and play the sympathy card.

"I can imagine how frightening it was for you, Mr. Smith, with all that poisonous gas and those shells exploding. It makes sense to keep the radiomen away from the action. Probably hard to keep men like you back from the front lines. Yet . . ." I rolled out that questioning "yet" to do double duty. Keeping suspects on the straight and narrow is the hallmark of a good sleuth.

"You got that right, little lady," Mr. Smith relaxed just a bit. "Shells and mortar bombs were falling at twenty a minute since daybreak. We could see Germans moving through the woods. We could have mown them down, but just before dusk Larry had gone ahead with a couple of guys."

Mr. Smith frowned. "I was for holding back and firing ahead to make it safer for us to move out. But I wasn't in charge. So we started off, using the trees for cover. That's where Larry was hiding. Beside a tree. With a Bosch."

He flushed a peculiar shade of red and corrected himself. "I was too far back to see exactly what Larry was doing."

I moved closer to him. "Yet, you *exactly* described the way that Larry was holding Lorenz's father. 'Cuddling an enemy soldier' is the way you put it."

"You are way out of line, missy. I said my say when I came back from the war. Best as I could to reduce the shame, for the Bresants and for you, Norma. I tried to soften up the facts by keeping the truth to myself. I didn't keep his name off the courthouse plaque. I'm not the guilty one."

"*Et tu, Brute.*" The Latin phrase from *Julius Caesar* tripped off Lorenz's tongue, as though he had responded on cue. "Pardon me, Mr. Smith. That's not from the play Papa said Lawrence talked about that night. I hope you will forgive me for adding my mustard," he spoke to Aunt Norma, not the rest of us.

"You mean putting in your two cents worth, Lorenz. That's how we say it," I patted Lorenz's arm to encourage him to continue his diplomatic put-downs that were charging the thread-like capillaries in Mr. Smith's cheeks to a near bursting point.

Ignoring me, Lorenz spoke only to Aunt Norma: "Lawrence told Papa that you lit up the stage the night your class put on *Romeo and Juliet*. These are personal things to hear in private. Lawrence told Papa his great wish would be hearing you say those beautiful words one more time." Lorenz turned and glowered at Mr. Smith. "I don't think you wanted Lawrence to hear Miss Norma say those words ever again."

"You are a lying Kraut. I said it once. I'll say it again. An escaped POW will face a firing squad. I've had enough of this! I'm going to find the Deputy Sheriff right now to report you!" Lester Smith shoved Aunt Harriet's prized Stickley chair halfway across the room and whacked me away as I tried to get between him and the parlor door.

Lorenz flung protective arms around me and shouted: "*Etappenschwein!*"

Manboy smiled slyly, as he shoved the parlor door wide for Mr. Smith.

"It means 'rear swine,' a name for soldiers who stay back from the action."

"Don't forget to take your stupid chicken coop," I screamed at his retreating back. "I don't like the way you fight wars. We don't need your help in this one!"

Aunt Harriet grabbed my arm, just as I headed down the hall after Mr. Smith. I had more to say to him: back-stabbing, betrayal, and, breach of trust. When I cranked into gear, I could fill a page of the *Oxford English Diction-ary* with what a friend should never do.

"'These hot days is the mad blood stirring.' Benvolio said that." Aunt Harriet's raised voice stopped me in my tracks as her grip loosened on my arm. "Luther, Felicity's husband, played Benvolio, Romeo's cousin. Of course, he wasn't her husband then. They were just seniors in high school."

Aunt Harriet flinched as the front door slammed, loudly enough to splinter the frame. "Benvolio was a pacifist. So was Luther. I never understand why he and Lawrence went to war. Lester was another matter; he was not cut from the same cloth."

"Lester couldn't act. That's why he did the stage and the props. He used too much black and red paint. He insisted that *Romeo and Juliet* wasn't about teenage lovers. He said it was a play about the Montague-Capulet feud." Aunt Norma's voice was lower and sadder than Aunt Har-riet's. They both seemed to be wandering hand-in-hand into a past where no one could follow them.

Bringing everyone back to the present was a special gift of mine.

"He might not have fired a bullet, but Lester Smith is responsible for Lawrence Bresant's death." Observing the shocked expressions on my aunts' faces, I added. "I think that's very clear."

No one said a word. I could feel a glacier creeping into the room, one of those slow-moving ones at no more than half a mile per year.

"I don't disagree with you, Clio, that Mr. Smith betrayed his friend, but in the midst of mass slaughter, military justice could be brutal, often a way of disciplining troops. They didn't hold tribunals. We may never know why . . ."

I interrupted Manboy: "I know why. Lester Smith was jealous of Lawrence. He had a thing for Aunt Norma so . . ."

"Clio, I think you've said enough. We all heard the same thing tonight. I never believed that Lester told me the truth all those years ago when he brought me Lawrence's journal. Sometimes the truth is unbearable. I suspect that it is for Lester," Aunt Norma's cheeks glistened under the soft glow of the finials on a glass-beaded chandelier overhead.

I turned my head so that she wouldn't see the sullen expression that I could not keep off my face. I had Lester Smith dead to rights. He's the one who accused Lawrence. Whatever happened to Lawrence had Lester's footprints all over it. If they didn't have a war crimes tribunal in Belleau Wood in 1918, we needed to have our own in Wolfe Flats.

Lester Smith was the jetsam of that terrible war. Some people might feel sympathy for him, but he had made a purposeful decision about his friend. Mr. Smith might be a sad sack man today, but Larry was a dead man. The scales weren't balanced yet.

"Lorenz, I need to get you back to Camp Houze. It's at least a thirty-minute drive. If we leave now, you can surrender, and I'll help explain why you left the camp. It won't be a good idea for the Deputy Sheriff to take you back." Manboy spoke with an authority that irritated me. This was my POW, not his.

"But I found Lorenz. I'm the one . . ."

"You're the one who will sit in the front seat with Manford while I sit in the back seat with Lorenz on the way to Camp Houze. We don't have much time, but I want to hear everything he has to tell me about Lawrence, everything his father could remember." Aunt Norma pulled me close to her and started toward the back door.

CHAPTER 30

As though he had planned for a quick exit from Wolfe Flats, Manboy's black Buick Roadmaster sat in his driveway next door. "Front seat, Clio. Your aunt and Lorenz have things to discuss in the back."

Things I wanted to hear. I reached for the lever that turned off the air control for ventilation, as Manboy swatted at my hand. "It's too noisy, Manboy. I can't hear a thing."

"At certain times, Clio, privacy is important." He cranked down his window so that a blitz of hot summer air drowned everything but the two voices behind us, speaking so low that they were incomprehensible.

After crossing the bridge over Red River into Texas, I could see only a few lights in the distance, hardly enough to suggest that Gainesville was ahead of us. The street-lights were turned off at a scheduled time to save electricity and hide the town from enemy bombers. As Manboy took a narrow road toward the west, I could see glaring lights ahead of me.

"I'll try to get us to Post Headquarters, but they probably won't let me drive inside the camp with you and Clio inside, Norma. The guards will take Lorenz at the gate, but I'll try to see the quartermaster or the NCO in charge tonight. We need to be sure they record that Lorenz returned to camp of his own volition."

The notion of "volition" went right out the door when we pulled up to the big fence with lethal-looking barbed wire twisted the length of it. Before Manboy could get half a sentence of lawyerly jargon out, Lorenz was traveling on tippy toes between two angry guards. I will have to give Manboy credit. Short as he was, when he flashed his ID and shouted with authority, one of the guards swung the gate wide and motioned him inside.

That left Aunt Norma and me waiting in a dark and silent car with nothing to do but whistle "Dixie," a song this Confederate-loving town of Gainesville held sacred. I felt like a dud, one of those bombs that doesn't go off but remains packed with explosives.

Once Lester Smith was exposed as complicit in whatever happened to Lawrence Bresant, it was only fair that he be confronted—publically. Otherwise, only my aunts, Lucinda, Manboy, and I would know the truth. One of us might talk a bit. One of us has a good friend at the *Wolfe Flats Messenger*, Sally Tolliver always needs an interesting story.

"Don't worry, Clio. Manford will see that Lorenz gets fair treatment. I don't think anything bad will happen to him. Not if I have anything to do with it." The assurance in Aunt Norma's last words seemed to shift the world back on its axis. When she spoke, people in Wolfe County listened.

So did the National Guard in Carter County when my mother trotted off with Jeremiah's father all those years ago.

Tonight, in this dark car, parked outside a POW camp with armed soldiers standing too close for comfort, I was unsettled. Like any self-righteous person at long last confronted with the truth, Aunt Norma should be plotting revenge against Lester Smith. She was breathing very quietly. Time to accelerate her pulse.

"What he did was wrong, Aunt Norma. Your friend didn't come back from the war because of Lester Smith. That man walks around this town like a rooster with that stupid cravat, selling his stupid victory chickens. Someone should get even with him."

"Someone did, Clio. Lester was once a friend of mine, and, of Harriet, and Felicity, all through grade school and high school. Not one of us continued that friendship when he returned from the war. I knew that he was hiding something; I just didn't know what. Now, I do," Aunt Norma's voice was as soothing as molasses. It really riled me.

"So it just goes on like it always did. You see him in church and don't speak? You sit there and listen to him sing in the choir? If someone caused the person I cared about to . . ."

"Over 100,000 Americans died in that war, Clio. Felicity's Luther died with no one really knowing what happened. Wars are monstrous. They bring out the worst and sometimes the best in people. Tonight was the first time in many years that I've spoken to Lester. It will be the last."

"But that just doesn't seem . . ." I couldn't explain. Agatha Christie could. Everything in her books is settled on the last page—actually, Miss Marple, her prize sleuth, nails the evil-doer in her own mind long before that.

I blurted out: "There's no conclusion here, Aunt Norma. The culprit just waltzes out the door. That's not supposed to happen."

"What you are looking for, Clio, is a denouement." Aunt Norma gave the term a nice French pronunciation. "It happens in literary works, rarely in everyday life. All the strands of the plot come together. All matters are resolved. Usually, in real life, we must settle for less."

The fragility of that word "less" brought tears to my eyes, so I turned to watch the soldiers watching us and tried to empty my mind of everything that felt so unjust in this world: Mother going off to war without a thought for me; seeing Aunt Norma crying over that journal at night; and, knowing that someone as guilty as Lester Smith would go on selling his chicken coops as a so-called war effort.

"Do you want to hear the words that my dear Larry asked to hear? I will only say them this one time and believe that he is somewhere listening. That's what I have to believe, Clio. It's what gets me by."

My head might have nodded, but I made no other movement as my ancient Aunt Norma spoke in the voice of a young girl, Juliet, so in love that her words have lasted for over three centuries.

"When he shall die, take him and cut him out into stars, and he shall make the face of heaven so fine that all the world will be in love with night and pay no worship to the garish sun."

Aunt Norma conjured up a living, breathing Juliet so intense in her grief that I was transported out of myself—or would have been if the scratchy upholstery in Manboy's Buick hadn't been torturing my bare legs.

Aunt Norma's were the last words that I heard that night. Oh, Manboy came back to the car and prattled on about how he would be meeting with someone or other in the morning and maybe Lorenz could get on the work detail for digging Lake Texoma now that he wasn't really a risk.

All I heard was a girl's voice that had tucked itself somewhere inside an old woman who wore thick, cotton stockings attached to a hideous girdle, a woman who could boss a rabid dog into submission, a woman who kept her secret-most thoughts away from the rest of the world.

By the time we drove back across Red River on Highway 77, Aunt Norma didn't say another word until Manboy pulled into our driveway. "You need to get to bed, Clio. It's very late." As she hustled me to the door, she turned toward Manboy. "I have no doubt that you will do your best for Lorenz. He really shouldn't have taken such a risk, even though he made his father a promise. Promises shouldn't weigh people down with guilt, but I value what that young man tried to do for me. I value it beyond words."

With no further words, she swept into the house like a duchess who holds sovereignty in her own right, knowing the duke will never return. At that moment, I realized that Aunt Norma's sense of missing Larry was too acute for ordinary words. She must have been consoled, knowing her friend better than anyone else would ever know him, the way that Juliet knew the only love of her life.

As I watched Aunt Norma heading up the stairs, I sent a limp wave in Manboy's direction and closed the door as gently as possible. Standing in the foyer of this big gloomy house, I thought of how sad Aunt Norma sounded in the car as she quoted Juliet's lines about Romeo.

At that instant, it became very clear to me. Aunt Norma's memory of what could have been set a standard that other people might never understand. For instance, my mother never loved my father the way that Aunt Norma loved and still loves Lawrence Bresant. Mother told me that she and my father were "ill-suited," whatever that means. She told me to always beware of infatuation. "It's a word that means short-lived, like my marriage." But then she'd grin, hug me, and add: "But my prize of a daughter made it worth the dance."

Over my head, I could hear Aunt Norma's footsteps, the firm closing of her door, then silence. Just for a moment, I thought that I understood the penalty she had paid for loving Larry's memory more than she could ever love the man he might have become.

CHAPTER 31

When the sunlight sidled through the heavy, olive velvet drapes in my bedroom the next morning, I couldn't hear a single noise downstairs. Before Aunt Norma got up to badger me about my piano scales or her summer reading list, I needed to do some serious mapmaking.

Ptolemy, the first recognized mapmaker, is a particular hero of mine, although his reasoning for making maps was a bit screwy. Doing horoscopes was his passion, and he wanted to be sure that the longitudes and latitudes lined up perfectly for identifying places of birth. He also was the first to flatten the planet so that he could get the globe on a piece of paper.

Not able to keep a smirk off my face, I conjectured that half the citizens of Wolfe Flats probably thought the world *was* flat. I reflected that my skill in mapping crime scenes had taken me on the road to a killer's house. Anxiety gripped me, just before a sharp pain in my solar plexus reminded me that an executioner of sorts had walked out of my investigation last night.

When we had headed home from Camp Houze last night, Manboy tried to lighten the mood when he said: "The *verräter* is in the *hundehütte*. The traitor is in the doghouse."

"The only house for Lester Smith should be a gibbet." I pictured him in one of those iron baskets that caged a victim outside and attracted carrion birds.

Manboy grunted; Aunt Norma didn't respond. *Methodists have their own torture—hard pews and long sermons.* I kept my mouth shut the rest of the way home.

This morning, before the sun got any higher, I needed to work. Rolling out a sheet of pristine paper, grabbing one of my favorite Venus drawing pencils and my trusty metal ruler, I started a new map, calculating the distance from our house to Jeremiah's farm and marking interesting intersections along the way. When I rode the horse home from Jeremiah's, I had noted everything of interest, even while perched precariously atop a trotting equine. With my attention to detail, I'm very much a student of Ptolemy.

I made a little dog house for Lester Smith's Feed and Seed Store on Second Street. Then, I drew a two-story building on Main Street for the Masonic Hall—with the Masons' clever symbol of square and compass (a mapmaker's favorite tools). When I first arrived in Wolfe Flats, I scouted out the Masonic Hall, because it had an impressive pool table on the first floor, and a long, empty room with chairs along the walls on the upper floor.

When I questioned Lucinda about the building, she hit the roof. "Men folks don't let the ladies join Masons, but the Eastern Star women meet up there with them Rainbow Girls, sashaying around in taffeta dresses. Can't join them unless you have a Mason granddaddy or husband or daddy. Norma and Harriet joined the Eastern Star so's that Delia could be a Rainbow Girl."

"A what?" My mother wouldn't be caught dead wearing anything brighter than a sparrow's plumage.

"Some preacher over in McAlester dreamed up a club for girls like them Demolay boys have—sort of a juvenile version of the Masons for boys and girls."

"I've heard about Masons, Lucinda. George Washington was one. So was Clark Gable—a man with wooden teeth and a man with Hollywood teeth." I pondered that image and moved on. "I think all those creepy handshakes and secret rituals are spooky. What does that have to do with my aunts joining something called the Eastern Star?"

"They was tryin' to get Delia to fit in with other girls when she didn't ever want to. Yer mama was what they call contrary. I think she did things just to get under the skin of your aunt. Norma made Harriet join the Eastern Star with her so that Delia could be initiated into the Rainbow Girls," Lucinda let out a snort that might have been an effort to smother laughter.

"Delia put on that plaid taffeta dress that Norma special ordered from Daube's in Ardmore. She pranced down the street with the other girls, heading for the initiation ceremony on the top floor of the Masonic Lodge." Lucinda paused and got this silly smirk on her face.

"And what?"

"Some of them Demolay boys was playin' pool on the first floor. Delia challenged one of them to a game and never made it to the Rainbow Girls' initiation. She said that flittin' around makin' little speeches about faith, hope, and charity would be a bore." Lucinda shook her head. "That ain't the real reason she agreed to join; she was just reelin' in Norma to get a new dress. When Delia found out that her friend Sally Tolliver hadn't been invited to join, she wasn't about to go up them stairs."

On the map I was making, I redrew the Masonic Lodge with one wall missing, so the pool table could be seen.

Then I drew lines from the back alley of Lewin's Department Store out to the Lewin home on the edge of town. Not every victim of a madman wants to revisit the crime scene, but a good detective puts down every bit of useful information to hone her skills. What went right; what went wrong; what should have been done differently.

I thought about the evening that Whitey Lewin stuffed an ether-soaked gag in my mouth and threw me in his well. His mistake was in tossing my bicycle in ahead of me, giving me spokes, fenders, and handlebars as a safety net.

If I made a mistake—and I don't admit that I did—it was in going out after dark alone to check the timing from place to place at the intersections on my map. How could I have known that Whitey owned high-powered night vision binoculars and was spying on me?

I don't believe that revenge is best served cold, so I helped a serial killer bite the big one. It wasn't me who steered Whitey's pickup into a tree, causing it to explode, but I was the one who took his bullet. I solved The Case of the Missing Girls.

Maybe I should write it down like Mrs. Christie, put some text with my maps. I could almost see the letters of my name tracing down the spine of a best-selling crime book.

The cover would need to be a bit garish, perhaps blood on a white background. That would be a subtle nod to Whitey's imagined albinism. Or, I could draw a big powder puff and surround it with tibias and fibias— as a reminder to his hostile mother that she bore some responsibility for Whitey's psychopathic personality by putting talcum on him as a child.

Aunt Norma would never let my book see the light of day. She had been downright rude to Sally Tolliver when news stories came out in the *Daily Oklahoman* and the *Ardmorite*, giving me credit where credit was due.

The smack of the lion's head doorknocker reverberated up the stairs into my room, creating a sense of foreboding. No one knocked on front doors this early, especially not Aunt Norma's door. It couldn't be Lester Smith. He and his chicken coop were long gone when we returned from Camp Houze last night. Maybe Lorenz had taken another runner, because he didn't like the prospect of digging up 93,000 acres of land for Lake Texoma.

Stepping into the skirt that coiled in a convenient circle on the floor, I tied a firmer knot in the rotten elastic waistband, slipped a slightly soiled blouse over my head, trotted down the long hall to the stairway landing, and looked down.

Aunt Norma stood by the front door, staring at an envelope in one hand and a piece of paper in the other. From between the rails circling the landing above her head, I could spot the pasted-on strips of a telegram. I could probably read the words with my eagle eyes, but I wasn't sure I wanted to know what they said.

Aunt Norma frowned up at me. "It's an odd telegram, Clio, from someone who identifies himself as a colleague of your mother. Over there."

Wouldn't you know the bouncy song from that *Yankee Doodle Dandy* movie would pop into my mind: "Over there. Over there. Send the word over there. That the Yanks are coming." But they weren't. Our Yank, my impulsive mother, wasn't coming home. Aunt Norma's face appeared to be frozen, as though she refused to accept what the telegram said.

Tearing down the stairs, I snatched it from her hand. "Advise Delia missing 2 wks. Possibly with FFI friends. Sorry. John N. Colleague"

"That must be her friend, John. That letter she sent two weeks ago mentioned someone named John with the BBC. What does FFI mean, Aunt Norma?" I rubbed the letters on the telegraph fiercely, knowing that they represented some horror, someone who had kidnapped Mother, definitely not friends.

"I think the reference might be to the French Forces of the Interior. Those are the French fighters who are resisting the German invasion of their country. Marshal Petain may have capitulated to Hitler, but he doesn't represent the French people. You don't suppose that . . ." Aunt Norma's voice dropped to a faint murmur before she belted out at the top of her lungs: "Harriet, get down here. Now!"

Within seconds, a dripping head appeared over the stair rail above us.

"I was in the bathtub, Norma. What in the world has happened?"

"That's it." Aunt Norma leaned forward eagerly, re-reading those scant lines and ignoring Aunt Harriet's question. "That foolish Delia did a minor in French. She has French aquaintences. The U.S. military won't let female correspondents close to the action. Delia's gone where they will!"

"Where who will what?" I shouted in frustration.

"Where desperate people will welcome an American reporter to tell their story," Aunt Norma snapped back at me.

"People with not much to lose under German occupation," a dripping Aunt Harriet chimed in, as she snatched the telegram.

"Do you remember the name of that French family that Delia met in Paris when she and that Lichtman fellow went on their honeymoon? It was in January of 1930. She sent us a postcard with the Louvre on it and a message for everyone in our post office to see: 'Hitched last week to Joseph Lichtman. Staying with Dubois family.'"

Aunt Norma's face had defrosted to a faint pinkish hue. I was busy doing math in my head, figuring that I was about a five-months fetus when my mother got "hitched." Mother didn't bother telling me that. She did tell me about her French friends, Marie and Guillaume Dubois. They exchanged letters often before the war broke out. Then, they didn't. When the Germans invaded Paris about this same time last year, on June fourteenth, I saw Mother cry for the first time ever.

At this moment, I began to blubber. Great, heaving sobs echoed around the foyer and into the kitchen where Lucinda's pans were silent. I knew about the French resistance fighters. Mother told me they were citizens who fought against the German occupiers of Paris and the Vichy regime in the south of France. The Germans did bad things to resistance fighters when they could catch them. Torture, firing squads, and instant burials. An icy chill went right up from my bare toes to the top of my head.

CHAPTER 32

A t the very moment when I thought that I might pass out cold, two warm arms encircled me and Lucinda whispered into my ear: "Yer mama will be all right, Clio. She's a girl who knows how to get herself out of scrapes. If somethin' bad happened to her, I'd feel it in my bones. We got a kind of psychopathic connection. Me and Delia."

For an instant, I almost corrected Lucinda to say "paranormal connection," but knowing my mother's risky behavior, I thought "psychopathic" nailed it. I remembered something else and blurted it out: "Marie and Guillaume Dubois are cousins of my father, maybe second cousins. Mother said they like her better than him."

"I don't think your father was French, Clio. That name Lichtman sounds a bit Jewish or maybe Russian. Preferably Russian." Aunt Norma smiled benignly, tossing the dice more favorably as she juggled my genes.

"Actually, Dutch. But his parents originally came from Russia. Mother said they spoke Yiddish in front of her. She couldn't understand a word of it, but they weren't saying nice things. She said their idea of a visit was right out of the Antebellum South—a year. We left before my grandparents did."

The vague memory of my father was not pleasant. My ears hurt when I think about him. I nestled against Lucinda. She was familiar, warm, and confident that Mother was safe.

Having only one parent made me doubly dependent on my mother, because my father was a ghost. Mother released information about my father the way that an octopus squirts ink—in brief, dark, obscuring clouds. That's where the comparison ends. An octopus has three hearts; I'm not sure my mother has one. She manages to hang on to her grudges for years.

I remember Mother explaining: "Joseph's father bullied his mother, but Mrs. Litchman was incapable of expressing her grievances against him, so she went after me like a fishwife. She let me know right after I met her that an educated, career-minded woman ranked up there with Jezebel. I brushed off her snide remarks until I couldn't. We had to leave, Clio." "Leaving" is probably Mother's favorite word.

Mother said she had developed a "protective crust" from years of living with Aunt Norma. She said that the Lichtmans' rudeness rolled off her "like water off a duck's back," until my father entered the fray. "Your father chose the wrong side. Fatal error when you're up against a Clower, Clio. Mae West nailed it when she said: 'Marriage is a great institution, but I'm not ready for an institution.'"

Mother loved quoting other people to hammer a point home. That way, she kept her protective crust in place, giving herself a spokesperson to describe how she really felt. I'm working on my own crust. Something thick and gnarly, like the bony plates on an alligator.

"Your father's family was a charmed circle, Clio. Doting parents and a spoiled son. Your father had that kind of self-possession that speaks of utter confidence; it lures in the unwary. Utter selfishness was what it really was. I was smitten at first, then repulsed.

Mother rarely talked about my father. Her set-in-stone face communicated her displeasure with that topic. She occasionally let things slip. "When Joseph's parents moved in with us, his mother called you Hadar. That was her name. She said the first daughter is always named for the grandmother." Mother forced a weak smile at that point.

"Your father told me that we should indulge his mother. Indulgence started with a name; it ended with a ruler." My mother looked ready to blow a fuse. "On your third birthday, Clio, you reached up on the counter to swipe the icing on your cake. Your grandmother hit you with a wooden ruler—hard. I almost . . . well, nevermind. We left." She patted my cheek, a bit regretfully, like someone about to leave the family pet at the pound.

"There are worse things in life than not having a father around, Clio. We have each other."

We did until Mother revealed her own selfish nature and dumped me in Wolfe Flats. Now she was somewhere in France, wearing one of those berets at a rakish angle and tearing around battle zones with those French resistance fighters. I stared at those words on the telegram that Aunt Harriet still clutched. "Possibly with FFI friends."

"If those French friends of Delia's were your father's relatives, I wonder if he could find them? Or, if he could be located, what he might be doing?" Aunt Harriet's questioning voice jogged my memory.

I knew what my father *did*. He taught languages at a private college in upstate New York. I didn't know what my father *was*. I had no composite picture of him—only that he had gone over to the dark side. That, according to my mother, meant he sided against her. No matter how often I wheedled Mother for information about my father, her response was the same: "Closed subject, Clio. He could have filed for visitation rights to see you. He didn't."

While I stood there thinking of my unnatural father, who never cared enough about his daughter to send her an occasional card, Aunt Norma marched over to the black, bakelite Siemens wall phone and dialed the operator.

"Rayleen, I want you to hook me up to the Office of War Information Services in Washington, D.C. No? Well. You find out and call me back when you have someone on the line. Someone with authority. If it's Franklin Roosevelt, I'll talk to him." She smacked the phone down and raised one eyebrow at me. "I intend to go to the top authority to find out exactly why someone named John, who doesn't give a last name, sent that cryptic telegram. Surely, someone in our government knows what's happening behind the scenes in France."

"Anybody here? I saw the boy from Western Union at your front door. What's happened?" Manboy's voice sounded tentative, as the back screen door slammed behind him. He stared at Aunt Norma, Aunt Harriet, Lucinda, and me, as though we were actors in one of those frozen tableaux that the Victorians loved to stage. Called "living pictures," they would depict a famous scene from history or art.

I could almost see the cogs turning behind Manboy's eyes: Aunt Harriet dangled a telegram with bad news; Lucinda clutched me; and, Aunt Norma stood glaring at a telephone that refused to ring and probably had no answers to give us. Our tableau would be called "Despair."

Thanks to the Office of War Information Services radio broadcasts on "This is Our Enemy—Germany, Japan, and Italy," we were kept up-to-date after a fashion.

Manboy told me that we had to keep our antennae alert, to listen between the lines of such broadcasts. I didn't need any advice from Manboy about listening between the lines. I guess that's what lawyers do in court when they are prosecuting someone, trying to trip them up by hearing what isn't said.

Listening to news on the radio these days could give a person ulcers. Bombings. Nazis gobbling up country after country. We could read the wire stories in the *Daily Oklahoman*, a day late, recapping what we'd already heard on the evening news. I preferred our weekly *Wolfe Flats Messenger*. My friend, Sally, did a bang-up job interviewing mothers with boys at the front. Since Wolfe County is awash with pig fat, she wrote a little sidebar story about the efforts of a local group that collects grease for bombs—with a special nod to Lucinda, who heads that group.

Manboy gently removed the telegram from Aunt Harriet's hand and read it quickly. "I'll try to reach the BBC office in London, see if anyone knows this John N. fellow, who didn't give his last name. It's about 3 p.m. in London. With restrictions on long-distance calls, I'm not sure Rayleen can get me through. Even if I'm lucky, it's unlikely that anyone will tell me much. Communications have to be so cryptic these days. Our enemies monitor the airwaves, our newspapers, and telegraphs. Probably our phone calls as well, but I'll try."

Just a tinge of relief crept over me as I watched Manboy's odd gait down the hall and out the back door. Mother's childhood friend had climbed down an old well to rescue me. When he said: "I'll try," I knew that Manboy would do everything in his power to find out where my mother had gone in France.

At the moment, I was sensing an emotional current running through Aunt Norma, Aunt Harriet, and Lucinda—a negative charge of electrons that might not respond to the positive charge that I was about to interject, but I needed to be out of this house of grief. "If I could visit Jeremiah, it would really take my mind off this telegram. He's supposed to be at Mr. Neboja's this morning. He gets paid," I added, hoping for a nickel for pulling weeds out of Aunt Harriet's zinnias—without having to ask.

The trace of a frown centered itself between Aunt Norma's eyes, and I could imagine her tallying how many books I had not read on her "enrichment list of literary works." But she surprised me and swung the front door open.

"Be back for lunch, Clio. Don't go near the forge."

CHAPTER 33

Spending the day last week at Jeremiah's farm was the best time I'd had since arriving like an unwanted orphan in Wolfe Flats. My second favorite place was the blacksmith shop. Mr. Neboja, his son Marek, and Jeremiah would all be there.

As refugees who left Czechoslovakia just before the Germans invaded, the Nebojas might know something about the French resistance. Marek had flown planes over France, so he might have an idea about where journalists hide. At any rate, I hadn't seen Jeremiah for several days. He'd be floored by my POW story. Looking back over my shoulder, I could see Aunt Norma standing in the frame of the open front door, probably watching to see if I followed the kindergarten intersection rule of looking left, right, and left again.

A painful thought stopped me in my tracks. Aunt Norma's story wasn't mine to tell. In Manboy's car last night, when her ancient voice became that of a young Juliet, reciting grief-stricken words for only me—and the ghost of Lawrence Bresant—to hear, I realized that some stories can never be retold; like a small insect trapped in amber for thousands of years, some stories belong to themselves.

I'd have to invent another reason why the POW hid in our garage. Whatever reason I dreamed up would feature me saving the leg of a frightened POW with my alcohol and Mercurochrome potions, like Clara Barton, that famous nurse, who founded the Red Cross,

The news about Mother was more important and mine to share, so I kicked up my pace to a comfortable trot. My best friend and I had more in common than we wanted to admit, ergo, disappearing mothers. But, that's where the similarity ended. Jeremiah's mother was on a pleasant tropical island; mine was hiding from Nazis.

Jeremiah worries constantly that his mother will catch jungle rot, so I delivered him a little treatise that trench foot wasn't a communicable disease. I suppose my description of cyanosis turning feet the color of a Blue-Footed Booby just before necrosis set in with a stench that leads to amputation might have been a bit over the top. Jeremiah was downright rude to me until he got a letter from his mother, telling him not to worry about her.

On much of the flimsy, pale blue sheet, the black ink of a censor bled through the page—except for the list of plants in Latin that she described as "my boy's special interest." Poking the indecipherable list with his finger, Jeremiah shouted loud enough for the Imperial Japanese Army to hear: "She's in Hawaii! These are plants endemic to Hawaii. I can stop worrying so much."

The serene expression on Jeremiah's face suggested that he might be thinking of grass-skirted hula girls, dancing around while his mother ate roasted pig at a luau, on a sublimely beautiful beach. It wasn't my duty to remind him that the Japanese Mitsubishi Zeros were only 3,859 miles away and might strike Hawaii again.

Unlike Jeremiah, I had not been constantly worrying about my mother. Except for the fact that she been in the British Isles, where bombs rain as routinely as a spring hailstorm in Wolfe Flats, I try not to use up all my worry hours on Mother. Our military keeps women reporters back from the front lines. Normally, I'd protest the gender prejudice that let men get all the good news stories, but not when my mother might be the target of an errant bazooka.

This morning's telegram saying that my mother had gone off the deep end with some French resistance fighters, just to get smack dab in the middle of the war, put me in a quandary. If American journalists had been given equal opportunity, Mother could be perched up on a tank, writing away—not on the run in the Nazi-infested country France had become.

From all accounts, Jeremiah's mother Sonya had the personality of a saint—forbearing, understanding, and forgiving, considering that she had recently sent a couple of letters to Jeremiah's father. My mother's notion of a good day was getting a news scoop ahead of her male counterpart. As for risk avoidance, she wouldn't lift her arm in a Heil Hitler salute with a gun at her head.

There was another major difference in our parental situations: Jeremiah's testy father kept him on a short leash, until every single chore was done. If he were lucky, Jeremiah could work at Mr. Neboja's blacksmith shop for 20 cents an hour but only in his spare time. At least, Jeremiah had a father waiting for him at the end of the day.

Mother dumped my father when I was three years old, because his mother, my grandmother, whacked me with a ruler. I don't remember that incident. I remember only a tall shadow of a man and lots of shouting. Mother went to a civil court in New York to get my name changed to her maiden name: Clower. "A foreign-sounding name like Licthman is a handicap, Clio. At any rate, you are a Clower through and through."

I didn't understand what she meant then, until she left me at her aunts' front door for an up-front looksee at the war. After a few weeks with Aunt Norma, I understood more about what being a Clower meant than I ever wanted to know.

You learn to sing like a Methodist, grow callouses on your knees from bedside prayers, pound on a resisting piano, and pretend that you are *not* better than anyone who isn't named Clower. That meant self-control, helping the less fortunate, and never, ever taking full credit for tracking down the worst serial killer in the history of Wolfe Flats.

With a self-imposed boost of confidence, I sprinted on down the block toward Neboja's Blacksmith Shop. A big orange Nehi pop would be waiting for me there, along with people who appreciated my particular kind of genius.

"Clio. We haven't seen you for week," Mr. Neboja waved at me from behind the forge where he held up a horseshoe, examined it, and clobbered it, while sparks flew. "We're shoeing horses today." He pointed out the large open back doors at a small corral, teeming with horses, circling one way and then another. "Grab a soda pop. Go talk to Jeremiah. He's learning to be a farrier."

Skirting the forge, I looked up at the soot-covered walls of this old converted cotton gin that Mr. Neboja and his son Marek had turned into a thriving blacksmith shop. Wisps of cotton clung to the roof trusses like little ghosts that refused to leave.

Marek had told me that the art of the blacksmith had been a dying craft until the war changed everything. "Factories only produce what's needed for the war—tanks, jeeps, airplanes, and munitions. Farmers need blacksmiths to repair tractor parts, tools, and plows. Horses and wagons are back in use because of gas shortages."

I had seen the "A," "B," and "C" gas stickers on car windows. Aunt Norma had an "A" on her Pierce Arrow. She said it meant she could have three gallons of gas a week. Manboy had a "B" sticker, so he got eight gallons a week. He was considered a "war worker" because of his interviews with the German POWs at Camp Houze. The Methodist preacher and Doctor Lontry had "C" stickers on their cars for all the gas they needed. Doc Lontry traveled all over Wolfe County delivering babies and pronouncing death. For the life of me, I can't understand why a preacher gets a special privilege to gad about when we're having a gas shortage.

As I had passed the corner filling station, a big window poster reminded people that they shouldn't buy off the black market. The blond woman in the picture held one hand aloft as though pledging on a stack of Bibles: "I pay no more than top legal prices. I accept no rationed goods without giving ration stamps."

Lucinda was a stickler about ration stamps, even though she wasn't supposed to use loose pages of stamps. She could crank out excuses faster than she could make butter in the Daisy hand churn. "Your aunts got enough shoes in their closets to keep a battalion in footwear. I trade shoe and red meat stamps for sugar and fuel oil, so as we can keep cakes on the table and heat in the upstairs bathroom. I figure it equals out. I ain't a hoarder. We use what we use and that's all."

No need for me to point out the error in that kind of thinking. Farming communities like Wolfe Flats produced their own meat, butter, and lard. Canning was a way of life here, so empty shelves of canned goods at the grocery weren't an issue. Jam and jelly went the way of rubber tires. There was none to be had unless you finagled extra sugar and boiled it with wild sand plums the way that Lucinda did.

Going out to the backside of the Blacksmith Shop, I spotted Jeremiah wearing weird leather chaps that came just below his knees. He appeared to be preoccupied with a horse's back foot and was butt to butt with the animal. I sidled up to him as he straddled the horse's leg and squeezed its back foot between his thighs. "Ease up to its head and hold him still, Clio. He's jumpy about getting this shoe off."

So I crept up to the head of the enormous draft horse and grabbed his halter, keeping to the side of a mouthful of blocky, yellow teeth that needed a good brushing.

Marek wore the same odd chaps and was working his way down a line of tethered horses, lifting hooves, picking at them, moving his hands down the front and back of the horses' legs, talking softly in Czechoslovakian. Wolfe Flats people were suspicious of people who spoke another language; but, the horses seemed right at home with it. The horses in Wolfe County were probably much more worldly than their backwoods owners.

With a loud grunt, Jeremiah yanked off the horse's shoe, dropped its hoof, and spun toward me with a grin. "First time I've used a shoe puller. Marek is letting me do the entire job: shoe puller, hoof tester, nippers, knife, and rasp. I'm learning to be a farrier." His smile drooped. "Mr. Neboja shapes the shoes on the forge. He won't let me near it. Ever since that stupid gear piece flew into my eye."

He winked at me. "Good as new, thanks to Lucinda and Doc Lontry. And my amazing constitution." He neglected to remember that I was the one who helped save his eye with my underwear. I had humiliated myself in public to get a clean cotton slip to stop the flow of blood, so I fixed a gimlet eye on him.

With a sneaky move, Jeremiah grabbed the Nehi I had helped myself to from the ice chest by the back door.

He took a big swig. "I'll teach you to use the rasp, Clio." He snatched up an over-sized file. "Just like filing your toenails. Girls know how to do that, don't they?"

"Learning farrier skills is not high on my list, Jeremiah," I answered, feeling as snarky as I sounded. Jeremiah, Marek and Mr. Neboja were engaged in some kind of male bonding ritual over horses' hooves. It seemed neither the time nor place to tell them about my morning telegram, to let them know that my disappearing mother had put me through the wringer once again.

I set a half-empty orange soda pop down on Jeremiah's workbox, among all his tools, turned, and walked away, feeling self-righteously alone, as his faint call of "Clio! Come back . . . I didn't mean to" faded behind me.

After circling ten city blocks and annotating every house, shed, sidewalk, and tumbled-down garage in my handy pocket notebook, I had enough information to map the southwest quadrant of Wolfe Flats. If there is one thing that Wolfe Flats needs, it is a good city map. When I asked the librarian for one, she looked at me as though I had a loose screw. "You can practically see from one end of Wolfe Flats to the other. Why would anyone need a map?"

That's a question that should never be asked of a Claudius Ptolemy devotee. Scanning the sky for German bombers, as I do every day, I trotted down the street thinking about those Second Century maps of Ptolemy. Without those, the Germans wouldn't know how old some of their cities were. Having that information didn't make them less greedy for grabbing more cities. Or make them less threatening to a mother who didn't have the good sense to stay on this side of the Atlantic Ocean.

By the time I reached home, Lucinda had anchored that odd meat grinder of hers to the cabinet and was cranking out her own special pimento cheese, ignoring me. Eyeing the Universal grinder that looked a bit rusty around the shank, I said: "*Staphyloccoii* can get into places like the teeth around the front of that thing, Lucinda. I hope you clean it well after you grind sausage with it. If there's anything we don't need around here, it's bacteria on the rampage."

"If there's anythin' you don't need, Miss Smarty Pants, it's your aunt on a rampage. It's one o'clock, and she told you to be home for lunch. She and Harriet are at the church puttin' together Red Cross parcels. You'd be well-advised to practice your scales or start workin' through that stack of books your Aunt Norma set out for you."

"Speaking of books, Lucinda, you wouldn't know how to get your hands on *Tobacco Road*, would you? The librarian wouldn't let me check it out. She said it was a book about turnips, and I wouldn't like it. That's not what Jeremiah told me." I turned an innocent face toward her. "He said it's about sharecroppers in Georgia, an interesting study about poor people."

"Huumph!" Lucinda's throat clearing could stampede cattle. "Poor white trash. That's what it's about. Our preacher tried to get it taken off the library shelf after his wife read it. She read it twice, he said, just to be sure she weren't wrong about the goings on in it. She weren't." Lucinda gave an extra hard crank to the food grinder handle to squeeze out the last bits of rat cheese and pimentos.

"You go tickle them ivories or pick out a decent book to read, Clio. Your Aunt Harriet brought you a stack of Grace Livingston Hill books. She's a nice Christian lady, writin' about things a little girl would want to read."

"I'd rather be boiled in oil, drawn and quartered, strapped in a Judas cradle, or stretched on a rack," I paused, thinking of those inventive medieval torture devices. I might have been over-stating my dislike of Grace's smarmy books. "Tell you what, Lucinda. I'll go work on my city map of Wolfe Flats. Aunt Harriet won't mind if I borrow her water colors."

Just as she turned away, I stuck one finger into the bowl of pimento cheese and scooped out enough to tide me over until dinner.

Chapter 34

When the front door knocker sounded at exactly five o'clock, I dashed down the hall ahead of Aunt Harriet and swung the door wide. A mountainous ruin of a man, with dark, bushy brows topping a hawk-like nose, stood in front of me. As he looked down at me, his cheeks paled, then flamed, like one of those tropical birds that change color to attract mates.

Without saying a word, he reached above his head and swung down a huge backpack. Then he became almost normal sized, but dressed as though he might be taking off for a climb up Mount Everest. His clumpy boots and layers of clothes were not typical garb for Wolfe Flats in June.

"Clio?" He flattened out my name so that it sounded like "Kleio," with three syllables, not two. He bent over and stared into my eyes. "Your mother and I didn't agree on the spelling of your name. I liked the Greek. She didn't. She won. She usually does."

I scooted backwards, bumping into Aunt Harriet, who stood like a noiseless wraith behind me. This strange man, talking about my mother as though she'd just left the room, seemed vaguely familiar, like the sharp odor of gasoline that hangs in the air long after the gas cap is screwed into place. Something was out of place here, niggling latent brain cells, trying to make a connection that I didn't want to make.

"Can I help you, sir? This is the Clower house," Aunt Harriet's weedy voice seemed unnaturally shrill.

"Yes. It would be, wouldn't it? Biggest house on the street. Queen Anne, with handsome ornamental cornices. The wrap-around porch is not quite right," the man asserted, with a broad grin.

I could almost feel Aunt Harriet's dander getting the best of her. She is a self-proclaimed student of Wolfe Flats architecture and considers her own home to be at the apex of good taste.

"In this climate, large shaded porches are desirable," Aunt Harriet said defensively. "Are you selling something?" She glanced at his over-stuffed pack. "We have a set of encyclopedias."

He flashed a startled glance at Aunt Harriet and winked at me. "I'm Joseph Licthman. Here to see my daughter, now that Delia has deserted her." He brushed his hand gently across my cheek. "I see that Delia managed to clone herself."

"You'd better come inside, Mr. Licthman. We don't air personal business on our not-quite-right front porch," Aunt Norma's authoritative voice behind me cut to the chase. She let this man who claimed to be my father know two things right off the bat: one) for a Clower, anything personal is private; and two) the invitation of a stranger into the house acknowledged his blood connection to me.

Aunt Norma pointed to the floor in the foyer. "Your bag can go there. We're just about ready to sit down to dinner. You'll join us, of course."

With an affability that had almost gone out of style, my self-proclaimed father took control. He examined family portraits lining the dining room walls and pointed to one of my Great-Grandfather Clower. "That Weiner is a fine portrait."

Aunt Norma looked pleased at that comment. He pulled out Aunt Harriet's chair with a flourish, as though currying favor with elderly women came naturally to him. My suspicion monitor put me on edge.

When Lucinda emerged from the kitchen, carrying a big tureen of soup, he sprang up and wrested it from her. "You're Lucinda. From Delia's description, I'd know you anywhere. She named Clio after you: Clio Lucinda Licthman. It was a mouthful, but Delia was determined to honor her friend."

"My name is Clio Lucinda Clower," I muttered sullenly. My newly found father appeared to be romancing everyone in the room but me.

"I know that Delia changed your last name to hers. That doesn't alter the fact that you are one-half Licthman. That tiny cleft in your chin is my father's legacy to you, my dear Clio." The huge hand that settled on the nape of my neck felt like a rock.

Lucinda glowered from the doorway, as Aunt Harriet said: "Lucinda is part of this family. Here, Lucinda. Sit by me. Clio's father is a special guest tonight."

She gestured to the chair that I usually sit in, leaving me on the other side of my father, but Lucinda stood as silent as the sphinx before blurting out: "I'm watchin' my soufflé. Has to come out of the oven at exactly the right time. I don't need to be part of this talk." She turned and marched back to the kitchen, her back as stiff as her upper lip.

"Whatever are you doing in Wolfe Flats, Mr. Lichthman? Not that we aren't happy to finally meet Clio's father," Aunt Harriet cushioned her abrupt question with what almost sounded like a euphemism, one of those will-of-the-wisp tags that make the question not so blunt.

"I'm on my way to Australia to work with the ATIS group." Seeing our blank expressions, he added: "Allied Translators and Interpreter Services, in Brisbane. My expertise is in languages—many languages. I'll be catching a freighter out of Galveston. My work will be vital to the war effort. I couldn't stay in my teaching job when my expertise is needed. And well compensated," he added smugly.

"How did you know that Clio was with us?" Aunt Norma went right to the heart of the matter.

The soupspoon heading toward my father's mouth halted mid-air. He placed it alongside his bowl and leaned back in his chair. "I guess I need to explain a few things before I impose on your hospitality. Just because I haven't seen Clio since Delia took her away doesn't mean that I haven't kept track of her. And Delia. I knew when Delia left for Europe, and I suspect I know where she is now."

No one around the table seemed to be breathing. I saw the shadow of Lucinda, just behind the archway leading to the kitchen.

"My cousin, Marie Dubois, is a Licthman, one of the 'inferior race,' according to the Germans. She speaks five languages and has an advanced degree in physics."

I made an unladylike guttural noise, clearing my throat. My father said he knew where Mother was, but here he sat, blathering on about his relative, while the rest of us waited for the bombshell about Mother. "So where is my mother?"

"Sorry, Clio. I know that you are worried about her." He extended one hand toward me gingerly, the way one might approach an unfamiliar dog that looked snappish. "My cousin Marie and her husband went underground the day that the Germans marched into Paris. Communications out of France are problematic. The Germans closed the Le Havre cable office, but the French Resistance cut phone lines, dug up cables, and dynamited repeater stations all over France to keep the Germans from communicating. However, the Germans can't control the radio. The BBC sends messages with hidden meanings regularly, and the French Resistance uses those very effectively."

Honestly, this father of mine was as gassy as Aunt Harriet when she gets wound up. I glared at him. He ignored me.

"Someone on a Jedburgh team talked briefly to Delia and got a message back to a guy I know at the BBC."

"Jedburgh what? Talked to her where?" I practically had to shout at this so-called relative of mine to get him back on track.

He frowned at me. "Patience wasn't a virtue of your mother's either, Clio." I smacked his arm before he could lift his soupspoon again.

"Jedburgh is supposed to be a clandestine activity, but it isn't. The Jedburgh teams parachute into France and use radios to get information out. The British Special Ops, the US Strategic Service, and Free French Intelligence all work together on this project." He paused, scooped up several spoonfuls of soup, then spoke to Lucinda in a normal voice, as though he wasn't in the least perturbed because she remained behind the swinging door to the kitchen.

"The leeks in this potato soup remind me of my mother's recipe. She was a fine cook. You probably don't remember your grandmother, do you, Clio?" He patted my shoulder in a perfunctory manner, as though calming an unruly child. "My parents moved in with us when you were a toddler, because we needed help. Graduate school in classical and modern languages was a full-time occupation for me, and Delia wasn't exactly the domestic type."

Carefully settling his soupspoon in the center of his empty bowl, my father smiled genially across the table at Aunt Norma. "Delia's life in Wolfe Flats was a well-kept secret. I had no idea that she grew up with all this." My father caressed the top of the dining table. "Chippendale?"

"Georgian," Aunt Harriet responded. "We rarely use the additional leaves," she added, as though the disclaimer would level the playing field.

My father lifted a single eyebrow and surveyed the room. "Delia let things slip occasionally, such as saying that our entire two-bedroom flat would fit inside her aunts' living room." He swiveled his head toward the adjoining parlor. "That's probably an exaggeration, but I suspect this house is what—6,000 or 7,000 square feet? Delia refused to give me any details, except to say her house was old and big. How big?"

"In this part of Oklahoma, we don't usually discuss the size of our houses, Mr. Licthman, except with the builder. It might be considered pretentious. That's the way Delia was raised. I'm not surprised that she didn't talk about inappropriate subjects," Aunt Norma's statement was surprisingly curt.

My father's face flushed, his eyes narrowed slightly, and he said almost too casually: "I hope that Delia is watching her tongue now. She could be in a difficult situation in France. Her accent is not very good."

Just the faintest self-satisfied twist of his mouth made me blurt out: "Why would you say something like that about my mother? Are you trying to upset us?"

"*Les carottes sont cuites.*" The French phrase rolled out easily. "The carrots are cooked, Clio. That's the literal translation. It means that there is no use in crying over spilt milk. Your mother made her own choice, a dangerous one, if you ask me. Delia is in France with the resistance. That's all I know."

"I rather wish we didn't know that much, Mr. Licthman. We could sleep easier when Delia was in England. At least, they have bomb shelters there. Safe places," Aunt Harriet added.

"I agree, Miss Clower, but Delia has always done exactly what she wants to do. Actually, she speaks French tolerably well—except for her accent. Comes with the territory, I guess." Again, he lifted one annoying eyebrow.

That set me on edge. He was doing it again. Here we were, sitting around a table covered with too much food, learning that my mother was in a perilous situation, and this upstart father of mine was making snide remarks about her speaking French with an Oklahoma accent.

Turning away from my glare that would melt a glacier in seconds, my father flashed his winning smile at Aunt Norma. "Delia told me that you have a large ranch and some other rural property. I grew up in a very populated part of New York. Farms are small. These wide, open spaces that I saw on the train intrigued me. How many acres do you own?"

I just started to spout out "Two . . ." when Aunt Norma's shoe smacked my shinbone. I knew the estate had over 2,000 acres. Aunt Norma had shown me her books in the little office off the kitchen.

"Enough for our cattle, Mr. Lichtman. If you need a place for tonight, we have a guest bedroom downstairs. The next train going south won't be through until about seven o'clock in the morning. We'd like to know more about the kind of work you do with languages. The Australian assignment sounds most interesting." Aunt Norma could turn a conversation on a dime. She was after information, not planning to offer any.

CHAPTER 35

For the next hour, I watched this man, trying to get a good take on him. He had been a bad husband, a neglectful father, and, obviously, a stretcher of the truth, but he had been blessed with the charm of a superb bullshitter. He praised the Sheraton chair he sat on. He assessed portraits of ancestors on the wall, as though a master artist had produced them, instead of an itinerant painter. He went into raptures over Aunt Harriet's knowledge about the local architecture, not that there was much of it to be seen. He commended Lucinda on her soufflé, until she banged pans in the kitchen to drown out the sound of his voice.

"Would you mind if Clio and I sit outside for just a while tonight?" He dropped his hand casually again on the nape of my neck. "I'd like to get acquainted with my daughter before I go down under."

I stiffened at his touch. He had managed to ignore me through dinner and focused most of his conversation toward my aunts, wooing them like one of those Seventeenth Century cavaliers. Aunt Harriet smiled too much and nervously. Aunt Norma's back was stiff as buckram. Lucinda's absence proclaimed her opinion of my father.

We sat side by side in the backyard glider. Spying a shadow by the garage, I wondered if my POW had escaped from Camp Houze again, but it must have been the wind moving the tree limbs.

My father began firing off questions about my school, my friends, and what I did for entertainment, interspersed with questions about the property my aunts owned. I muttered answers in single syllables. Why did this would-be father take such an interest in me now? Or my aunts? Or their property? Nine years had gone by without so much as a birthday card from him. I pushed the rusty glider to make it screech and drown out the silence between us.

"I'm very charming by nature, Clio. It must be my manner that offends you."

"Not necessarily," I answered. "Your nine-year absence can't be easily explained."

"It can. You know your mother. She didn't want me around. It was her decision," he responded.

"She didn't want to live under the same roof with your parents. She told me that they weren't nice to her," I added testily.

"They're old country, Clio. They have certain expectations. Delia simply didn't try to meet them. I think that growing up with your aunts had a negative impact on Delia. She doesn't like rules. She doesn't like meeting other people's expectations. Frankly, marriage didn't agree with her."

He let out a rueful sigh. "Your aunts do seem rather rigid, Clio. Your mother would never tell me why she left Wolfe Flats; she refused to say why she had never returned. Your aunts' attitudes could have been an issue. Although I tried hard to win her over, Lucinda was downright rude to me tonight. Seems to hold a grudge, even though I have never met her before today."

The back porch light of the Mullers' house flashed on, lighting up the side yard. We could see Manboy heading out toward the back fence with bags of garbage.

"That must be the dwarf that Delia used to go on and on about. He's an odd-looking fellow. Delia always attracted strange friends," he mused, shifting closer to me. "I wish I'd stepped in before she left for Europe. Delia shouldn't have left you to the mercy of your great aunts and a handicapped neighbor."

"Manboy Muller is my friend. He's not a dwarf. He just has short arms and legs. He saved my life. Probably saved Mother's too, years ago. He's a very capable lawyer. He interviews POWs for the government."

Just to set the record straight, I launched into an abbreviated recital of how Mother got hit on the head when she was a senior in high school by someone who would become the Wolfe Flats Serial Killer. Manboy had found her atop Devil's Kitchen Tower near Lake Murray and taken her to the hospital in Ardmore. I left out the salient details about Mother and why she left Wolfe Flats. It was not the business of her ex-husband.

Just a few weeks ago, Manboy, Jeremiah, and I had dispatched Mother's attacker to perdition. If I emphasized my role as a super sleuth and a tracker of a serial killer tonight, I felt justified. This long-absent father of mine needed to know that I could take care of myself without any help from him. So, I let it rip.

"Whatever were your aunts thinking?" he exclaimed. "Letting a child put herself at risk, tracking down a killer? He threw you in a well? I can't believe all this. Does Delia know? Surely, you are letting your imagination get the best of you, Clio."

"I can show you the newspaper clippings, if you don't believe me. I'm a hero of sorts in this place. My aunts didn't know what I was doing. A good detective doesn't broadcast her activities," I added peevishly. "Mother had enough to worry about with bombs falling everywhere in England. My aunts said that we shouldn't distract her, so we didn't."

I glanced up at the canopy of stars overhead. With not much ambient light, the skies in southern Oklahoma were brilliant. I should be feeling comforted that my father had arrived, but I didn't. I shivered in the warm June night air.

My father's arm snaked around me. "A spirited young girl like you must be a challenge to ladies as old as your aunts. Delia named them as guardians when you were born, but they're even older now. What would happen to you if they weren't around? Where would you go?"

"Manboy is my successor guardian. Aunt Norma told me. I'd stay right here until Mother comes back. I've gotten used to this place. I have some good friends." I clicked off the names of Jeremiah, Mr. Neboja, his son Marek, and Sally Tolliver, hoping all those syllables would add up to a cluster of more friends than I actually had.

"Regardless of that name-changing business that Delia got through the court, you are my legal child, Clio. Make no mistake about that. A father has rights. You are of my blood."

I eyed him suspiciously, wondering how much of his blood was in me. At a height of five feet, four inches and a weight of 102 pounds, I figure I have about seven pints of blood. If I lose three and a half pints, would that be Lichtman or Clower blood?

"When your aunts die . . ." My body stiffened with those words. "And, if anything happens to Delia, you're the only Clower left. You'd have a considerable estate to manage. That kind of situation can attract the wrong kind of people. A father could help."

Although he cloaked his suppositions in a warm, concerned voice, my father's comments chilled me to the bone. The foul odor of mendacity settled around me. I could feel myself shrinking back from him, even though I tried to remain perfectly rigid in his embrace.

"I'm not trying to frighten you, Clio. I'm sure your aunts are perfectly healthy. Your mother is probably with my cousins in France. They'll look after her. They like her much more than they like me," he laughed harshly at that admission.

Stretching out his long legs, he pushed the glider back and forth, encouraging the rusty springs to wail into the silent night, setting my nerves as much on edge as Aunt Harriet could do with her piano scales. "I did a little walkabout earlier today."

"A what?"

"A walkabout. That's what the Australians say when they walk into the bush, away from civilization. I wandered around the streets in Wolfe Flats before I came to your aunts' house this evening. I needed some socks, so I went into Lewin's Dry Goods Store and met the strangest woman."

"Hedy Lewin. She's Whitey's mother. The serial killer's mother. She's not an albino. Neither was Whitey. His grandmother was." I was doing my best to shift the conversation away from the Clower estate.

"What are you rattling on about albinos, Clio? I was telling you about an interesting conversation I had with the owner of that store. The minute I asked Mrs. Lewin about the Clower family, she spewed out information faster than a broken gas jet. She pointed out buildings they owned down the street. She said they owned more acres of farmland than they should. That woman really has it in for your aunts."

Grabbing both my hands, he spun me around to face him. "Mrs. Lewin told me that the great-niece who had come to stay with them needed to be sent to a reform school," he chuckled uneasily. "I now know what 'turning the air blue' means. According to that woman, you're the worst villain around. I couldn't get out of her store fast enough. I wanted to deck her for saying such things about my daughter, but I don't hit women. I'm very calm around them."

Another whiff of mendacity hit me. I might have been only three years old, but I vividly remember a red-faced man shouting at the top of his lungs at Mother, not once, often.

"My intention, Clio, when I stopped off in Wolfe Flats, was just to check on you before I left for Australia. With Delia out of . . . contact, things have changed," he paused uncomfortably. "This war could go on for a long time. You need one of your parents looking after you. That leaves me. I think Australia is a safe place."

I believe in getting all my ducks lined up when I state my argument. "If you can avoid kangaroos, hungry crocodiles, and hostile aborigines that have every reason to resent people taking over their country, the greatest threat now is from Japanese submarines off the coasts of Australia. Wolfe Flats doesn't have a coastline. I guess you have forgotten that the Japanese bombed Darwin earlier this year and killed over two hundred people. I'm perfectly safe here with relatives and friends who want to look after me."

"You might be safe from Japanese bombers, Clio, but getting thrown into a well by a serial killer doesn't make a very good case for your argument. You need a parent to look after you. Now that General MacArthur is in Brisbane, Americans will be settled there. I'm sure that your aunts won't put up too much resistance to you being in a safe place with your father. With a bit of persuasion, they'll see it the way I do. Sweet-talking is one of my talents." My father turned his million-watt smile under a new moon toward me for what he clearly saw as a magic moment of consent.

His self-assured tone nettled me. If my father tried to take me to Australia, Lucinda would bloody well kneecap him with the .38 Special she keeps in the glove compartment of her old pickup. Aunt Norma would call out the National Guard. Aunt Harriet might need her smelling salts. Manboy would cite every legal precedent in over one thousand years of jurisprudence to keep my father at bay.

"I'm not going with you. I like it here. This is where I belong." Even in the darkness, I could see a flush rising from my father's neck up to the black-brush rim of hair above those thick eyebrows. "My aunts would never give up their guardianship. I know that for a fact," I added, although I wasn't sure that they wouldn't be relieved to have me out of their hair.

"You might be right, Clio. Your Aunt Norma is a harridan of the first order. She didn't answer any of my questions directly, but she certainly asked me for more information than I wanted to provide."

"You shouldn't call Aunt Norma that name. She's had a great sadness in her life. She's a very conscientious person. She'd never call you a name," I snatched my hand out of his grip.

"No. I shouldn't. Harridan comes from the Old French. It meant 'old horse.' I just meant that she seemed a bit bossy. Your mother said that she was very domineering," he chuckled. "I suspect that Delia had it coming.

That may explain her flighty nature, her risk-taking in heading to France."

He paused and said defensively: "What you know about me is second-hand—from your mother who was angry with me. I'm going to Australia to serve a patriotic purpose. That should carry some weight with your aunts."

Harboring suspicions about the motives behind both of my parents' wartime efforts set my nerves on edge. Mother coveted the fame of bylines. My father had let it slip at dinner that the Australian job was lucrative.

He leaned his head close to mine and whispered: "Here's what I'm thinking. An adventurous girl like you could not resist this exciting opportunity. You'll have the experience of a lifetime seeing a new part of the world, but your aunts and Lucinda might try to keep you here. They're probably friends with the local sheriff."

I could have told him right then and there that I had gotten the local sheriff fired, after he threatened me about the death of Whitey Lewin when I was in the Ardmore hospital. Only an incompetent deputy roamed the streets of Wolfe Flats these days. But, I kept quiet to see where this was going. My father was a big man. He could probably gag me and take me out of town with no one the wiser.

"When they think about it, they'll understand that you should be with your father. We don't want to upset your aunts unnecessarily. When you go up to bed, just pack whatever you think you'll need. We'll have a long trip on the ship. You should write your aunts and Lucinda a nice note, saying that your father wants you to live with him in a safe country until your mother returns to claim you. Tell them that you'll write often and that you're very grateful for their hospitality. You don't want to burn any bridges with those three."

He locked his thumb and forefinger onto my chin, turned my face toward him, and stared into my eyes. "You will be with a father who is concerned about your best interests. Not another word, Clio. I've made a decision. It's the right one for both of us. We deserve time to make up for those lost years, Sweetheart."

When he said the word "sweetheart," the pang that struck my heart caused an ache that I'd never felt before. I think it ached from a paucity of feeling. A father who had made no contact for years shows up with a covetous eye—not aimed at me but at my aunts' property. Oh, he'd put up with a troublesome daughter for a pot of gold he imagined owning if Mother didn't make it back from France.

That's when he threw in a zinger: "I might be able to contact my relatives in France about your mother. I'll have connections in high places now that General MacArthur is Supreme Commander. Together, we'll figure out how to locate your mother." His conspiratorial smile was almost convincing. Almost but not quite.

With a hushed, secretive voice, he said, "Meet me outside on the street at midnight. Your aunt is wrong about the train schedule. There is a train at one o'clock in the morning to Ft. Worth. We'll be on it. Pack your suitcase. I'll be waiting for you at midnight."

CHAPTER 36

"Mr. Licthman? Clio? Are you still out there?" Aunt Harriet's voice sounded like the sweetest wind chimes I'd ever heard. "It's past Clio's bedtime. She'll want to see you off before seven o'clock in the morning when you catch your train for Fort Worth, Mr. Licthman. Lucinda will fix you a nice breakfast before you leave."

A vise squeezing my arm couldn't have communicated more effectively. My father was a big, muscular man. Both of my aunts were elderly women. Lucinda had probably gone home for the night. Strong as he was, Manboy might not be able to rout a man the size of my father.

Without relaxing his grip, my father kept me plastered to his side as we walked through the back door, down the hall, and into the parlor where my aunts sat next to the big Zenith radio with its bands of flamed maple dancing under the Tiffany lily lamp atop it.

"Clio and I have been making up for lost time. We've had a wonderful visit. I can't express enough gratitude for your hospitality—to me and, especially, to my daughter.

This little scamp has probably made a nuisance of herself. She's certainly disturbed your peace, if what she tells me is true about Mr. Lewin," he laughed.

"Clio is family, Mr. Licthman. Our home is her home. It's not a hospitable act to care for your own family. She's only been here a few months, but we can't imagine our lives without Clio," Aunt Norma responded curtly. "As for what she might have told you about Mr. Lewin, you shouldn't question that it happened just as she described. That was a bad chapter in our lives, but it's closed now."

I glanced up at my father's face. By the hue of his skin, he didn't appear to be accepting this rebuff very graciously, but his smile was ear-to-ear. "I'm sure that Clio told me the truth, but, frankly, I'm stunned that she was allowed to put herself at such risk, with a serial killer at large."

"Lester Lewin wasn't 'at large,' as you said, Mr. Licthman. We all believed that he was an upstanding citizen and a devout member of the Methodist Church. Three young women had disappeared over a considerable period of time. No one linked those events to him. Then Clio did. We would never have allowed her to put herself at risk if we'd known what she was doing. Never!" Aunt Harriet might as well have been on a podium in Hyde Park. Her usually quiet voice cracked the night like a thunderbolt.

"I'm sure that Mr. Licthman knows Clio is safe with us, Harriet," Aunt Norma's voice was carefully controlled as she eased up from her chair. "I'll just walk her upstairs to say goodnight. She'll be up to have breakfast with you before you leave in the morning. The news will be on in five minutes if you want to listen to it before you retire."

Never was I so happy to have my arm grasped firmly by Aunt Norma. Never did her droopy beige cotton stockings look more like a fine fashion statement than they did at that moment, as she marched me up the stairs.

When she pushed open my bedroom door, there sat Lucinda on my bed, her face as dark as a raincloud. "That father of yourn has a loaded gun in his backpack. I looked while you wuz outside with him. I took them bullets out." She held out her palm toward me and showed me six, shiny brass bullets. A suspicious lump with a pointy end nestled in her apron pocket.

"Lucinda eavesdropped. When your father said he was taking you outside for a visit, she slipped out the back door, hid next to the garage, and listened," Aunt Norma whispered, almost shame-faced by her words. "Actually, she slipped through the alley and talked to Manford. Apparently, your father had been busy today before he showed up at our front door."

"Busy doing what?" I questioned.

"Pokin' his nose in where it don't belong," Lucinda piped up.

"Manford got an interesting call from a friend of his in the County Clerk's office in Ardmore this morning. She said a stranger came in inquiring about records of real estate and land deeds of the Clower family. She knew about some of the buildings we own, but didn't tell him. She told him he had to have proper identification to look at someone else's records. Later, Manford called Wolfe

Flats County Clerk. The same man had been in that office asking questions."

"When you seen Manboy takin' out the trash tonight, he was checkin' on your pa." Lucinda patted her pocket. "I got my gun out of the pickup. Never know when it might be needed."

"Hush that kind of talk, Lucinda. We don't hold with violence around here," Aunt Norma's whisper was sharp with anxiety. "We know that your father is putting pressure on you to leave with him, Clio. He has no right to take you. Your mother named Harriet and me to be your guardians for a good reason. Your father hasn't been in your life for nine years. Your mother took the measure of him in the nick of time."

Pulling the door ajar, Aunt Norma spoke in a louder than normal voice: "I'd better get back downstairs to show your father to his bedroom, Clio. Sweet dreams. I'll wake you early so you can see him off."

I crawled up onto the tall four-poster bed and snuggled close to Lucinda, on the safe side, away from her gun. Just a month earlier, I'd been shot in the arm. I don't have a gun fetish like most people in Wolfe Flats. Guns give me the willies—or woollies if you want to be correct about the derivation of the word.

Lucinda drew in a long, shuddering breath and pulled me so close that it was hard to breathe. "I need to confess a secret, Clio. I never tole yer aunts. It would be hurtful to them. While yer ma lived in New York City, we had a set time to talk. Me and Delia. Onct ever month, on a third Sunday mornin' when Norma and Harriet go to church,

Delia called me at the house here. I always attends evenin' prayer on them Sundays. No sermon."

"Why did she call you? She never told me that she did."

"Delia left home in fury. Angry with her aunts over that time she was hurt real bad at Lake Murray. They didn't tell the police. Yer mama can hold a grudge longer than about anybody, Clio. Don't make it right. She never forgot to ast me about her aunts. She told me about everthin' that happened to her and you and that pa of yourn."

I eased away from her and said: "Tell me."

"Yer mama didn't want you to have bad feelings about yer pa. He coulda visited you. He didn't pay you no mind. He was interested in his own doins'. Delia tole him she grew up in an old house in Wolfe Flats, but said that she let it slip that she did barrel racin' and kept her horse at the family ranch. That caught his attention. When they first met, she told him she lived in an old house with spinster aunts. And me. She told him about me. That's all she wanted him to know about her past."

Lucinda shifted her considerable bulk against the headboard of the bed. "When your pa's folks moved in with 'em when you was about two years old, Delia said he changed for the worst. He shouted her down afore his own folks, and they never said nothin', 'cept for his ma, who called you by her name. She said that a Gentile woman wantin' to do a man's job at a newspaper weren't the right kind of wife fer her son."

Feeling the tension in her body, I knew that it graveled Lucinda to talk about anything unpleasant about my mother. "So Mother just walked out with me?"

"No. She grabbed a ruler from her mother-in-law and done somethin' unfittin'. Then, she left with you— that was fittin'. Before all was said and done, Delia paid your pa a sizeable sum to agree to a quick divorce and no legal right to you, includin' changin' your last name to her maiden name."

Rolling carefully off the bed, and avoiding Lucinda's grasping hands, I tiptoed across the thick red Bohara rug and cracked the door. I could hear my father's voice and Aunt Harriet's giggles. No doubt he could be very entertaining. Like a cobra winding his way out of a basket, my father was mesmerizing my aunt. At the same time, he was plotting to take me so far away that my aunts might promise him anything to get me back. Or not.

I crept down the hall to peer over the railing that Aunt Harriet called the balustrade so that I could hear more clearly. Aunt Norma's voice sounded artificially bright and friendly. "We're early risers, Mr. Lichtman. You've probably had a long day with your train journey— and a longer one ahead of you. Lucinda will fix breakfast at six o'clock. Clio will be down to have breakfast with you; then, I'll drive you to the depot for the seven o'clock train to Fort Worth."

"Too kind, Miss Clower. I said my goodbye to Clio this evening. Let her sleep late in the morning. She's had enough excitement for the day. I don't eat early. I'll just be on my way without making too much noise. You'll never know how grateful I am for your courtesy and hospitality. I'm very comforted to know that Clio will be in such a good home while I'm breaking Japanese codes in

Australia. War puts strange burdens on us. But we soldier on."

Well. That was pretty little speech. My father laid out a plan to keep anyone from checking on him the next morning. He wove a nice web of lies about appreciating my "good home." And, to top it off, he cast himself as a code-breaker par excellence, bearing up bravely under the burden of war. Somewhere out there my mother might be hiding in a barn in France, desperately trying to rig up a Type B Mark II radio, to send an SOS. Yet here sat my long-absent father, furtively going against my mother's express wish for me to live with my aunts.

I studied the craggy features of what must have been a very handsome younger man. No doubt, he could deal with colleagues in a friendly manner. All that sorting of sounds coming from the enemy, trying to make sense of what skullduggery they were plotting. My father would be in his element.

His conversations with my aunts and me had been a kind of clearinghouse for practicing those small cruelties that Mother had occasionally let slip: phrases that put him in a better light; an ooze of flattery to capture the unwary; and the casual clutch of a hand that might be just a bit too forceful.

I could hear both my aunts walking side-by-side up the stairs, making loud clomping noises. Bedroom doors opened and closed. The toilet flushed twice. The silence terrified me. I could imagine my father downstairs in the guest bedroom, checking his gun, reloading the bullets, and packing away the family silver.

CHAPTER 37

A sliver of hall light entered the room as my aunts, fully dressed, inched into my bedroom. Both held up warning fingers until the door clicked behind them. "We're staying in here with you and Lucinda, Clio. I have no idea what your father will attempt if he tries to take you away and is thwarted in the process. Manford is on alert."

Aunt Norma picked up a spindly Sheraton armchair and put it against my bedroom door. Sitting upright with both hands tucked into her armpits, Aunt Norma looked exactly like the ancient Greek Sphinx, a winged lion with a woman's head. Except that my aunt had an expression that meant she wasn't there to solve a riddle.

Aunt Harriet moved over to my desk and began looking at my maps. "These are really quite good, Clio," she whispered. The steeple on the Methodist Church is a bit lopsided, but the perspective is good."

Aunt Harriet doesn't get my maps. I purposefully and subtly insert my opinions in my maps. The Wolfe Flats Methodist Church is more than "a bit lopsided." It harbored a serial killer for years and watched him pander to old ladies while he was slaughtering the young attractive ones.

I crawled back up on my bed close to Lucinda, who was already snoring quietly. Through my open window, I could hear the static rise and fall of a nightjar's churr. Those dumb birds sit in the middle of the street at night, not in the least concerned about danger. I had brought danger to this house. Half of my gene pool was downstairs plotting to take me to Australia—probably just long enough to get my aunts to pay him a substantial sum for my return.

Sleepless, I relived my father's re-entrance into my life. My absentee father didn't know a thing about me—not that I was devoted to Ptolemy, the greatest map-maker of all time, or that I was a natural sleuth and subscribed to Sherlock Holmes's method. My father had his eye on a prize. It wasn't me. He exposed his greed the moment he walked into this house and began assessing the furniture. His eyes rolled like cherries in a slot machine, as he ticked off Sheraton chairs, a Jacobean library table, and a Chippendale Bombe chest.

In a dark corner of the best parlor, a small painting of a woman with flowing reddish hair and roses by her neck had caught his attention. "That isn't . . . that can't be . . . is that a Renoir?"

"Yes. Not an exceptional one, but my mother liked it, so my father bought it in Paris years and years ago," Aunt Norma said, dismissively. She'd rather be wrapping bandages for the war effort down at the Methodist Church than observing the greedy expression on my father's face.

Giving him the benefit of doubt earlier in the evening, I thought that he had been a bit overwhelmed by this "old house" that my mother hadn't told him about. I'm sure she described it like the inside of a barn: steam heaters that didn't work right; tall ceilings that made rooms the temperature of an icebox in winter; and, a dreadful clutter of heavy, dark furniture, except for the spindly chairs.

After I recovered from the shock of seeing him on the doorstep, my first impression had been that he was better looking than Jeremiah's father, George, with whom Mother might or might not have been smitten. As I watched him circling the room, the undeniable glint of rapacity appeared in his greenish eyes, followed by a yellow tint of covetousness.

Spotting the silver tea set on the end of the table, my father had caressed it with both hands. I was just about to tell him not to touch it, because it makes tarnish marks and sends Lucinda into a dither, because she has to polish it with a cloth and no tarnish remover.

Aunt Norma's politeness intervened before I could send up a warning shot. "That's Crichton. George the Fifth. My father liked silver. I find it a bit tedious, with all that polishing. I prefer a porcelain teapot with no taste of metal."

The taste of metal can be caused by a disorder of the nerves or lead poisoning or pesticides like DDT. Lucinda keeps a can of DDT under the sink to discourage ants. Tonight at dinner, Lucinda's soufflé had a suspicious metallic taste. I noticed that she put an enormous helping in front of my father. However, I cast out those bad thoughts when I watched Lucinda glaring at my father, while refusing to sit at the dinner table with us. Lucinda is no Lucrezia Borgia poisoner. Her weapon of choice is the lethal lump in her apron pocket; she dozes, innocent as a lamb on my bed.

While we were all clustered in my bedroom, almost two hours passed before we heard the faintest scrape of the front door's soft closing. I poked Lucinda. She sat up with a jerk, pulled the .38 out of her pocket, and twirled the cylinder as though she knew exactly where six shots would go if she tickled the trigger.

Aunt Harriet gasped softly and clung to the side of my desk as though it might be the only life raft left to her.

I pulled a heavy drape aside and reported just as Sherlock would have: "Suspect is by the curb. Has his backpack on. Is watching the house. Not a car in sight. All lights are off in the Muller house. No sign of Manboy. No reinforcements in sight."

"Thank you, Clio. Stay back from the window. We have no idea how Mr. Licthman will react when you don't appear with your suitcase in hand." Aunt Norma stood, turned toward the door and put one knee upon the chair bracing the door knob. "We'll just have to wait him out."

Watching my aunts trying to hide their distress in their own fashion and seeing Lucinda's stony face as she fiddled with her gun touched me in a very sore spot. I had brought them to this night—or my mother had. She had chosen an avaricious husband. Perhaps, I could have avoided this set-to if I had been more forceful about not going to Australia with him. When he made his smoke and mirror pitch about finding Mother through his connections to the Supreme Commander MacArthur, he raised my hopes and silenced my protest.

The truth is that my interest had been piqued by the thought of Australia. Over the radio, I had heard one of those big, hollow didgeridoos that the aborigines play. The sound is so guttural and strange. It carries for miles. I could learn to throw a boomerang. It spins about an axis perpendicular to the direction of flight and returns to the thrower. That marvelous little weapon can fell a kangaroo and has been in use for 50,000 years, so much classier than Lucinda's .38.

CHAPTER 38

No one in my bedroom said a word, but the room hummed with unspoken sentences—about a houseguest who had broken the rules of propriety by trying to insinuate himself into the bosom of my family for a dastardly purpose. His motive had set a collision course with my better judgment when he dangled the plum of Australia before me.

If I had disappeared down under with my father, it might have given Mother a little taste of what desertion feels like, nevermind an opportunity for me to check out wombats and platypuses. No. I would be willfully abandoning my aunts and Lucinda. If I got on that ship to Australia with my father, I'd be resurrected into his daughter. I didn't know who that girl would be. She wouldn't be me.

By moving the velvet drape just an inch, I could see my father's dark mass silhouetted against the night sky. His surprise visitation had put my aunts and Lucinda in danger. My father was a big, strapping man with a gun and a temper that he managed to keep under control as he tried to flimflam my aunts and me.

If I left quietly now, they would be safe. I could write to them on the sly, telling them not to give my father a penny of their money. At the bottom of the letter, I could quote those famous words of General MacArthur when he left the Philippines for Australia: "I shall return."

What if I couldn't return? Japanese subs trawled the coast of Australia constantly. Although huge, with its barrier reefs and ancient lava tubes for hiding places, it is not my home. New York City was my home for over eleven years; in less than two months with no explanation, Wolfe Flats has latched on to my heart. I looked at my aunts and Lucinda, beside themselves with dread. Maybe it had to do with them.

Fists pounding against the front door and a siren wailing down the street made a breathtaking cacophony of sound in a town where only colicky babies and ill-tempered roosters dare to disturb the nighttime peace. My aunts and Lucinda crowded against me at the window; not one of them seemed to be breathing.

With his red lights flashing, the deputy spun his car against the curb, creating an ear-splitting sound. His door wouldn't open more than a foot. Like one of those Moray eels, flattened on both sides and hesitant to emerge from a coral reef, the deputy sheriff eased out of the driver's seat sideways, crushing his Stetson. His lanky body unfolded joint by joint and reassembled itself atop the curb.

After engaging in a bit of fancy footwork to avoid Aunt Harriet's marigolds, he eased his Wesson .357 Magnum out of his holster and cut across the sidewalk.

Manboy circled alongside the porch with a shotgun looped casually under his arm.

I have to give credit to my father. Under the porch light, his face looked like one of those self-righteous Medicis out of a Fifteenth-Century painting—arrogant and imperious.

"You are disturbing the peace, Mister Whatever Your Name is." The deputy kept his hand on his gun and stopped halfway down the front walkway.

"His name, Deputy, is Joseph Licthman. He's Clio's father, but I'm not sure why he is banging on the Clower house at this hour in the morning," Manboy's carefully enunciated words should have been calming. They weren't. With a flip of his wrist, the shotgun appeared to be an extension of his arm.

"Well. Well. Delia's dwarf. And armed. I'm unarmed, and you are threatening me with guns? What's wrong with you people? I'm simply taking my daughter to the train station. We will be leaving this backwater town without any interference from either of you." My father's voice soared with confidence that I was sure he wasn't feeling.

Manboy spoke with no apparent hostility, but I could sense tension in his wide-legged stance. "You're not her guardian, Mr. Licthman. Her aunts are. Then, I am. You have no legal right to take Clio anywhere. I suggest that you get into the back of the deputy's car. We'll drive you to the station and see you off on the train. There are elderly women and a child in the house. Your actions are making them very nervous."

Irritated by being lumped in with "elderly women" in their so-called "nervous" state, I would have a bone to pick with Manboy when the dust settled. Edginess, along with a kind of desperate forboding, was what I felt at that moment—like watching Hopalong Cassidy leap from a balcony and imagining the pain of landing astraddle his horse Topper.

Manboy edged left and then right, like a riled cat stalking its prey, as he moved closer to the front door. The deputy stumbled over a loose brick in the walkway, recovered his footing and shouted: "You heard Mr. Muller. Move over to my vehicle. You been disturbing the peace. It ain't allowed in this neighborhood."

I watched slack-jawed as that stupid deputy bounded forward and grabbed my father. Within seconds, a judo toss sent him right into Aunt Harriet's dahlias, the ones she had propped up with little bamboo sticks, where he wallowed around like a victim of Japanese torture.

Just as my father whirled toward Manboy, he found himself looking into two chambers of a double-barreled shotgun.

"This isn't loaded for turkeys, Mr. Licthman. You don't want to experience a short-range shot. You need to get into the back seat of the deputy's car. You are no longer welcome in Wolfe Flats. You could be charged with assaulting our deputy and spend the rest of the war in Big Mac, our prison over in McAlester. Or, you can be on the train and off to Australia to help with the war effort. Which way do you want Clio to remember you?"

I only remember the dark form of my father in the backseat of the deputy's car, with Manboy riding shotgun in the front. Neither of my aunts or Lucinda said a word. From my upstairs bedroom window, we watched the car speed down Choctaw, turn onto Main, and disappear.

Part of what should have been mine—a past and a future with my father—was vanishing with the deputy sheriff's taillights. Maybe my father's motives were mixed and ambiguous, not totally selfish. He might have been trying to protect me, to ensure that I'd be safe for the rest of this war.

Just as I moved away from the window, thinking that I could easily get to the depot before the southbound train arrived, skepticism planted its sturdy foot in front of me. A concerned, loving father wouldn't wait nine years to visit his daughter. He wouldn't check out her future financial assets with the local county clerks' offices before he knocked on the door.

Next, a finely honed sense of anger settled on me. The careful touches and the guarded expressions of concern were the worst kind of treachery. Fathers didn't love daughters because of what they might inherit. In Dickens's *A Christmas Carol*, Bob Cratchit is poor as a church mouse but can't wait to share a tiny plum pudding with his daughter. Jane Austen's Mr. Bennet, in *Pride and Prejudice*, would never agree to let his beloved Elizabeth marry for money.

After my aunts and Lucinda left my bedroom without a word, I crawled up on my enormous bed, scooted under the covers, and tried to put myself to sleep by turning the tables. What if my father had lots of money, so that greenbacks could never be an issue in our relationship? A gloomy thought intruded. Shakespeare already worked that plot to its bitter end. King Lear decides to give his fortune to the daughter who claims she loves him best— he goes stark, raving mad when he makes the wrong choice. Just thinking about my father wandering around the moors shrieking like Lear with guilt put me to sleep.

Several times during that long night, my door would ease open and one of three worried faces would briefly appear. Images of aborigines troubled my sleep. Standing like storks on one leg and pointing to somewhere in the distance, small brown men seemed to be asking me a single question that I couldn't answer, because I couldn't bear to hear the question.

CHAPTER 39

The morning after my mendacious father high-tailed it out of Wolfe Flats, I could hear ungodly wailing coming from the kitchen. The sound was unfamiliar in a house where emotional outbursts were viewed with the same repugnance as dangling modifiers. The crying was urgent, unstoppable. Lucinda sat at the table with both arms tucked so far into her favorite, shabby sweater that she might have been a double amputee. Aunt Norma perched next to her, hesitantly patting her back.

Lucinda blurted out: "To hear Amaday tell it, her Opal was supposed to be safe as houses in that field hospital in the Malinta Tunnel under Corregidor. Way down underground so no bombs could hit. When MacArthur took off in that sub, they was so many American and Philippine troops left behind that Amaday and me figured they'd keep the nurses safe in that tunnel. Not on one of them Bataan forced death marches. Opal shoulda been safe." Like one of those old shellac records with a sizeable crack, Lucinda's voice wavered every time she said "safe."

Lucinda lifted a plaintive face toward me, as I edged into the room. Still unsettled about my father's *forced march* to a train out of Wolfe Flats early this morning, I expected to be the center of attention today. I felt a bit disgruntled that Lucinda's tears were for a neighbor's daughter that I didn't even know.

"I been bearin' up about Delia takin' off for France, so as not to upset Clio no worsen she is. Then that worthless ex-father of hern upsets the entire household last night. I coulda shot him outa puredee spite, but I controlled myself," Lucinda sniffed self-righteously, before her next volley.

"Opal Terrill's been special to me ever since I seen that little carroty head of hers come out bass-ackwards. One leg out first, then t'other. Me and Doc Lontry had to put a cast on the leg of a newborn. That was a first for both of us." Lucinda's chest puffed up with what might have been self-importance or just an extra deep breath.

The startled expression on Aunt Norma's face convinced me that the old stork delivery myth was foremost in her mind, as she tried to gloss over Lucinda's colorful description of Opal's birth. "The Gainesville hospital has a nice maternity ward now. Very antiseptic. When Opal was born, twenty years ago, things were done differently."

Just as I was about to ask how differently, Lucinda heaved a mighty sigh and said, "Sometimes this war is too much for folks at home to bear. That's bad business about the Philippines. Some generals takin' off in subs to Australia. Other generals surrenderin' without a second thought for what might happen to Opal." She shoved her chair back and shook her fist in the direction of the front door—as though the ghost of an unwanted visitor lingered.

"To top it all off, we had to put up with Clio's long-lost pa tryin' to kidnap her to Australia. That foreign country is gettin' on my nerves. Makes a body lose hope."

"Lucinda, I don't understand why you are in such a state this morning. It's been two months since the Japanese invaded Corregidor. General Wainwright surrendered on May 7th. You remember that we listened to his dreadful radio broadcast. You went over to Amaday's house to comfort her, after she got the telegram from that friend of Opal's that her daughter wasn't on the plane that made it to Australia. Is there new information?" Aunt Norma's expression was of a person who wanted to be hopeful but didn't dare.

I dared. Lucinda's fresh onslaught of sobs shocked me into action. I jumped right in there. I follow war news as religiously as that ace reporter Edward R. Morrow, who broadcasts out of London.

Except nobody ever listens to me. They should. I'm on top of important historical events through my mapmaking. Without cartographers to map the stars or ancient cave mappers to make little triangles representing mountains, humans would be wandering in endless circles.

On Mercator's splayed-out globe, tacked to the red-flocked wallpaper in my bedroom, I move colored pins to track events. I knew that two Navy PBY seaplanes took off from Corregidor on April 29 with some nurses aboard. One of the planes made it to Australia, without

our neighbor Opal Terrill on board. The other plane went
down in Mindanao, in the southern part of the Philippines, with those on board, supposedly, captured by the
Japanese.

A possibility struck me with a kind of hopefulness
that might comfort Lucinda. "That other seaplane. The
one that went down in Mindanao. Opal was probably on
that one." I grabbed a kitchen towel and began wiping
Lucinda's streaming cheeks to set her aright. Lucinda had
never been a weeper.

"Really, Clio. This is not the time for your wild sur-
mises. Every American in the Philippines is now a prisoner of war or in internment camps. They are well treated
under the terms of the Geneva Convention—we have to
believe," Aunt Norma tagged on that last bit, as though
she questioned her own assertion.

"They didn't sign it!" I retorted. "In 1929, the Japanese didn't sign. Mother told me that we're just whistling
past the graveyard if we think the Japanese will observe
the Geneva Convention." Watching Lucinda's face fall
again, I wished I weren't so blessed full of information
that I just can't wait to share. I tried to make amends. "I
read that General Wainwright did everything he could
to get good terms when he surrendered to that Japanese
General Homma."

"Skinny Wainwright ain't to blame cause no one
come to help when the Japs took the Philippines. But our
little Opal may be on her own in that jungle. That's what
her nurse friend might be tellin' us, but this is hard to
read with them marked out parts." Lucinda unrolled one

damp fist; the thin, blue envelope she held blossomed like a forget-me-not.

I snatched the blue envelope with scribbles on the other side and announced: "It was posted from Melbourne, Australia. See APO 501." Struggling to read the crimped, smeared ink, I read the signature aloud: "Milly Simpson."

"She's the gal that sent a telegram to Opal's ma when her plane got to Australia safe and sound. Milly said that some nurses were loading on a second plane, but she wasn't sure if Opal got a seat. They was some discussion about important military gettin' captured and civilians who shoulda gone earlier. You'd think they could work out transport before the Japs got there."

Lucinda turned an up-to-speed face toward Aunt Norma. "You know them Simpsons out by Burneyville? Them's the William Simpsons. They's another branch. Les Simpson owns land you can see from Bishop's Bottom over to the Texas side of the river, not too far from our ranch. Milly's one of them Simpsons. She and Opal didn't know each other afore the Philippines but hit it off right away, beings Corregidor was a strange place for them gals."

Lucinda was obviously diverted from her emotional outburst by helping Aunt Norma sort out the Texas neighbors' relationship to a nurse who escaped to Australia. Meanwhile, I was trying to make out Milly Simpson's cramped words on the wrinkled blue paper—words that the censor hadn't marked out. "Milly says that some information came to the base from Filipino Freedom

Fighters on Mindanao. A few people on the plane might have escaped into the jungle. They can't name them or any other Americans that might be in the jungle."

I held up the flimsy airmail page and stabbed at one corner of it. "This is a line that the censor missed in trying to mark out Filipino Freedom Fighters, but the letters bled through. Someone drew a heart and something that looks like a carrot on the side of the page."

"Carrot top. That's what Opal's pa called her! It's a secret message," Lucinda exclaimed.

Like a mechanized doll, Aunt Norma continued to stroke Lucinda's heaving back, as she lifted a cautionary eyebrow toward me. "Lucinda is a bit distraught by the letter Amaday got this morning, Clio. She's always been close to Opal."

"Now them Japs is close to her," Lucinda sputtered through a fresh onslaught of sobs. "She just had to join them Army nurses and go to a foreign country. They's plenty of work for nurses at the Ardmore hospital."

"After the Japanese invasion of the Philippines, there's been somewhat of a news block," Aunt Norma offered optimistically, as though no news was good news.

Lucinda glared at Aunt Norma as though she might be the enemy. "They's been no good news since MacArthur skedaddled off to Australia. Maybe he'll run into Clio's pa, and they'll have a little conflab. With the aborigines. He probably speaks their language too."

I wiggled uncomfortably on my chair and eyed the bare kitchen table. No buckwheat cakes. No sausages. No eggs scrambled so that the slimy whites hid from view.

Lucinda had been the most stable part of my life in Wolfe Flats. For her to get hysterical over a missing nurse—even one she'd brought into this world, one leg at a time—was not the Lucinda I knew. Her comments about my father set me on edge. Finding a father and losing him within eight hours had put me in a sour mood. I expected kindness and consideration and buckwheat cakes this morning. I was winding up a clever retort when Aunt Harriet beat me to the punch.

"The news block from the Phillipines happened when General MacArthur gave his speech in Melbourne. He said: 'I came through, and I shall return.' Those are reassuring words, Lucinda."

Lucinda waved a crumpled envelope. "Not when Milly Simpson says otherwise. It's clear here that she tried to tell us more bad things, but that censor won't let her talk about them Jap soldiers. I guess it wouldn't be fittin' for Clio's ears. Worse 'n what the Yankees done."

Desperate to enlighten everyone about the nameless Japanese atrocities that had upset Lucinda, I explained: "The Second Sino-Japanese War against China started before our war with Japan. Mother and I keep abreast of history. She never censors my reading. No surprises there," I added brightly, reaching for the letter again.

Aunt Norma swatted my grasping hand. "Then you won't be surprised that the censors in this house don't approve of children reading anything they can get their hands on. That includes *Tobacco Road*, Clio. The librarian told me you had wheedled her mercilessly, but she stood her ground."

Also standing her ground, Aunt Norma boosted Lucinda to her feet. "Let's go visit with Amaday to reassure her. Nurses are in great demand in wartime. Like doctors, they treat all who are wounded. The Japanese would know their value—although Clio may disagree, they surely observe the Geneva Convention guidelines."

Just as I tried to stand up to go with Aunt Norma and Lucinda on a reassuring trip to a neighbor I hardly knew, a hand clutched my collar—not a friendly one. "Sit, Clio, and please reflect before you speak. I don't think our neighbor Amaday needs anything but comfort now. Her only child may be in a concentration camp. Frankly, I'm disappointed that Opal's colleague would send such an upsetting letter to her mother. Serves no purpose. Better not to know." Aunt Harriet echoed Aunt Norma's philosophy about blocked news in four words.

I looked at Aunt Harriet gravely. In two minutes, she'd be at her piano playing Chopin's Nocturne in E flat major. That song is sadder than the funeral march.

As Lucinda and Aunt Norma marched hip-to-hip down the hall to the front door, I opened my mouth to shout "Bushido" to correct Aunt Norma's naive assumption that Japan would treat prisoners under the Geneva Convention rules. I know for a fact that the old Samurai code was in play here. Before we took the train to Wolfe Flats, Mother took me to a lecture by the anthropologist Ruth Benedict. She didn't have positive things to say about Japan's "shame culture."

Sitting unfed at the kitchen table with Chopin rattling the rafters, I felt out of sorts. My rock-solid Lucinda seemed vulnerable in a way that was totally unexpected—just because our neighbor got a letter from a nurse in Australia, without much concrete information.

For all the martial music and flag-waving that pumped people into patriotic bluster, evil rode in on the coattails of every war. When I was showing off, quoting the Seven Deadly Sins: pride, greed, lust, envy, gluttany, wrath, and sloth, Mother told me that fascism is the worst sin. She said fascism is a platform for dictators and nationalists, like the Nazis, to destroy the world, as we know it.

I knew now that the war to end all wars, WWI, changed Aunt Norma's world forever—and Felicity's too. Aunt Norma's bond to her first and only love had locked her into a painful, private place for over two decades. She relinquished her privacy for only one rare moment in the back of Manboy's car when she quoted Juliet's speech. Now, I shared a different kind of bond with Aunt Norma.

She could torment the bejesus out of me with her fixation on turning me into a model Wolfe Flats citizen, but we had an undeniable connection. I now understood my blood-kin obligation. I'm not sure Mother ever did.

CHAPTER 40

The summer rain lashed my bedroom windows with an early-morning fury. Downstairs, Aunt Harriet switched from Chopin and pounded out Beethoven's "Ode to Joy," which should have been a cheerful song. It wasn't. She seemed to be trying too hard. Or maybe Beethoven had. My piano teacher told me that Beethoven was deaf by the time he wrote the *Ninth Symphony*. I thought about all those notes rattling around in his head, unable to reach his ears. That would account for the testy expression on those statues of him.

Tired of waiting for Lucinda and Aunt Norma to return from their compassionate trek over to Amaday Terrill's house, I mulled over the scenerios they might discuss about the plight of her daughter Opal: one) they could whitewash what life in a Japanese internment camp would mean—probably nothing scarier than captors with Oni demon masks to frighten them; or, two) they might describe a tropical jungle paradise, where Opal could wait out the war, eating bananas off trees. With the war, Lucinda says that bananas are scarcer than hen's teeth in Wolfe Flats.

Hearing voices downstairs, I rummaged through a drawer of dirty clothes and yanked on some blousy shorts that Lucinda had stitched up for me. The legs were supposed to cling to my upper thighs, but these ballooned out from my knobby knees like half-deflated parachutes. "Cause of this war, can't buy nothin' but rotten elastic at Lewin's," Lucinda had complained before Aunt Norma sent her a warning glance. The Lewin name didn't come up in polite conversation, since I had managed to roast the family heir.

Sauntering downstairs, I tried to make my face resemble one of those plaster death masks from the Middle Ages so that no one in this house would forget yesterday's drama. I could write that story, newspaper style, in three sentences. Mother would be proud. Long-lost father finds daughter in backwoods town. Plans to shanghai said daughter to Australia. Is foiled by aunts, an inept deputy, and a short lawyer.

"We missed breakfast, havin' to spend over an hour consolin' Amaday. Yer Aunt Norma is real good at quotin' Jeremiah. Downright upliftin' for our neighbor," Lucinda assured us.

Recalling that Jeremiah is known as the "weeping prophet," I would wager that enough tears flowed in Amaday's parlor this morning to turn the Sahara into a jungle.

"To keep us on track, I fixed breakfast for our noon meal. Just out-of-the-oven cinnamon rolls, Clio." Lucinda slid a yeasty bun, dripping with powdered sugar icing, next to a stack of buckwheat cakes, swimming in maple syrup, in front of me. I plopped into my usual place at the long refractory table that stretched the length of the kitchen.

Aunt Norma looked over the tops of her bifocals at me. "Lucinda, I doubt that Clio needs that much sugar this late in the day. Not healthy."

Unwinding the steaming cinnamon roll, I dangled it above my gaping maw and said: "Fungi. The yeast in this tasty roll. Do you know that yeast is one of the earliest domesticated organisms, Aunt Norma? Jeremiah's mother is studying fungi somewhere in a jungle. She's not likely to run into Opal. Too bad, because she could point out the mushrooms that are safe to eat."

I don't know why I had to bring up the topic of a missing mother or the misplaced daughter of our neighbor. My mother might be in a desperate situation in France, unable to speak French without an Oklahoma twang. And just last night, my father had been sent packing on the fastest train south. All the cinnamon rolls in the state of Oklahoma couldn't make the empty feeling inside me go away. So, I made a daring attack on another cinnamon roll and waited for Aunt Norma's reprimand.

"We have a little outing planned today, Clio. We intended to get an earlier start," Aunt Norma said with an unusual lilt, as though the tone of her voice could lift the smog-like heaviness in this house.

I lifted one eyebrow, propped my elbow on the table, and swooped an oversized bite of pancakes into my mouth—three not-so-subtle gestures designed to annoy Aunt Norma. Then I added a fourth: "Like an outing to unravel wool sweaters or smash tin cans at the church? That kind of fun war-effort stuff?"

"Actually, no. We're taking you out to our ranch. Our manager, Mr. Blake, and his wife live in our old home place now. Harriet and I spent every summer in that house when we growing up. In the Territory days, some people had houses in town and in the country. The best of both worlds—rural and urban."

My jaw dropped. Aunt Norma must be joking. New York City was urban. Wolfe Flats was . . . Well, it was what it was. You could fit most of the Main Street stores into Bergdorf Goodman and still have half of a building left over. Still, I mused optimistically, Wolfe Flats had a dandy crime rate and, lately, one very interesting, escaped, German POW. Crime with a personal touch is hands-down better than screaming police sirens chasing up and down New York City streets.

"So what are we going to see?" I mumbled with my mouth full to further irritate Aunt Norma. "Cows? Wheat pastures? Peanut fields?"

"A surprise." Aunt Harriet's high tinkling voice whispered just above my left ear.

"I don't know if I can take anymore surprises after yesterday," I muttered, trying for a sullen expression. I didn't want my aunts and Lucinda to think that I'd forgotten how they'd taken my future into their hands, by jettisoning my father, so to speak. I might have liked an ocean voyage to Australia. I might never get another opportunity to see a duck-billed platypus or kangaroos boxing.

Blithely ignoring my bad mood, Aunt Norma grabbed her driving gloves, smashed a practical black straw hat on her head, and announced: "I'm backing the Pierce Arrow out of the garage. I told Mr. Blake that we'd be there around ten o'clock. We'll be late. He has other things to do than wait on us."

"You can ride shotgun, Clio. Lucinda and I will sit in the back with our picnic for later," Aunt Harriet said, swinging the back door closed, as I crawled into the front passenger seat.

Grinding the gears, Aunt Norma stomped on the gas, clipped the corner hedge, and dropped the right tire off the curb as she pulled onto Choctaw Street, without looking left or right.

"Leaf-spring suspension," she exclaimed to no one in particular. "The Pierce Arrow can hop curbs without disturbing the passengers."

Had I not experienced Aunt Norma's erratic driving patterns in the past, I might not have remembered to keep my teeth clenched and my tongue safely nestled between my jaws as she pulled out of the driveway.

Heading out of town, Aunt Norma kept the car equidistant from both sides of the road. That meant, she straddled the centerline of Highway 77 for about five miles, and then swerved onto a graveled side road, with no other marker than a tin mailbox.

The terrain changed from what appeared to be miles of wheat pasture to large stands of trees. In the distance, I could a river snaking alongside thick clusters of willows.

"The big trees are pecans. Papa planted some of the first paper-shell pecans in this part of the county. The natives have a better flavor, but they're not a good cash crop," Aunt Norma pointed toward a stand of trees in the distance.

When she said: "The natives have a better flavor," I almost made a catty comment about cannibalism, but there was a kind of unspoken festive spirit in the car that restrained me.

Rolling down the back window, Aunt Harriet said eagerly: "Next curve, Norma. Stop so we get the best view."

A weathered two-story, board house tucked itself into the only hill within sight, companionably claiming the shelter of a friendly knoll. Hollyhocks thrust toward the morning sun all along the edge of a wide porch.

If Hopalong Cassidy had a double, it would have been the silver-haired cowboy who moved across the front yard as soon as the Pierce Arrow ground to a halt.

"It's been a coon's age since you ladies have paid us a visit. The missus made a berry cobbler. Come on into the house. Lucinda, don't let me forget that we have a basket of early garden produce to send back with you."

I slid out of the front seat, hugging the fender, feeling out of place, still a bit irritated about some so-called surprise that hadn't materialized. Maybe these people thought that berry cobbler was a good surprise. Not.

When Mr. Blake eased the back car door closed, he spotted me. "My Lord. If I didn't know better, I'd swear I was seeing Delia. Spittin' image. No question about that."

"This is Clio, Delia's daughter. She's living with us while Delia is in . . . Europe . . . working as journalist." Aunt Norma's voice dropped to almost a whisper, as if she didn't pinpoint exactly where my mother might be in Europe, she could ensure her safety.

"I never saw such a likeness. Your mother used to spend lots of time out here in the summers, Clio. She had her own room in the house. Did lots of barrel racing back then. Mostly at the local rodeo. Not many girls did the rodeo circuit back then. I did, but it was different for a man."

I wanted to ask him why, but Aunt Norma interrupted with questions about the impact of morning rain on the wheat and yield per acre, one of those dull-as-dirt conversations that could only titillate a farmer. Aunt Harriet and Lucinda were going into spasms over Mrs. Blake's double hollyhocks. I dropped down on the edge of the porch and eyed a blue tick hound, tethered to a stake in the yard. We spoke the same language.

At the moment, my emotions were holding me hostage. After having only vague memories of my father, seeing him materialize on my aunts' doorstep yesterday had shaken me to the core. Gobsmacked me. Shifted my emotional universe. Turned my tear ducts into miniature waterspouts.

To irk Aunt Norma, I took a big swipe at my nose with the bottom of my blouse and waited for her reaction. Lucinda had one: "We are torturin' this child of ours. We promised her a surprise, but we're just standin' around waggin' our tongues."

Mr. Blake held out a hand toward me. "Come on, Clio. The surprise is in the big barn. Miss Clower, you ladies lead the way. I don't intend to steal your thunder."

We wound past two hen houses, a drift of young pigs in a pen, and a sizeable garden before we came to corrals, with a huge barn adjacent to them. My aunts and Lucinda trudged through what might have been mud or not, while I leapfrogged from dry patch to dry patch in my sandals.

Standing inside the barn with scissors of sunlight whacking through slightly musty bales of hay, I felt as though I had just entered a kind of rural cathedral. I was standing in the middle aisle. Instead of chapels at the transept, I saw mostly empty stalls. There was a hushed, almost magical sense of something unexpected waiting in this giant, silent barn.

Sunlight poured in a direct stream from a high window in the upper hay loft directly into a stall ahead of us. Mr. Blake swung the gate wide and beckoned us forward. "Clio, meet Hopkins the Third."

"She has more freckles than Jeremiah!" I exclaimed, stretching my hand toward the horse's reddish face.

"She's a strawberry roan. Good lineage through Oklahoma Star," Mr. Blake said proudly. "Hard to get a good strawberry roan. Our third one since your mother's first mare, the original Hopkins."

"Actually, a chestnut roan," Aunt Harriet corrected no one in particular.

A shadow moved against the backside of Hopkins, stepped forward, and head-butted me. "And her filly, born two days ago, who has no name," Mr. Blake grinned at me. "She likes you, Clio. She's not the least bit afraid. That's a good sign."

The short, bushy tail on that little filly moved like a metronome as she latched onto her mother. Aunt Norma, Aunt Harriet, and Lucinda spoke separately, but harmoniously. I wasn't sure what I was hearing.

"They're yours, Clio. The mare and the filly. Your surprise. This mare is the granddaughter of Delia's barrel-racing horse."

Hopkins the Third lifted her head out of a bucket of oats and blew a snotty mix down the front of my blouse. It was a baptism of sorts. One of the file cabinets in my brain popped open. Mother and I had been sunning on a bench in Central Park when she reached over and touched my nose: "You're getting more freckles than my strawberry roan, Hopkins, Clio." Mother rarely talked about Wolfe Flats or my aunts or her childhood—and never about some freckled thing called a roan.

I remember feeling annoyed, swatting her hand away and protesting: "Don't say that. I hate freckles."

Mother had laughed and said, "Gerard Manley Hopkins wrote the most beautiful poem in the English language about freckles. "'Glory be to God for dappled things.' I named my horse for him."

"What are you going to name this little filly?" Mr. Blake asked.

"Her name is Glory. It's Glory."

Somewhere in a safe and secret place in France, where brave people outwitted the evil Nazis, my mother, who loved horses and poetry, heard me and smiled.

The End

Acknowledgments

Many thanks to my friends and relatives for their critiques, especially Lily, Kathy, Wade, Janet, Joann, and Sharon.

A special thank-you to Debbie O'Byrne for her cover design.

www.ingramcontent.com/pod-product-compliance
Lightning Source LLC
Chambersburg PA
CBHW061538170626
46811CB00001B/20